Published by: GladEye Press
Interior Design: J.V. Bolkan
Cover Design: Sharleen Nelson
Copy editing: GladEye Press
ISBN-13: 978-1-951289-07-2
Library of Congress Control Number: 2023937622

Printed in the United States of America.
10 9 8 7 6 5 4 3 2 1

The body text is presented in Garamond 11-point for easy readability.

Faith, Hope, Dying

PATRICIA BROWN

DEDICATION

For all the dogs I've ever loved—Shep, Peppy, Molly, Zeke, Ollie, Belle, and Lucy—just to name a few.

Eleanor Penrose sat on her deck and looked out over the broad expanse of the Pacific Ocean. Despite the blue cloudless sky she was filled with a deep and inexplicable melancholy. How was it possible that someone could feel this way when the sun shone overhead and birds sang as they flitted from tree to tree? The waves that washed upon the shore would still roll in with the changing tide when she was dead. The birds would go on singing after she was gone and the sun would set and rise again after she had taken her last breath.

It wasn't unusual for someone over seventy to contemplate their own death or assess the value of her being, but Eleanor wasn't one to dwell on such things. She sighed and stood up. She was tired of depressing thoughts. What she needed was a stimulating walk on the beach. An ache in her bones told her to go inside and take a nap, but Eleanor knew the more she moved, the faster that ache would subside.

Feathers, her African gray parrot, flew to her shoulder and murmured in her ear, "I love you, Ellie." He spoke in the voice of her late husband, Walter. If she were being honest she would admit to missing Walter today as one season blended into another. Autumn, with its cool foggy mornings and dry crackling leaves, was always her favorite until she compared it to the seasons of her life. Everyone knew what followed: the final season of winter, and then death. She stroked Feathers' smooth back and gave him a sunflower seed treat before leaving the house.

Once down the hill that lead to the shore, Eleanor could see a group of hang gliders at the top of the point preparing to fly over the ocean and catch the wind blowing from the west. They would sail inland over trees and roads that led to who knew where. The thought of flying that way aroused a desire for adventure and excitement within her that was negated by the fear of diving into the water or falling onto power lines. Eleanor knew her limitations. There were opportunities closed to her now that might have been open just a few years earlier.

It wasn't the first time Eleanor envied the strong physicality of youth. A gust of autumn wind sent a chill through her so she picked up the pace to warm her aging body. Three hang gliders circled overhead and soon turned to red and blue specks then disappeared over the trees to the east. Eleanor continued along the water's edge—her eyes always searching for treasures among the stones and ocean's debris. Few others shared her beach midweek now that fall had arrived. Children returned to school and Eleanor's grandchildren too were now involved with their studies, friends, and sports activities leaving her with a great deal more time to pursue her own interests— and dwell on her relevance in an ever-changing world.

During the summer months, Eleanor's beach house had become the place for visits from those who loved the sea, boogie boarding, castle building, volleyball games, and bonfires with marshmallow roasting, and all the other fun stuff of sunny days. Elise, the oldest of Eleanor's grandchildren, and her friends had driven often to Sand Beach and brought with them the joyful exuberance of youth. Of course, it was delightful, but it couldn't last. Perhaps that was the reason for the empty ache she felt. She anticipated the day when her grandchildren went off to college and forgot about the gramma living alone along Oregon's breathtaking coast.

Eleanor turned back toward home and lifted her eyes to the point that jutted out into the ocean. Now that the trees had lost most of their leaves, she could make out parts of the grand old house that sat on high like an aerie. Reverend Strong lived there. She knew he had suffered a stroke and his daughters had come home to care for him until his death. They hadn't made much of an appearance in the village, but rather, had holed up in the big house on the hill. Eleanor wondered where they had been and why they had stayed away so long. Maybe she would stop in at Suzanna's and see if the Do Nothings had anything to report on that front.

Mavis and Sybil sat at their usual table drinking coffee. The Do Nothings had dwindled to two but today they were joined by two women Eleanor did not recognize. At first glance and in her dark state of mind Eleanor thought one represented life; the other death.

"Eleanor, it's so good to see you," said Mavis, "Please sit down and join us."

Eleanor sat obediently and Sybil poured her a cup of coffee from the table's carafe. "You remember Reverend Strong who lived at the top of the point," Sybil said. "These are his daughter's Faith and Hope."

Eleanor smiled as she studied the two women sitting at the table. Faith was the older sister by a good ten years, maybe more. She was tall and lean with a serious countenance. Her brown hair was pulled harshly away from a face that might have been pretty if it weren't for the thick dark brows that resembled check marks over eyes obscured behind granny glasses and the thin line that passed for her mouth. Faith gave off an aura of chilly rage and simply nodded as a way of greeting.

Hope, on the other hand, could not hide her youthful beauty. Even without makeup, her skin glowed and her large brown eyes twinkled with unbridled curiosity. Her chestnut hair could hardly be contained in the bun that was coming undone at the nape of her long neck. Rosy cheeks and pouty lips completed the portrait of a woman in the prime of her life. Hope's smile was full of warmth, which contrasted wildly with that of her sister.

"It's nice to finally meet you both," Eleanor said. "I'm sorry about your father."

"Thank you." Faith lowered her head. "It was a difficult death, a massive stroke. I'm afraid he suffered a great deal. Such is the lot of sinners, but now he's at peace with the Lord."

It was clear to Eleanor that Faith's austerity had a religious base and assumed it was something instilled in her from a strict upbringing. She noticed Faith drank her coffee black while Hope poured three portions of cream and sugar into hers. Faith's bony fingers closed over Hope's elegant hand as she reached for another piece of coffee cake that sat on the table.

"'Their destiny is destruction, their God is their stomach, and their glory is in their shame.'" Faith quoted.

"Sorry," Hope said, withdrawing her hand and bowing her head meekly.

"So what's your story, Faith? Where's your home?" Eleanor asked.

"We've been living in a small town in . . ." Hope began before Faith interrupted her.

"How does this concern you?" Faith inquired. "Where there is no wood, a fire goes out, and where there is no gossip, contention ceases."

"I didn't mean to pry," Eleanor said unapologetically. "I find most people interesting and often willing to share their experiences."

"We should be going. Hope and I have many things to do. Father's house is full of material things that need to be discarded or given to the less fortunate among us. Good day." Faith stood and strode to the exit on long legs, her skeletal frame in sharp contrast to Hope's voluptuousness. Hope followed quickly behind like a faithful puppy.

Eleanor raised her eyebrows and widened her eyes as she looked to Mavis and Sybil for some kind of confirmation that something strange had just happened.

"Yep, that's Faith Strong and no, Eleanor, you were not prying," Sybil reassured her while shaking her silvery head.

"I didn't mean to chase them away," Eleanor said.

"It's hard to have a conversation with her. She's locked herself behind a wall of religious platitudes," added Mavis. "We couldn't get much out of her either."

"How did you get her to sit with you? She's certainly not a friendly person." Eleanor found it difficult to imagine anyone colder.

"She and her sister were sitting at our table when we got here, so I guess we just sat down uninvited," Sybil explained. "Don't let it bother you Eleanor. I'm sure it's nothing personal. Rumor has it that Faith had a falling out with her father years ago and she's been away living who knows where taking care of her little sister."

"I'd guess her life hasn't been a happy one considering her attitude," Mavis noted.

"Do you think they'll stay?" asked Eleanor.

"It's hard to say. Faith didn't say anything about her plans other than cleaning out the house. Her father was a recluse for the last few years. He gave up his ministry in Waterton and just shut himself up in that house. Who knows what condition it's in now or how much is stored in there," Mavis continued. "He could have been a hoarder for all we know."

"I'd forgotten it was even there," admitted Sybil. "The house is the last one on the road that winds to the top so you wouldn't go up there unless you were visiting Reverend Strong. Most of the time it's hidden by trees and brush that's grown up over the years."

"Surely his parishioners came here to see him," Eleanor ventured.

"Maybe they did, but I think they were happy to get that new young guy with the face of a movie star and the body of Adonis," Sybil said. "He came with fresh ideas and the little church had a renewal. Young girls flocked to church on Sunday mornings just to look at him."

"Is he still here?" asked Eleanor, who didn't keep up with the latest church news.

"Surely not, Waterton was too small for him. He had big aspirations. I don't know who's at that church now," Mavis said. "For all I know it dissolved like so many do these days."

"What are you up to, Eleanor?" Sybil asked, evidently tired of the current topic.

"Just out for a walk, nothing exciting to report," Eleanor sighed.

"You must be missing Angus," Mavis sighed. "If I had a man like him in my life, I'd never want him out of my sight. When is he coming back?"

Angus McBride was a retired homicide detective and Eleanor's close friend. He and his son had gone hunting somewhere in the eastern part of the state where there were few cell towers and reception was poor, making communication difficult.

"I haven't heard from Angus for days. When he'll come back is a mystery to me." Eleanor didn't want to admit his absence was the cause for her funk. She liked to think of herself as an independent woman who didn't need a man to make her life complete. "What are you ladies doing today?"

"We're off on an adventure to the big city this afternoon. We both have appointments for mammograms and then we're shopping. Want to come along?" Mavis offered.

"No, I have errands to run and should get going. You two have fun." Eleanor stood and walked to the post office to pick up her mail.

Sand Beach felt deserted as she began the climb up the hill to her home. As she passed Angus' house she realized how empty her life felt without him and his frequent visits and dinner conversation. She hadn't cooked a real meal in days and she loved to cook. There wasn't anything she was looking forward to and that needed to change. Her thoughts swirled with ideas to make her life more meaningful.

"If you aren't happy, a change is in order. Do something to help someone so you can't dwell on yourself," she scolded. As she made a mental list of possibilities she noticed a change in the air. The sky was overcast and the sun had disappeared. On the horizon Eleanor could see dark clouds approaching. In her hurry to get home before the rains fell, she tripped and took a tumble. It gave her whole body a jolt as she landed hard, scraping her hand and knees on the jagged little rocks on the road. She sat up slowly assessing the damage. Blood oozed from her palm and was running down her arm, and her pants were torn at the knee, but it could have been worse she thought as she struggled to her feet. What if she had broken something and couldn't walk home. Eleanor wondered how long she would've sat in the road until someone noticed her if something worse had happened. She imagined herself wet and miserable waiting for help that didn't come and felt the uncertainty of those who live alone. Fortunately, Eleanor was able to pick up her mail and make her way painfully back up the hill and inside her house where her useless parrot pet greeted her by flying to her shoulder.

"Go away, Feathers!" she admonished. All she wanted to do was clean up and lie down.

After a shower and two aspirin, Eleanor lay on her bed and watched the rain pelt the windows as the wind blew and the ocean churned. When she woke from a short nap she could barely move. The fall must have caused her lower back to go out of alignment, just like a car when it hits a pothole. She knew she needed to see Dr. Baxter, her chiropractor. She picked up her phone and made a call.

It was still raining when Eleanor pulled into the parking lot of the Lumbar Yard. As she got out of her car she felt a sharp pain in her back that took her breath away but straightened her spine in an attempt to look as though nothing was wrong. She was reminded of a dog she once owned when her children were young. The golden retriever would limp until they got out of the car to go to the vet. It must be a survival instinct. If they can't see any signs of weakness they won't shoot you she thought. She had been to see Dr. Baxter before and knew he would only make things better.

Dr. Baxter was a tall muscular man in his mid-forties. He kept his light brown hair short and out of his line of vision presumably enabling him to see his clients more clearly. What was clearly visible to Eleanor that Dr. Baxter did not seem to notice was the look of adoration his receptionist Vivian gave him as he strode into the waiting room to greet Eleanor. Although Eleanor hadn't been in for some time, she couldn't ever remember noticing that look on Vivian's face before, nor had she noticed Vivian dressing as provocatively, wearing her long dark hair down, or wearing quite as much makeup as she did now.

Dr. Baxter had never married as far as she knew, but rumor had it his one and only love had left town and become an obsession for him years ago—a sad tale for someone like Vivian who must have fallen under the handsome man's spell.

"Bone jour," said Dr. Baxter in an attempt at chiropractic humor. "I was hoping that would crack you up."

Eleanor hobbled into the examining room and explained the situation to Dr. Baxter. Her sense of humor was lacking at the moment. "Nothing 'humerus' today," she quipped. "I think it's more backbone."

"I forgot to put that bubble wrap under the table," he said as he wrapped her arms in front of her and cracked her back. "I know how satisfying it is for you to hear that popping sound."

"Next time, I just might put potato chips in my pockets," Eleanor teased. "That should give you a start."

After several adjustments, Eleanor stood and tentatively moved her body in several directions.

"Be sure to ice it when you get home," he cautioned, "and don't do anything strenuous for a few days. If it gives you anymore trouble, give us a call. Sometimes it takes more than one adjustment. Remember I've got your back, Eleanor." Eleanor simply nodded and left the office giving the lovely Vivian a wave on her way out.

"Bone giorno," she heard Dr. Baxter say as she closed the door.

As Eleanor drove home the wind continued to blow and the rain fell sideways. All she could think of was getting back to her snug home and out of the weather. Thank goodness for Dr. Baxter. If she had gone to Urgent Care there would have been hours of waiting in uncomfortable chairs, followed by a visit to the pharmacy to get a prescription for a muscle relaxer, and her back would still hurt. Usually, Eleanor didn't make use of what some considered alternative medicine. When she had asked her regular doctor about seeing a chiropractor, she had warned her not to let him adjust her neck—something about the manipulation causing a stroke, but Eleanor's pain was in her lower back, and it was already feeling better as she hurried home.

Eleanor obediently iced her back and sipped a cup of lemongrass tea as she snuggled under a plush throw by the fire. Outside, the wind raged and the rain pelted the windows in an angry attempt to get inside. Eleanor felt safe and lucky to have the shelter and warmth her home provided. She picked up the latest selection from her book club and began to read the first chapter when the doorbell rang. Feathers flew from his perch near the window to investigate while Eleanor gingerly went to see who could be out in this weather.

On the porch stood the dark figure that was Faith Strong, rain water dripping from every strand of her windblown hair, down her face onto her raincoat and pooling at her sensible black shoes.

"Faith, please come in out of the rain," Eleanor said with concern.

Faith stepped carefully inside while Eleanor quickly shut the storm out and took her guest's drenched coat and hung it out of the way. Feathers took one look at the visitor and quickly flew back to his window perch. He obviously preferred watching the raging storm outside to the icy expression on Faith's face.

"What brings you out in this weather?"

"I needed to speak with you about a pressing matter."

"Please sit down, Faith," Eleanor motioned to a seat near the fire. "I was having tea. Would you like a cup?"

Faith pursed her lips and rubbed her bony hands together as she sat and contemplated the offer the way an ascetic might consider something as simple as a warm cup of tea a sinful pleasure. Then she nodded.

Eleanor brought the tea and a plate of cookies and sat across from Faith wondering what in heaven's name this pressing matter could be that would bring Faith Strong to her door.

Faith took the tea and wrapped her cold hands around the cup ignoring the fat chocolate chip cookies whose sweet aroma wafted in the air.

"I need a place to live. Someone told me you own Mattie May's house and it's vacant. I'd like to rent it." Faith took a sip of tea and waited for a response.

Eleanor wanted to know why Faith would need a place to live when her father's massive house sat empty on the hill but she was reluctant to ask given her earlier experience with this woman. Perhaps her father left the house to someone else or maybe it needed repairs. There were several reasons and Eleanor didn't need to know. Mattie May had left the house to her and it was vacant. There was no reason not to rent it to Faith.

"I'll get the paperwork," she said and went into her office for the necessary forms. If Faith was surprised by Eleanor's lack of curiosity she didn't show it. They quickly came to an agreement on terms and Faith left with the keys to Mattie's house and Eleanor was left with a check and an uneasy feeling.

That Friday, Eleanor met her friends for coffee at the Boat House. They sat at their usual table by the large river rock fireplace and ate their usual breakfasts. Cleo always ordered scrambled eggs and bacon. Dede had one egg over easy, one piece of bacon and toast. Josephine enjoyed one piece of dry toast with peanut butter and blueberries on the side while Pearl ate the Piggle Wiggle sandwich without fail.

"What do you know about the reverend Strong and his family?" asked Eleanor.

"I heard he died," said Cleo. "Why do you want to know about him?"

"His daughters are renting Mattie May's house from me. I guess I'm just curious." Eleanor said. She knew if anyone had information worth knowing she would get it from someone in the coffee group. They had lived in the Waterton/Sand Beach area for decades.

"Why do they need to rent a place?" Pearl asked. "Didn't their father own a big house in Sand Beach?"

"I don't know and didn't want to pry," Eleanor said. "I met them briefly at Suzanna's. Faith seems to be a very private and super religious person."

"Maybe the house is haunted," said Cleo with a gleam in her green eyes.

"That may be truer than you think," added Josephine adjusting her intricate white hairdo. "From what I remember, that family wasn't a happy one. The house may hold some memories they don't want to revisit." Eleanor wondered if Josephine knew more than she could tell considering her vocation as a therapist.

"Faith was never what you might call normal. I remember her as a child—quiet, strange, always alone. Hope was born when she was a teenager and then her mother left—just walked out on her family without a word. The rumor was she'd run off with another man. Faith ended up taking care of Hope and then she disappeared too taking her sister with her. Reverend Strong didn't have much to say about it. I guess he expected women to leave him. He was so dedicated to his flock he didn't have time for the girls," Dede said. "It was a scandal at the time, but passed quickly. No one wanted the reverend to suffer any more than he already had."

"Was she one of your students?" Eleanor asked knowing that Waterton's mayor had once taught first grade and knew just about everyone in town, and their stories.

"No, I think she was homeschooled for the first few years, but she did go to our school later. Wasn't she in your class, Pearl?" Dede asked.

"Yes, but she was so quiet I hardly remember much about her," Pearl answered.

"What makes you say the family wasn't a happy one?" asked Eleanor.

"Reverend Strong was very strict. I've known several children of ministers and religious people who just couldn't live up to the expectations of their parents. It's not uncommon for them to rebel," Josephine added.

"If Charity left him because of his unrealistic expectations, why would she leave her girls behind?" asked Eleanor.

"Faith rebelled and Charity couldn't handle her," Dede said. "She must have thought her husband could, or she just didn't want them around cramping her new lifestyle."

"I knew some very religious kids in high school," Cleo said. "Everyone thought they were extraordinarily good. They weren't allowed to dance or watch television, but at night they would drive around and smash people's mailboxes."

"Everyone has a shadow self," Josephine said. "No one is perfect and when you deny that aspect of yourself, it comes out in unexpected ways."

"Right, we don't always know what goes on behind closed doors. The reverend and his wife may have been dealing with some awful behaviors from Faith. Maybe she was into drugs, sex, and rock and roll. Who knows? There was plenty of gossip back then. They certainly wouldn't want to air their dirty laundry to a congregation that expected perfection," Pearl said.

"That might account for her super religious lifestyle now," Josephine said. "She may be trying to atone for her past behavior."

"I always thought it was odd that a girl as wild as Faith would take her little sister with her. If I remember correctly, she was at least ten or fifteen years older than Hope," Dede said.

"It's possible Faith went to live with relatives somewhere else. No one ever really knew where she went. It was all speculation," Josephine said.

"I bet someone around here knows what kind of person Faith Strong was as a teen. She must have had some friends. Who would she be doing drugs, sex, and rock and roll with?" asked Cleo thoughtfully.

"This is not a mystery, Cleo," chided Pearl. "Sometimes it's better to let the past stay buried."

"Did Charity ever turn up?" asked Eleanor.

"Not that I know," offered Dede. "Reverend Strong was always a righteous man. He probably didn't want to pursue a wanton wife."

"I hope I don't regret my decision to rent to them." Eleanor sighed.

When Angus McBride knocked on Eleanor's door that evening he wasn't alone. Feathers flew through the house alerting Eleanor in his usual way whenever Angus visited. "Intruders, intruders!" he squawked. "Murder!" he added when he saw the creature that accompanied him because when Eleanor opened the door a shadow leaped up attempting to lick the surprise off her face.

"Down boy," Angus ordered. "I told him you didn't allow kissing on the first date, but he just doesn't listen."

"Angus, what have you done?" laughed Eleanor as she kneeled down to the dog's level and wrapped her arms around him in an attempt to control his unbridled enthusiasm.

"Eleanor Penrose, I'd like to introduce you to the newest member of the McBride family who is still nameless at this time. Nameless, this is the famous poet and illustrious food magician, Eleanor Penrose. Now sit," Angus ordered. The black lab did not respond but continued to wriggle and lick as Feathers flew around the house in distress. When the pup finally took notice of the gray bird he lost interest in Eleanor and began to bark and chase the bird from room to room with Eleanor and Angus in hot pursuit. Eventually, Angus captured the dog and Eleanor closed Feathers in her office.

"Welcome home," Eleanor said. Angus tried to include Eleanor in an embrace but could not hold her and a wriggling pet. "I'll get you a drink. I can't wait to hear how this transpired."

While Eleanor was in the kitchen, Angus made a bed for Nameless with Eleanor's fleecy throw and ordered him to lie down, but of course, he had other ideas and followed Angus into the kitchen.

"I missed you, Ellie," Angus said as he nuzzled her neck and wrapped his arms around her and began to cover her face with kisses.

"You know you are kissing a face that is covered in dog slime Eleanor reminded him. "There's no telling where that tongue has been."

"Ahhh darn," he groaned as he looked down to see Nameless relieving himself on his shoe. "I think this little shit is going to need some training."

"I hope that isn't going to be his name," Eleanor laughed.

After Angus and Eleanor finished eating the perfectly cooked tenderloin steaks, potatoes au gratin, and green salad she had prepared for dinner, they snuggled on the couch with the dog on Angus' lap.

"He seems to be exhausted," Eleanor noticed.

"I don't like that name any more than I like Little Shit," Angus joked.

"You know Dede's daughter got a small brown dog and named it Dog Martin," Eleanor said. "I think that's very clever."

Angus was not impressed. "At least she didn't name it Father Brown."

"How do you like Shadow?" Eleanor offered.

Angus shook his head. "Too long. I want a short, easy name like Rex or Spike."

"I've always wanted a dog named Scout," Eleanor said.

"I like it." Angus looked down at the sleepy pup the way he used to look at Eleanor. "I'd better get Scout home to his bed. Thanks for dinner, Ellie." Angus rose and put on his coat. "Do you want to go walking tomorrow? We can introduce Scout to the sand and salt of the beach."

Eleanor had a vision of a wet dog covered with sand tracking through her immaculate house. She nodded while Angus pecked her on the cheek and left with his new love. It didn't go unnoticed that for the first time Angus had come to dinner without flowers, or wine, or candy.

The following morning Eleanor stopped by Angus' house on her way to the beach. The sky was clear and the gulls circled while their cries filled the brisk fall air. It was perfect beachcombing weather and Eleanor was eager to watch Scout's reaction to a new environment. When Angus answered the door evidence of the pup was everywhere. Fragments of the morning newspaper were all over the living room, items of laundry were strewn about the floor, and one lonely slipper lay on the bear rug where Scout was blissfully sleeping.

"What happened?" Eleanor asked as she peered closely at her friend who appeared unshaven and bleary eyed.

"We didn't get much sleep last night," Angus explained. His thick brows spoke a language of their own and relayed his unhappy state. "It seems Scout is a night owl and can't sleep unless he's in my bed. We had to go out several times during the night and there was a great deal of whining and whimpering. Now he's exhausted."

"Who exactly was doing the whining and whimpering?" Eleanor seemed amused by the whole affair. Angus only lowered his heavy brows in a scowl that defied humor of any sort. "I know exactly what is needed," Eleanor said with authority. "Let's get him tired out on a long beach walk. Then you can go into town and buy him a big stuffed animal to sleep with and a comfortable bed of his own. By the looks of things, he needs some chew toys too. I read somewhere that there are no bad dogs, only bad owners."

"Great," Angus growled. "You take him on a walk while I take a nap."

"Come on," Eleanor urged as she picked up a sock and threw it at a reluctant Angus. "I'll get Scout while you put on your shoes."

Once exposed to the cool sea air and the roar of the surf, Angus got a second wind. He set Scout free to run to his heart's content while he and Eleanor delighted in watching the playful pup explore his new environment. Afraid at first of the foamy waves that rushed at him he later became intrepid, charging into them and barking to keep them at bay.

"Do you regret getting a dog?" Eleanor asked. "They take a great deal of energy."

"I did this morning after a sleepless night, but now I think he may be just the kind of company I need to keep me from becoming a couch potato," Angus confessed. "Why? Don't you think I'm up to the task?"

"Of course you're up to it, but having a pet can be constraining. You have to get a dog sitter whenever you want to go somewhere." Eleanor knew from personal experience that having a pet could cramp your lifestyle. Fortunately, she had many friends and family who offered to look after her bodacious bird.

"That's why I keep you around." Angus raised and lowered his thick brows and smiled revealing his perfect teeth and deep dimples. Eleanor didn't think that was funny and worried if Feathers would ever accept having a dog in her house.

"You didn't tell me about your hunting trip. Were you able to harvest anything?" she asked as they walked hand in hand.

"Nope, I'll just have to continue eating at your house this winter," Angus said, giving her hand a gentle squeeze.

"What about Michael? Did he shoot anything?" Eleanor regretted asking as soon as she saw the look on Angus' face.

"Even a blind squirrel finds a nut once in a while," he said sullenly. She knew the subject was closed until Angus wanted to talk about his son with whom he had recently discovered through a DNA service. She suspected that things were not going well on that front. Michael had retired from the Seattle Fire Department and had an extramarital affair with a private detective named Delia Parker. Eleanor knew Angus disapproved but was reluctant to give fatherly advice to a grown man whose relationship was still in the early stages of development.

"We should probably head back," Angus said looking at the dark clouds that gathered on the horizon. As they headed back, Angus whistled for Scout who unexpectedly responded by bounding toward them with wild puppy enthusiasm. The only problem being that he continued to run past them without stopping.

"Scout, come back here!" Angus began to jog after him while Eleanor quickened her pace. It wasn't long before the black dog was out of sight and neither one of them could keep up with him as he headed up the hill toward Angus' house. "I hope he knows where he lives," Angus panted as he and Eleanor made their way up the steep incline.

"I don't see any sign of him," Eleanor said as they reached Angus' house. "Do you suppose he's gone to my place?"

"There's nothing to do but chase him down," Angus replied. They hurried to Eleanor's huffing and puffing the entire way. With no sign of him there, they continued up the hill. Angus looked again at the encroaching clouds. "Maybe I should go get my truck. He travels a lot faster than we do." Eleanor nodded in agreement. There was no way she could run uphill after an energetic dog.

"I'll keep going," Eleanor said. "Maybe he's just around the next corner." By the time Angus drove up beside her she had covered a great deal of ground without a sign. "He could have left the lane, Angus. I'm afraid he could be anywhere."

"He isn't familiar with this place," Angus said, worried that he had already lost his newfound friend.

"Wait, I hear barking," Eleanor said as she climbed in the pickup. Angus followed the barks up the winding road that led to Reverend Strong's house at the top of the point. They stopped and left the truck at a wide spot in the road and continued on foot, following the sound of what they hoped was the lost dog. When the barking turned into a painful yip, Angus ran ahead where he came face to face with an angry Faith Strong wielding a shovel. It was obvious to him that she had been chasing Scout and probably had used the shovel as a weapon on his baby.

"Hey," he yelled. Upon seeing Angus, Scout ran behind him and growled menacingly at the shovel-wielding witch.

"Is that your beast?" Faith asked, pushing the shovel into the ground. "There's an ordinance in this county that requires he be on a leash."

"There's a law against hitting a dog with a shovel," Angus replied angrily. "It's called animal abuse."

"You best keep control of him. He tried to bite me. I was just defending myself," Faith replied.

"He's a pup and no threat to you," Angus said.

"The Bible warns to beware of dogs and evil workers, beware of the concision," Faith spoke as she walked closer to Angus until she was literally in his face. "As a dog returneth to his vomit, a fool returneth to his folly."

Angus could feel her hot breath on his face as she glared into his eyes but refused to give an inch. "You should get some help," he spoke calmly.

Faith's eyes widened as if seeing a truth newly discovered. "You have a demon," she hissed accusingly.

"You want to pet it?" he asked moving closer. Faith Strong recoiled as if struck by fire. When she backed away he easily scooped Scout up and walked quickly down the lane where he saw Eleanor hiding behind some brambles. "Did you catch all that?"

"I sure did," Eleanor said. "I didn't want to complicate matters by showing my face. I think it's better that I'm not on her bad side."

"Does she have a good side?" he asked.

"I don't know her very well, but she's renting Mattie's house from me," Eleanor admitted.

"What? How did that happen?" Angus was incredulous.

"I'm not sure." Eleanor related her experience with Faith and Hope at Suzanna's and her surprise visit from Faith during the rainstorm.

"I hope you don't regret it,." Angus said. Just as they climbed back into his pickup, the rain began to fall. "I need to give Scout a bath. He's covered with mud."

"What do you suppose she was doing with a shovel? It's not really the time of year for gardening," Eleanor said.

Angus shook his head. "I think she hit Scout with it. She reminds me of the Wicked Witch of the West. I expect to hear her theme song any minute."

Neither of them noticed Scout drop the bone he carried in his mouth or saw it roll under the car seat.

Eleanor made herself a cup of coffee and sat down with the crossword puzzle. Feathers perched behind her and cooed words of encouragement. "Twenty down, twenty down," he squawked. When the telephone rang, Eleanor was ready for a break.

"Hello, Mrs. Penrose. This is Megan Fields. I know you offered to watch my baby and I'm calling your bluff. I've got a dentist appointment today and my babysitter has bailed on me at the last minute. I'm sure it will only be for a couple of hours and I wouldn't ask, but I'm desperate. I've had a toothache for several days and I really need to take care of it."

Eleanor knew Megan. She lived in the yellow cottage on Ocean Street and Eleanor had indeed offered to watch her baby boy in a pinch knowing how difficult it was for a mom to get away. "Of course, I'd be delighted," she said.

"I'll bring him right over."

By the time Eleanor took her coffee cup to the kitchen and cautioned Feathers to be on his best behavior, Megan was at her door.

"Thank you so much, Mrs. Penrose," Megan gushed. "He's been fed and I should be back before he needs more to eat. Diapers are in the bag. I'll be at Dr. Larson's office if you need to contact me."

Out the door she flew leaving baby Willy staring into Eleanor's startled blue eyes. Before he could gather the energy to complain, Feathers flew to Eleanor's shoulder for a closer look at the tiny human. Willy's eyes grew even wider, and his pudgy fingers reached out to grab the gray parrot who began a litany of strange sound effects. Willy was mesmerized.

"It's been a while since there was a baby in this house," Eleanor informed Willy who must have been about three months old. If she remembered correctly, babies slept a great deal. "This should be a snap, Feathers." Willy could not take his eyes off Feathers who continued to click and chortle. It didn't take long before Feathers lost interest in the child and flew to his perch by the window and Willy nodded off in Eleanor's arms. It felt good to hold the warm bundle but Eleanor decided he would sleep better if she put him in the middle of her big bed. She surrounded him with a pillow barrier but remembered to lay him on his back to prevent suffocation—just the opposite of when she laid her own little ones down. Then she returned to the kitchen to finish tidying up. When the doorbell rang she wasn't surprised to find Angus on her porch with an energetic Scout eager to come inside.

"Want to walk with us?" Angus asked as he stepped inside.

"Of course," Eleanor said, wiping her hands on a dish towel. There was a cry from down the hall.

"Ellie, are you entertaining someone in your bedroom?" Angus asked in mock indignation.

"Well, yes," she answered mysteriously. "Follow me and I'll introduce you to Willy." Eleanor led the way with Angus, Scout, and Feathers following close behind. Eleanor picked Willy up and then quickly put him back down on the bed. "I think Master Willy has soiled himself," she said, wrinkling her nose. She rifled through his bag and proceeded to change his dirty diaper while Angus began to babble in baby talk. Eleanor had never seen this side of Angus—big, masculine Angus cooing nonsense words of comfort to a tiny baby.

"You better let me do that," he said, interrupting his infantile conversation as he watched Eleanor navigate Willy's nether regions. She simply looked at him with raised brows. "You're not familiar with that equipment," he continued.

Eleanor could not believe her ears nor her eyes as Angus gently nudged her out of the way and cleaned Willy's bottom with a wet wipe. "I certainly know how to change a diaper," she declared indignantly.

"Well, you broke yours off," he said and smiled wickedly.

Eleanor wanted to throw the dirty diaper at him but broke out in hysterical laughter instead.

Willy was a big hit with everyone, including the pets, and they were all sad to see him go when Megan came to collect him but they had put off their walk long enough. The wonderful gift of retirement was that walks could be put off and there was always time to be charming because there was always time.

"Let's walk the trail," Angus suggested. "I'm already tired of sandy dog prints everywhere."

Eleanor didn't have the heart to warn him of muddy dog prints and fur that would adhere to everything he owned. Of course, that would come later when the temperature rose, and Scout began to shed his winter coat. Then there was the ever present scent of wet dog that would soon emanate from every corner of Angus' man cave. Eleanor held her tongue and wondered if she could hold her nose when the odor became too much. There was always the possibility that Angus would keep Scout well- groomed and avoid the pitfalls of doggy ownership, but something told her this wasn't in the cards.

As they walked east on the trail the ocean continued to roar and the moist marine air condensed leaving little beads glistening in their hair. Angus released Scout from his lead and watched as he ran ahead to sniff every tall blade of grass and mark his territory.

"He's not really a puppy," Eleanor noted as she watched the gangly canine. "How did you get him?"

"Well, he's a lab so he'll be a puppy for at least three years," Angus said. "He belonged to Michael, but he couldn't keep him."

Eleanor waited silently for Angus to offer more.

"Michael left Angela and moved in to an apartment that doesn't allow pets. Angela refused to keep the dog. I think she's royally pissed." Angus sighed. "I can't blame her. Michael's having a midlife crisis. He took early retirement from the fire department, sent his boys off to live their own lives, had an affair, and now he thinks life with Angela is boring. He doesn't know what he's giving up."

"So is he still seeing Delia, or are you calling her the other woman now?" Eleanor asked.

"Yes, but he's not committed to her. He's free now and wants to play the field. The two of them want to go into business together. Delia's invited Michael to work in her private detective agency," Angus laughed. "I'm sure it was Delia who got Michael the dog and named him Sherlock Bones."

"Clever," Eleanor said. "Why didn't she keep the dog?"

"Neither of them wants the responsibility a dog requires. They don't think things through. They saw a cute little ball of fur and then found out it needed to be fed, walked, and cleaned up after. As old as they are they still act like children," Angus said.

"So why did you come to the rescue?" Eleanor asked.

"I like the little guy. I've got the time to be there for him and he's good company. Sometimes I get a little lonely," Angus admitted.

They had walked almost to Mattie May's house when Scout's furious barking alerted them to the fact that he might once again be in trouble. Angus broke into a jog with Eleanor following his lead. Before they reached the gray shingled cottage's white picket fence, Scout came running toward them at warp speed and Angus saw the front door closing behind a dark figure.

"I hope that's not Faith going after her gun," Angus said. "Come, Scout, let's get out of here before she realizes you're the dog whose owner has a demon." Eleanor glanced quickly in the direction of the house and noted Mattie May's old Lincoln Town car parked out front. She wondered if Faith and Hope were driving it, and if they had officially moved in. When she gave Faith the keys to the house, the car key was also on the ring. Perhaps she decided to park her own car in the small garage and leave Mattie's out in the weather. Being a landlord was new to Eleanor and she had forgotten about the vintage car. She didn't relish the idea of bringing it up now. Perhaps she would have to store the car somewhere else. In the meantime, Scout continued to run back in the direction of Eleanor's house as if his tail were on fire. Angus and Eleanor hurried after him.

"Maybe I'm not up to having a young dog," Angus said as he realized Scout was once again out of sight.

"It's good for him to run off that excess energy," Eleanor responded. "It won't hurt either of us to get our hearts racing a bit. I'm more afraid of Faith than of losing Scout."

Angus slowed to catch his breath then whistled three short blasts. They were both surprised when Scout appeared around the bend in the lane, but even more so when they saw that he carried something in his mouth.

"What did you get into now, boy?" Angus bent to retrieve the item while Eleanor frowned as she recognized what it was.

"Angus, is that a bone?" Eleanor asked.

Angus managed to extract it from Scout and studied it closely while Scout danced around jumping up in an attempt to get it once again. The bone was old and covered with mud much like the small bone Angus had discovered on the floor of his truck when he had gone into town.

"It looks like it could be a rib bone from some animal. I guess Sherlock Bones is a good name for him after all."

Eleanor took the apple pie out of the oven and placed it on the counter to cool just as the telephone rang. "Ellie, there's a big storm coming in. I'm going into town to get supplies. Is there anything you need?" Angus must have smelled the apple pie. Eleanor knew Angus had a gift of showing up right when food was ready. She quickly made an inventory of staples.

"I could use some vanilla bean ice cream," she said, "And some coffee creamer. There's bound to be a power outage so I'll make a pot of stew." She thought a bit. "Bring me some cold cuts and a loaf of crusty bread."

"I'm on it."

Something disturbed her peace of mind. She remembered Mattie's vintage Town Car sitting outside and knew she had to move it out of the storm. A car like that might leak and there was nothing worse than a sour smelling old automobile. Eleanor made her way into her garage, moved a few boxes to make room for the beast and hurried to Mattie's house to collect the car. As she walked along the lane she could feel the threat of the storm approaching. There was a flurry of leaves and the branches of the large hemlocks waved overhead. The sky darkened as clouds moved in from the southwest and swirled above her. She didn't relish the idea of seeing Faith Strong again, but Mattie's car was special and Eleanor put duty ahead of her distaste. When Hope answered her knock, Eleanor was relieved.

"Hi, Mrs. Penrose." Hope seemed delighted to see her. "Please come in. I've just put on a pot of coffee. Would you like a cup?"

"Oh no, thank you," Eleanor declined. "I just dropped by to pick up the car. It totally slipped my mind that it was in the little garage and you might need the space for your own car. It belonged to a friend of mine so I'll just move it to my place if you'll get the key for me. It was on the key chain along with the house key."

"Oh yes." Hope went immediately to a bowl on the kitchen counter, plucked the keys out, and began to slip the car key off the ring.

"How do you like the house so far?" Eleanor asked as she watched Hope's perfectly manicured fingers at work.

"It's very cozy here. I love it." She said with enthusiasm. "Daddy's house is big and cold. This is much better."

"Well, be prepared for a storm. I understand we're in for a doozy and the power is often out here and cell service is sketchy," Eleanor warned as she took the key. "You may want to bring in your garbage can and get some candles handy."

"Oh, I'll be sure to do that. Good bye, Mrs. Penrose."

Eleanor was out the door just as a gust of wind slammed the screen door against the house. She managed to get in the car and sat for a while wondering how Mattie maneuvered this boat of a vehicle down the narrow lane. If Mattie could do it, so could she. It was a close fit into the garage, too, but once inside Eleanor gave a sigh of relief, closed up the garage, and went inside her cozy nest to hunker until the storm passed.

While Angus drove to town with her list of supplies, Eleanor made a pot of beef stew, built a fire in the fireplace and read two chapters in her book club selection. It was dark and the wind was joined by a fierce rain that obscured the lights of the village. Feathers frantically flew through the house and finally perched on the back of the sofa where he pretended to read over Eleanor's shoulder.

Angus and Scout blasted through the door along with the raging wind. Eleanor quickly closed the door behind them just as the lights went out leaving the glow from the fireplace the only illumination in the room.

"Boy, I'm glad to get out of that!" Angus found his way into the kitchen and deposited two bags filled with necessities, including vanilla bean ice cream. "We may be forced to eat the ice cream before it melts if the power stays out."

"Not a problem," Eleanor reassured him while she dried Scout with a towel and wiped his muddy paws.

Together they turned on Eleanor's battery operated lantern, dished up bowls of tender beef stew with savory carrots and potatoes along with crusty bread and fresh butter and dined by candlelight. Neither of them noticed Feathers picking beefy tidbits from the pot and feeding them to Scout. When the two became friends was a mystery no one really cared to explore.

In the morning, Angus and Scout did a walk around Eleanor's house to check for storm damage. "I didn't find anything serious," Angus reported. "One of your flower pots was knocked over by a branch that broke off a nearby tree. I'll take Scout home and we'll check out my place."

"I need to get some exercise," Eleanor said. "Let me take Scout for a walk."

Angus looked skeptical. "Don't lose him now, and don't make him fall in love with you. He's supposed to be mine."

Eleanor only smiled as she put on her walking shoes and headed toward the beach with Scout. The day had dawned with a clear sky. The wind and rain had washed away what was left of summer. Fall was here and winter was not far behind. Eleanor often walked the shore after a storm looking for gifts left by the sea, but today she was leery. The ocean seemed angry and reluctant to give up its rage. The tide was out but coming back in and she could see several children standing on a driftwood log surrounded by the surf. She was alarmed and began to run toward them yelling a warning as she went.

"Get off that log," she cried and waved her hands over her head in an attempt to get their attention. A man on the beach trying to capture the group in a photo watched in dismay.

"What's the matter?" he asked.

"Did you know there's a sneaker wave alert? That's very dangerous! The ocean is powerful and can lift that log and roll it over on top of them."

The man reluctantly signaled to the children to abandon their perch and the group moved along laughing. Just then a sneaker waved rolled in carrying the log and causing everyone to scamper quickly out of the way. Eleanor decided today was not a day to trust the sea and left to walk a different path. As she and Scout ascended the hill, she turned and saw yet another group of people had climbed on the log. "Flatlanders," she muttered to herself shaking her head as she continued on her way. She reluctantly released Scout who was pulling on the leash in a desire to run.

Passing Mattie's house Eleanor slowed and noticed how dark and empty it looked. There didn't seem to be any damage that she could see. Scout had rushed ahead and was sniffing around. Eleanor hoped he wouldn't do his business here. She had no desire to run into Faith and was suddenly glad that the house looked empty. Nevertheless, she hurried by calling to Scout as she fled hoping he would follow without an incident. He blitzed by her in a flurry of puppy playfulness. Eleanor looked up and noticed the top of a huge hemlock tree had blown off and lay along the lane. It could have done some serious damage if it had fallen over the lane or in a different direction. Two large limbs hung tenuously from its trunk waiting for some unsuspecting walkers to pass underneath before falling on them and possibly breaking their necks. Suddenly Eleanor wanted to be home where she felt safe. She whistled to Scout and he came once again with something in his mouth. This time he refused to let her see what it was, and she had to chase him as he teased—first getting close, his head down, paws stretched in front and puppy tail in the air and then running away. Finally, she was able to grab his collar and pry what appeared to be another bone from his mouth but this one was different—it had teeth.

The mysterious jawbone lay on a piece of newspaper on the dining room table while Eleanor Googled photos of human skeletal remains to prove its origins as she waited for Angus to return from his trip to town. Some shingles from his roof had blown off during the storm and he had gone to Waterton's building supply to get materials to fix it. Eleanor had found a note on his door when she went to return Scout. Patience was not one of her virtues. Her mind was spinning with theories about this bone and she needed to share them with her coffee friends. She wrapped the newspaper around the jawbone, put Scout in the car, and drove to Dede's house to meet with them. It was urgent.

"Do you think Faith Strong has anything to do with this? Scout was in her yard," Eleanor said thoughtfully. Four heads leaned in to better view the evidence that now sat on Dede's dining room table.

"Those do look like human teeth," said Josephine.

"It's gross and disgusting," said Pearl. "How old do you think it is?"

"I think it is Charity Strong's jawbone. Maybe she was murdered and never ran off with another man after all," Cleo opined.

"It could be anyone's for all we know. How did Scout get it? Eleanor, you're not sure where he picked it up. Perhaps it's just an animal bone," reasoned Dede.

"The other day Angus and I were walking when Scout ran to Reverend Strong's house. Faith was there with a shovel. Angus thinks she meant to strike Scout with it. She could have been digging up a body," Eleanor said.

"Now you sound like Cleo," Pearl accused. "She could have simply been digging up her dahlias."

"It's the second time Scout brought back a bone. The first time Angus and I were near Mattie's house where Faith and Hope are renting when Scout had something that looked like a rib bone and then today, he had this when we were in the same area."

"It sounds more and more like someone dumped an animal carcass near there and Scout is returning to get the bones," Dede said. Every time he heard the word bones, Scout looked up expecting some command. He and Dede's Doogie lay on the floor experiencing doggy ennui.

"Maybe," said Josephine, "but this bone has been buried for a long time. Just look at the discoloration and how the dirt is packed between the teeth. And then there's this clean part where it must have been recently broken." Once more the heads leaned over the bone to observe it more closely. It was obviously a piece of the lower jaw that had been snapped in the middle with two incisors missing near the break.

"Does anyone recognize these teeth?" asked Cleo as she used her napkin to rub some of the grit from a lower molar revealing a glint of gold.

"I don't know any animals who can afford gold crowns," said Dede.

"These are definitely human remains," Josephine agreed.

"Ewww," said Pearl. "I have a very bad feeling about this."

"It looks like we have another mystery to solve." Cleo rubbed her hands together in delight.

"I'd better call Angus," Eleanor said and picked up her cell phone.

Angus studied the jawbone closely as it sat on Dede's table. "He could have picked it up anywhere," Angus said. "You said he was out of sight and off the lane for a while."

"Yes, but he was also in Mattie's yard sniffing around." Eleanor couldn't let go of the feeling that Faith Strong was involved in some way. "I guess I'm suspicious because Faith had that shovel the last time we saw her near Reverend Strong's house," Eleanor said. "What was she digging up this time of year?"

"We will leave that up to Officer McGraw," Angus said with authority. He knew Eleanor and her meddling coffee club friends would be all over this. "This is a cold case, ladies. It could be evidence in a murder investigation or a missing person's case. The bone is old. You don't have the skills or the equipment to solve it, so let it go." Angus gave each of them his sternest detective scowl. It was difficult to argue with the man when he used his impressive eyebrows to punctuate his command.

She knew he was right and he was. As soon as Angus and Scout left with the jawbone to take it to the police, Eleanor and her friends began speculating about the evidence. "I'll put on a fresh pot of coffee," said Dede.

"So what do we know for sure?" asked Josephine as she took out her pen to make a list.

"Scout found a human jawbone somewhere in the vicinity of Mattie's house that is now being rented by Faith and Hope Strong," Eleanor offered.

"The jawbone had a gold crown," added Dede.

"Eleanor saw Faith with a shovel at her father's house," Cleo reminded them.

"Charity Strong disappeared over twenty years ago," Pearl said.

"And the bones appeared after Faith and Hope returned to Sand Beach," Josephine said. "I don't think that's a coincidence.

"We can't say for sure that the bones belong to Charity but I think they do," Cleo said. "My theory is Reverend Strong killed her and buried her body somewhere in Sand Beach and Faith dug them up after he died."

"Why would she do that?" asked Pearl. "It's not like anyone was looking for Charity or suspected any foul play."

"Perhaps her father confessed on his deathbed," Cleo persisted.

"Maybe Reverend Strong didn't kill her. Maybe Faith killed her and she wanted to move the evidence because she was afraid someone would find the body if she sold the house," Dede speculated.

"That makes sense, but why would Faith kill her mother?" asked Eleanor. "If Charity was going to leave her husband, he might kill her, but what would Faith's motive be?"

"So far we don't have any facts to go on," Josephine said. "We need to make another list—a list of information we need to learn."

"It would help to know why Faith was digging," Pearl said.

"What exactly was going on back then between Faith and her parents?" Josephine pondered. "That kind of information would give us insight into a motive."

"If we can find out who Faith's friends were at the time, they might tell us if she was on drugs or doing other things that her parents wouldn't condone," Cleo said.

"We could also ask Charity's friends. Maybe she said something about a lover or her desire to leave her husband," said Pearl.

"I remember there was a lot of gossip about her disappearance. We'd have to tread carefully. It would be easy to get misinformation from the wrong people," Dede cautioned.

"Yes, but where there's smoke there's often fire, so even bad information can lead to a clue," Cleo said.

"Do any of us know who Charity's friends were?" asked Josephine.

"Someone from her church might know something," Dede said, "Although they might be reluctant to gossip."

"I doubt Charity would share information about a lover with anyone in her husband's church. They would tell their husband and then it would get back to Reverend Strong," Cleo said.

"Maybe that's what happened," suggested Eleanor. "I wonder how the rumor about her leaving him got started."

"Faith was in high school when Cary was teaching there. I'll ask him if he remembers anything unusual," Pearl said. "My husband has a remarkable memory and he also has a collection of yearbooks."

"I can find out what Faith plans to do with her father's house. She *is* renting from me so I can simply ask as an interested landlord," Eleanor said.

"We have a lot of work to do," said Josephine.

When Eleanor returned to Sand Beach, she noticed a police car parked near Angus' house. Evidently the ladies were not the only ones on the case.

Eleanor walked quickly down the lane carrying a large wrench. The last thing she wanted to do was draw attention as she visited Faith Strong. She had called ahead and told Faith she needed to check the hot water heater after the power outage to be sure it was functioning properly. Truthfully, Eleanor had absolutely no knowledge of hot water heaters whatsoever.

"Come in, Mrs. Penrose," Hope greeted her with a warm smile.

"Please call me Eleanor," she replied.

"I just baked some oatmeal cookies. Would you like one?" Hope offered.

"Yes, they smell delicious." Eleanor's least favorite cookie was oatmeal but she made the sacrifice in order to get the information she needed.

"Please sit down and I'll get you a cup of tea," Hope continued. "It's so very seldom that we get company."

"Is your sister at home?" asked Eleanor.

"I think she's reading her Bible. Sometimes she sits for hours in her room reading and praying. She is the most pious person I know," Hope said.

"Really . . . does she have any other hobbies? I noticed the other day she was digging near your father's house. Does she garden?" Eleanor pried.

"Not really. That must have been when she was moving the roses. Our mother loved roses and planted several bushes in a small garden by the house. Faith didn't want them damaged when the crew comes to work on the house, so she moved them to a bed farther away."

"Oh, are you remodeling the house?" Eleanor asked.

"Yes, I thought Faith told you when she rented this place." Hope seemed surprised. "Faith is turning the house into a church. She plans to start her own church right here in Sand Beach."

"That's an interesting concept. What kind of church will it be?" Eleanor probed.

"It will be a very Christian church. Faith will be the minister so I'm sure it will follow the laws and tenets of the Bible very strictly," Hope explained. "She's going to all call it Faith Christian Church."

"I see. Does Faith have a following already? Does she plan to appeal to her father's congregation?"

"I don't think so," Hope lowered her voice to a whisper, "I'm fairly certain she will be the only one holy enough to attend."

"'The words of a whisperer are like dainty morsels to some but to others are like deadly wounds.'" The solemn voice that came from the doorway startled both Eleanor and Hope.

Faith, standing straight as a board and dressed all in black, was holding her Bible.

Hope put her hand over her pouty lips in a gesture that said she wished to put her words back. Eleanor didn't pause or apologize. "Your sister is a very good baker."

"I thought you were here to check the water heater," Faith said without emotion.

"Yes, of course." Eleanor found the water heater and tinkered with some knobs making as much noise as she could with her wrench, then returned to the kitchen after what she hoped was a convincing time span. "Everything seems to be in order. If you have any difficulties, don't hesitate to call." As she walked away from the house she felt the steely gaze of Faith Strong on her back but she was not intimidated. Looking down on the gravel driveway her beachcombing eye caught sight of something unusual. She bent to pick up what she thought was a milky stone, but on closer examination proved to be a tooth.

Angus and Officer McGraw had spent several hours searching the brush along the lane near Mattie's house and had come up empty-handed. Even with the expert assistance of Scout, alias

Sherlock Bones, they were not able to turn up anything of interest.

"I can't believe *you* found more evidence," Angus said incredulously. After all he was the trained professional. "Tell me exactly where the tooth was."

"I think you should just breathe and settle down, Angus." Eleanor's mock concern just made him more frustrated. "Let me get you a drink."

Angus tilted his head to the side as he looked at Eleanor beneath his lowered brows. "A drink would be good."

"I found the tooth in the gravel in front of Mattie's house." Eleanor handed Angus two fingers of his favorite Crown Royal.

"What were you doing at Faith Strong's house?" he asked suspiciously. "I can't imagine she invited you to tea."

"I was just checking to make sure everything was okay after the big wind," Eleanor said. "I am a landlady now and I take the responsibility very seriously. Would you like to stay for dinner? I'm making lamb chops with feta cheese."

Angus sipped his drink and smiled. He knew Eleanor wanted to know something and he also knew he was going to tell her.

After Angus put the last bite of roasted butternut squash with garlic and parsley in his mouth and wiped the residue of marinated cheese from his mustache, he sighed and leaned back in his chair and looked lovingly at Eleanor who sipped her wine. What was it that made her so lovable?

"Do you have room for dessert?" she asked sweetly.

"What kind of dessert?" he asked with a twinkle in his eye.

"Lemon chiffon cake," said Eleanor as she rose from the table.

With catlike swiftness Angus stood and caught her in a tender embrace and delved deeply into her blue eyes. "I swear you are a witch. Just what magic are you practicing, Ellie? What do you want from me?"

"Angus, you're so dramatic. Let me go and help me with these dishes before you upset Feathers."

Feathers had been unusually quiet. He had not alerted Eleanor of Angus' arrival or given him the stink eye. It seemed as if the feisty bird had made an uneasy alliance with the black dog and the two were plotting some diabolical plan as they loitered in the kitchen.

Angus couldn't conceal his disappointment. He was sure Eleanor was fishing for clues about the mysterious bones and he wanted to please her. He began to babble giving away information about the bones. "We couldn't search the Strong house or grounds without a warrant, but it's in the works. I showed the rib bone to Andy McGraw as soon as I found it and he sent it to a lab for testing, along with a bone I found in the truck, so we should know more in another day or so."

"You found a bone in the truck?" Eleanor was surprised.

"I didn't think much about it at the time, but I think Scout brought it along with him that first time we encountered Faith with the shovel. It looks like another rib bone," Angus said. "The jawbone is definitely human and by the look of it, it belongs to a small woman. The new evidence of the tooth that you found in the driveway gives us reason to get another warrant to search Mattie's place."

"Can't I give you permission to search Mattie's?" asked Eleanor. "The property *is* mine."

"No, the renter has to give permission," Angus said.

"Do you think it's Charity Strong?" asked Eleanor as she loaded the dishwasher.

"That would be my guess," Angus admitted.

"Were you here when she went missing?" Eleanor asked.

"Yes. There was never an investigation. Reverend Strong never filed a missing person's report but convinced everyone she left him for some man she met at a retreat. No one ever doubted it." Angus said. "Later, when Faith left with Hope, he told his congregation the girls were living with relatives in Alaska. No one questioned that either. I guess we were gullible."

"Wait a minute." Eleanor hurried to her office and returned with the check she'd received from Faith for the rental house. "This check is from a bank in Alaska. Maybe Charity isn't dead. Has anyone asked her daughters if she might be living there?"

"Not yet, my guess is the police don't want to tip their hand. There hasn't been a positive identification, but this bank could give us some information that might be useful." Angus jotted down the name of the bank on a piece of paper and put it in his pocket.

"So if the bones are Charity's, do you think her husband killed her?" Eleanor asked.

"It seems likely, but I'd never presume that. It depends on what the bones tell us," Angus said. "We need to know for sure they belong to her, and we need to find out where they are buried and what's left of Charity Strong to learn the truth." Angus didn't mention that he planned to send Michael and Delia to Juneau to check up on the Strong sisters and make sure Charity wasn't living there.

Eleanor was satisfied. She had information to report to the coffee group. Angus was satisfied in other ways. Both of them were too sated for dessert but later when they went to the kitchen for the lemon chiffon cake they found it partly eaten and two very guilty looking pets lounging on the kitchen floor among crumbs and lemon curd. There was no mystery there.

Friday came and Eleanor was eager to learn what her friends had discovered about the Strong family. She pulled into the Boat House parking lot and realized everyone was there ahead of her. This was a first considering Dede was almost always late.

"Am I late?" asked Eleanor as she sat down at their usual table near the stone fireplace.

"No, we just got here too," Cleo stated.

"I did make an effort to get here early since I brought these," Pearl said pointing to four volumes of the local high school's yearbooks. "These are the years Faith Strong would have been in high school."

"Have you checked out her photos?" asked Josephine taking charge of the first yearbook titled *A Picture in Time*.

"I bookmarked a few pages, but she's not in very many," Pearl said.

"Oh my," said Cleo, "She was definitely into something grunge or goth or whatever it was that involved black hair, black lipstick, tattoos, and piercings."

"You can almost feel the anger emanating out of that photo," Dede observed.

"Was she in any clubs or organizations?" asked Josephine.

"Not that I can see," said Cleo as she studied the appendix. "But here's a picture of her sitting next to other girls at what looks like a pep rally."

"That looks like Megan Fields," Eleanor noted.

"I think it's Megan's older sister, Martha," Dede said. "She died that year in a car accident."

"I wonder if Megan remembers Faith. Maybe she knows something her sister told her." Eleanor was already rehearsing her inquisition of Megan Fields.

"She doesn't appear in the second book at all," Josephine said. "Was she homeschooled?"

"Cary remembers people talking about her. They said her parents sent her to a special school because they couldn't control her. Something like residential care. Evidently, she was behaving promiscuously and hanging out with a bad crowd," Pearl said.

"I wonder if they considered a lobotomy," said Cleo. "That's what they used to do to wild young girls who couldn't be controlled."

"That and incarceration in mental institutions where they treated them for nymphomania," added Josephine who had just finished watching a miniseries set in the Victorian era.

"So we were right about the sex, drugs, and rock and roll," said Dede.

"Does Cary remember who else was in that crowd?" asked Eleanor.

"He mentioned a couple of names, I don't remember now. Two guys . . . Donnie Gold and Jude something.

"Jude Thorn," Dede said. "He was a thorn in everyone's side back then, but grew up to be a hard worker. He still lives just outside of Waterton—works as a carpenter. Donnie Gold runs the sanitary service and the recycling center. He turned out to be a savvy businessman. I can't imagine why they would hang out with Faith. They were both out of high school by the time she got there."

"Maybe they were getting something out of a relationship with a troubled young girl they couldn't get anywhere else," Pearl suggested.

"That must have been a very effective residential care facility for Faith," Josephine said, picking up the third book and pointing to a picture of a totally different looking person. "She looks like the girl next door." Gone were the spiky dyed hair, black lipstick, and piercings. There was no makeup at all and her hair was styled in a low ponytail. "She was beautiful."

"Wow, what a transformation!" Cleo said.

"I'd like to know where that facility is." Josephine knew she couldn't get that kind of information. She had too much integrity to violate the rules of confidentiality.

Eleanor leafed through the fourth yearbook. There was a senior photo of Faith that showed a very serious girl with her hair pulled tightly away from her pretty face. Eleanor could already see the beginnings of the Faith that she knew. "She joined the choir her senior year, and here's a photo of her at a homecoming football game. Is that her mother?"

The ladies all leaned in to study the picture. A petite woman was seated beside Faith holding a little girl on her lap. The photo was grainy but it was clear that the woman's chiseled features and high cheekbones were perfect and there was no denying her happiness in the moment.

"Yes, I'm sure that's Charity Strong," said Dede. "I forgot she was so small and lovely."

"Isn't that Dr. Baxter sitting beside her?" Eleanor asked.

"Hmmm, I think it is," said Pearl. "Boy isn't he a hunk!"

"Reverend Strong must be this old bald man sitting next to Faith. He looks years older than Charity or maybe this picture is a bad likeness," Eleanor noted.

"No, that's what he looked like. It was always curious that Charity married a man so much older than she was especially when she was such a beauty. She could have had any man she wanted," said Dede. "People often mistook her for his daughter."

"Strange that we don't wonder why the Reverend married a girl so young," commented Eleanor.

"We don't always know why people are drawn to each other," Josephine said. "Sometimes there are wounds that need healing. Charity may have had issues with a father figure that she needed to work out through her relationship with her husband."

"I learned that Faith and Hope were living in Alaska. She paid her rent with a check from the First Bank of Alaska in Juneau. Angus is checking to see if Charity might be living there. Also, Faith is turning her father's house into Faith Christian Church," Eleanor reported. "Hope told me Faith was moving her mother's rose bushes to protect them from the workmen. Oh, and I found a tooth in the driveway of Mattie's house. Angus and Officer McGraw searched the area along the lane but didn't find anything and are waiting on a warrant to search the grounds of the Strong estate."

"Why don't they just ask Faith about her mother?" asked Cleo.

"They want to be sure it's Charity's bones before they start asking questions that might put suspects on their guard," Eleanor clarified. "At least that's what I understood."

"Doesn't Angus think someone already moved the body?" asked Josephine. "It seems obvious that bones appeared after the two sisters returned. Faith was digging. Connecting the dots isn't rocket science."

"The police always need proof," Dede commented. "If Faith *did* move the bones, she might get rid of them right away if she knows the police are on to her. Who knows, maybe she just found them when she was digging up the roses and left them there."

"If she was innocent, wouldn't she alert the police after finding a skeleton in the flower bed?" asked Cleo.

"Maybe she thinks her father killed her mother and she wants to protect him," Pearl speculated. "After all, both her mom and dad are dead. What good would it do to dig all this up now?"

"If that is true, she'd have to choose whose reputation to clear. If her father killed her mother, he's a murderer and she's a victim, but if she leaves everything as it is, her mother seems like a wanton woman and her father is the victim," Dede said.

"Or her mother *was* a wanton woman and he *was* a murderer who killed her rather than let her go," Cleo argued.

"Maybe Faith killed her and moved her bones so the workmen wouldn't accidentally stumble over them during the remodel," Eleanor added.

"An investigation might delay the building of her church," said Pearl.

"What about the mystery man? Maybe he killed her and buried her there to implicate her husband," said Cleo.

"Maybe it *is* rocket science," sighed Josephine. "Did anyone learn who Charity may have confided in about a lover?"

"I tried to talk to someone from her church, Prissy Sullivan to be exact. She was very defensive. I think she and Charity were close at one time. She denied knowing anything about the scandal but was interested in the fact that the sisters were back. She claims she and Charity had an argument over some petty issue involving church funds and she never heard from her again," Dede offered. "She said Charity didn't have any special friends. She treated everyone as if they were her sisters."

"I didn't expect to get any dirt from that holier than thou group," grumbled Josephine. "My guess is she kept her secrets secret and if she was having an affair she only confided in her lover."

"Who would know the identity of her lover?" asked Pearl.

"Waterton is a small town, someone must have known," Dede said.

Eleanor immediately thought of Gladys Reyburg who kept the history of Waterton County well preserved in her magnificent ninety-year-old brain. Even though she lived at the Riverside Retirement Home now, she was still an excellent resource when it came to learning the facts of unrecorded social events.

"I could visit Gladys," Eleanor offered.

"Excellent!" They all agreed and finished their breakfasts.

Eleanor was no stranger to Riverside Retirement Home. She often visited there and read to Gladys whose eyesight was failing. At ninety plus years, Gladys Reyburg still had an enormous amount of style and grace. Her face lit up when she saw Eleanor walking down the hallway and she greeted her with a hug.

"I haven't seen you in a while," she said. "Have you been behaving yourself?"

"The summer is always busy, Gladys. How have you been?" Eleanor asked.

"Well ninety is hard, but I'm persistent. I just keep breathing. Would you like to have a cup of coffee with me? I was just going to the café."

"Yes, that sounds delightful."

They got their coffee and sat at a small table in the corner. Eleanor looked around at the various residents that shared the space. Many of them were in wheelchairs or used walkers. Some of them seemed sad while others were totally out of it. Four ladies sat at a nearby table and giggled uncontrollably. A couple of people waved at Gladys as they made their way out of the café.

"What's on your mind, Eleanor? It's not like you to drop in unexpectedly. I suspect you need some information," Gladys said.

"You need to keep what I'm about to tell you to yourself. I found some bones that may belong to Charity Strong and I want to know what you remember about her. Her daughters have come back from Alaska and are living in Sand Beach." Eleanor wasn't sure how much she should tell Gladys but she didn't want to deceive her and trusted she could keep a secret.

"This news makes me sad. I always hoped she was living a happy life somewhere, but feared the worst for her. Charity Strong was a dear sweet girl. I say girl on purpose because she was naïve and pure of heart. I don't remember anything that she ever did that wasn't for the betterment of others, but she was very pretty too. Her kind of beauty can cause jealousy in some women. She didn't have many friends that I can remember, and spent most of her time at church or home with her family. I heard the most vicious rumors about her cheating on her husband and running around with other men. There was a clique of young women who were mean spirited. I think they were afraid that their boyfriends found Charity attractive and so they spread those rumors to smear her. I'm afraid they did the same to her daughter as well. I'm sure their menfolk were flattered by the thought that Charity would welcome their advances. Charity was small and looked younger than she was causing many to think she was the reverend's daughter and not his wife. Anyway there was an ugly scandal. Tonya Blakely was the one I remember most. She was newly married to a decent man, Gavin Blakely. I never could see what he saw in her. He was kind, sensitive, and years older than she was. Tonya had a mean streak. Maybe that's why he left her, but when he disappeared, she claimed Charity had destroyed their relationship and run off with him. It didn't help that Charity went missing about the same time and just added credibility to Reverend Strong's tale of a faithless wife. I never believed she would leave her girls." Gladys sighed.

"Do you think someone may have killed her?"

"Not physically, but she was such a gentle soul I'm certain the gossip may have killed her spirit. I can only imagine what might have happened to her. Perhaps she injured herself and died in the woods. She liked to hike. I don't think anyone searched for her back then because of the reverend's story. Maybe those are her bones scattered after all this time by animals. It's hard to think anyone would have murdered her and even more difficult to accuse her husband or a thwarted admirer."

"So did Tonya Blakely's husband ever come back?" asked Eleanor.

"No, and I don't blame him. He was a gentle man with a poetic nature—more mature and much kinder than Tonya deserved. She never admitted it but I think she was in contact with him. She must have divorced him because she married some other poor dope."

"Is she still in town?" Eleanor asked.

"As far as I know she still lives out by the high school. Her last husband died years ago . . . suicide." Gladys didn't need to say more.

"Is she still Tonya Blakely?"

"That was her first husband's name. I think her name is Jones now, unless she took her maiden name, Gold."

"Do you remember any of the other women?"

Gladys thought for a minute. "Vivian Thorn is the only other one that stayed in Waterton. She married Jude Thorn but they're getting a divorce if all the rumors are true."

"Is that the Vivian who works in Dr. Baxter's office?"

"Yes, that's the one." Gladys said.

Things were starting to come together in Eleanor's mind. She just didn't know what they meant.

Gossip is a horrible characteristic of a small community. Eleanor didn't remember hearing about other people's failings when she and Walter lived in a larger city in California. It seemed that everyone in Sand Beach and Waterton, for that matter, knew everything about everybody's business. There was a positive side to this, of course. When you walked down the street here, you could wave to everyone and when there was a misfortune, the kindness and support of neighbors was a comfort.

Eleanor walked along the beach and pondered the pros and cons of small-town living. She and Walter moved here over a decade ago. They spent years planning a retirement in a small town by the sea where they could be close to their children and grandchildren. Their life here was good and she never regretted the move. Even after Walter became ill and died Eleanor welcomed the generosity of her friends. Now she sometimes worried about those who gossiped about her relationship with Angus, but she was at an age where gossip didn't matter to her as much as pursuing her own happiness, and Angus definitely made her happy. Lately she found herself thinking seriously about his marriage proposal and wondered if he still wanted her after all her earlier protests. He was careful not to mention it again and she fretted that she might have let a golden opportunity pass. Now he had a dog.

Eleanor popped into Suzanna's and saw a different opportunity—a chance to get information from Mavis and Sybil who sat at their usual table drinking coffee.

"Good morning, ladies," Eleanor said.

"Eleanor, please join us," said Sybil. "What's new with you?"

"Not too much, Angus has a dog," Eleanor shared.

"Don't worry, dear, I'm sure the dog can't cook, so you won't be replaced," said Mavis with a laugh.

"I remember when Stanley and I were still married and he brought home a dog," began Sybil. "The dirty animal insisted on sleeping between us in our bed. It was the beginning of the end of intimacy."

"Did the dog growl at you?" asked Mavis who seemed to be in excellent spirits.

"I think it was my growling at the dog that may have been the issue," Sybil said.

"Well Angus' dog has a knack for finding bones. He's brought some interesting finds to our attention. And now I'm trying to find out if you two know anything about Charity Strong and her disappearance twenty years ago," Eleanor whispered.

"How fascinating!" said Sybil, "But I wasn't here twenty years ago and really don't know anything about Charity Strong except the stories I've heard."

"What have you heard?" Eleanor asked.

"I think we all heard the same story, dear," Mavis said. "A young unhappy wife married to an old, overbearing husband falls in love with a young buck and runs off with him—The End."

"That's about all I know too," admitted Sybil. "I'll be the first to admit how unfair that is since I didn't know her at all. She may have been the salt of the earth. Do you think the bones belong to her?"

"That would put a different spin on the story," Mavis said. "Where were these bones discovered?"

"We aren't sure since the dog brought them to us. They could have come from anywhere near the Strong property all the way to Mattie's house," Eleanor said. She began to feel that she had given away too much information with little return.

"They may not even be her bones. What makes you think they are?" asked Sybil.

"Just a hunch," Eleanor said.

"That's not much to go on," Mavis added. "The discovery of bones coinciding with the return of the Strong sisters is freaky. If they turn out to belong to Charity, it could mean something sinister happened to her. Perhaps the reverend wasn't all he's been cracked up to be."

"Are you investigating a cold case with Angus?" asked Sybil.

"Not really, I guess my imagination is getting away with me." Eleanor knew these women were smart enough to see through her dismissal.

"Well if you find out more, keep us in the loop," Sybil said. "Life has been quite dull since Mattie left us."

"I've taken a page out of Mattie's playbook to make my life more interesting. A little romance can really spice up a person's day to day so I've been corresponding with someone on line," Mavis confessed.

Eleanor's eyebrows rose in surprise. "Really, who is this someone?" she asked. Sybil simply sat with her mouth agape.

"His name is Phineas Fox. He's a retired navy captain who lives in San Diego. His wife died ten years ago and he's looking for a companion," Mavis reported. "I know what you're thinking. I'm not much of a catch, but really he's seen my photo and is still interested."

"Mavis, you're absolutely a catch," Eleanor said. "How did you meet him?"

"He friended me on Facebook," Mavis said. "I must admit that I was flattered that a man would want to be my friend, so I accepted and we've been conversing ever since. He's very handsome in his uniform."

Sybil sat dumbfounded.

"How long have you been communicating with him?" asked Eleanor.

"I think it's been a couple of months, but the good news is that he's coming to Sand Beach to meet me in person." Mavis clutched her scarf and sighed. "I'm just a little nervous. I didn't want to tell anyone because I was afraid you might convince me to stop corresponding with him because he might be after my money or other nonsense, but believe me when I tell you . . . I have the best feeling about where this is headed. I've been very happy lately and I know it's because of him."

"When is he coming?" asked Eleanor.

"We haven't worked out the details yet." Mavis stopped to check the time. "Oh, I almost forgot, I have an appointment with Dr. Baxter. I really must go. I'll see you later." With those words Mavis Bench was out the door leaving Eleanor and Sybil sitting in amazement.

"Wow that was quite a bomb she dropped!" Eleanor said.

"I can't believe it. I just can't believe what is happening. We have been the Do Nothings for fifteen years at least. We prided ourselves on our independence and our ability to be happy without men and now Mattie is gone and Mavis is having a fling with some sailor." Sybil blew out a long-held breath.

"I'm concerned that he may very well be trying to take advantage of her," Eleanor said.

"You and me both," said Sybil. "Every day I get a friend request on Facebook from some man I've never heard of before and I just delete them. I'm sure they're fishing for a lonely old woman so they can rip her off."

"I can understand why Mavis didn't want to tell us," Eleanor said. "Mattie found Artemas and spent happy hours in his company before she died." The vision of Mattie and Artemas lying naked in each other's arms flashed through

Eleanor and Sybil's minds. It was a scene they weren't meant to see, but one they had accidently come upon during a snoop.

"It's difficult to erase the memory of them together," said Sybil.

"Indeed," said Eleanor. "I think I'll do a little investigating on our Captain Fox."

"What do you have in mind?" asked Sybil.

"I know a couple of private investigators who might be willing to dig up some information about him. We don't have to let Mavis know unless it's something unsavory."

Sybil nodded.

Eleanor set the table for a family dinner. She used her finest linens, china, and crystal glasses. Flowers graced the table and candles were lit giving the dining area a warm and welcoming feeling. The aroma of hearty steak and potatoes with balsamic cranberry pan sauce filled the house. She poured a glass of cabernet and wandered into the living room where a fire's glow warmed the room and created the cozy home Eleanor enjoyed providing for her family and friends.

Amy and Tyler Ash arrived early with Eleanor's three grandchildren: Elise, Addie, and Wesley. Erin and Ben came soon after with Ruby and Mitch. After hugs were given and wine was poured the children gathered in the living room around the Bosendorfer where Elise entertained them with her medley of Billy Joel tunes. Eleanor and her daughters listened to the sounds of young voices singing old songs from the kitchen as they finished dinner preparations and sipped their wine. Tyler and Ben carried dishes to the table and discussed current political issues.

Feathers flew to the door when Angus arrived but there was no scolding or warnings of intruders. He simply landed on Scout's shoulder and greeted him with a polite parrot, "Hello, hello." Scout wiggled all over in doggy delight as the children left their music and welcomed this new addition.

"He's so cute," cooed Wesley, accepting a slew of wet doggy kisses.

"What kind of dog is he?" asked Elise.

"Where did you get him?" asked Addie.

"Does he bite?" asked Ruby cautiously.

"I wish we had a dog," said Mitch trying to pet the muscle in motion.

Angus answered each question in turn and watched as the children lavished his pet with loving strokes.

"Give the man a break," said Erin.

"Welcome, Angus," said Amy. "Would you like a drink?"

Angus stepped out of the fray and into the kitchen where he was greeted by the other grown-ups and a glass of his usual Crown Royal. He quickly pecked Eleanor on the cheek and offered her a sweet bouquet of yellow chrysanthemums. "Something smells mighty delicious."

Eleanor was more than pleased. She thought the days of wine and roses might be over.

Questions about the dog came up again during dinner.

"What do you call your dog?" asked Ben.

"Scout," answered Angus.

"But he used to be called Sherlock Bones," added Eleanor.

"Isn't it bad luck to change a dog's name?" asked Erin.

"I think that only applies to boats," Angus said. "Now that is very bad luck."

"Why?" asked Wesley.

"Sailors and fishermen are extremely superstitious," explained Amy who prided herself on understanding human behavior.

"Right, there is no eating bananas or whistling on a boat either," Angus shared.

"I had no idea," said Eleanor. "Are you superstitious, Angus?"

"Not at all or I never would have taken you out on a boat. Women are bad luck on board too, especially redheads."

"I'm not a redhead," objected Eleanor patting her silver hair.

"But you're definitely a woman," noted Angus.

"Keeping women off ships makes more sense than not," said Ben. "They would most likely distract the sailors."

"I think it's okay to change the dog's name from Sherlock Bones to Scout," said Elise. "Scout is short. Of course you could just call him Bones."

"Speaking of bones," Eleanor said, "have you learned anything new about the bones Scout found?"

"Scout dug up some bones?" asked Tyler. "Maybe his previous name is totally appropriate."

"They're human bones," Eleanor added.

"Where did he get them?" asked Mitch who was strangely interested in the macabre.

"We're not sure. He got away from us and returned with a bone." Angus was reluctant to say anything more about it and wished Eleanor hadn't mentioned it.

"We were walking around the old Strong house up on the hill," Eleanor continued until she caught Angus' eye and realized she was talking too much. Maybe it was the wine that loosened her tongue. She didn't remember Angus saying anything about keeping it under wraps.

"Was it Reverend Strong's bones?" asked Elise.

"No one knows who the bone belongs to yet," Angus said.

"Knock knock," said Wesley.

"Whose there?" asked Mitch.

"Skeleton."

"Skeleton who?"

"Why'd you ask when there's no *body* there?" Wesley chuckled.

"How much does a skeleton weigh?" asked Mitch.

"I don't know," said Ruby.

"One skeleTON," said Mitch.

"Why is a skeleton a bad liar?" asked Addie.

"Because he's a bonehead," said Elise.

"No, because you can see right through it." Addie smiled showing her perfect white teeth.

"Is there anyone living at the Strong house?" asked Elise.

"No, only dead people are up there," laughed Wesley. "Bhwaaaaaaa!"

Elise silenced him with her evil clown look. "Really, is the house deserted?"

"Faith and Hope Strong are renting Mattie May's house while they remodel their family home," said Eleanor. "They're turning it into a church."

"Faith Strong was one strange girl in high school," Tyler commented. It hadn't occurred to Eleanor that Tyler might have known Faith.

"What do you mean?" she prodded.

"Well, she was a wild thing if you must know. There were lots of boyfriends, parties, and drinking. It's a wonder she lived through it all. She had a reputation. We all thought it was because she was rebelling against her father's strict religious edicts."

"It's a wonder any of us lived through our teenage years," Amy said.

"Remember the night we drove over to your friend's to toilet paper her house?" Erin asked. "We were dressed all in black."

"Yes, we went inside to scare her because she was home alone and when we came out someone had gotten in my car and toilet-papered my car with my own toilet paper. I knew who it was too because I saw him drive off. I'm sure he was stalking me," Amy laughed.

"That wasn't the end of it," Erin continued. "We made so much noise that an old man came outside in his bathrobe. Of course, we thought he was a pervert and screamed. He saw us all dressed in black scurrying to get back in our car and suspected foul play. Someone said 'gun'. I'm sure he was the one who called the police."

"I remember that reverse 911 call as if it were yesterday," Eleanor said. "Your father answered the phone and I only heard one side of the conversation. 'Yes, I own a black Ford Focus. Yes, I know who is supposed to be driving it. Yes, she's my daughter.' I was sure you had been in a terrible accident."

"The police pulled us over and asked us if we were in the car willingly. I guess he thought Amy kidnapped us," Erin said.

"Fortunately, he let us go after confirming our identities, but our night of mischief was spoiled," Amy lamented.

"At least that night was," Erin said.

"There's no need to confess everything," Amy warned.

"Is anyone ready for dessert?" Eleanor asked. "I made Sinful Chocolate Brownies."

Eleanor woke from a dead sleep. Something wasn't right. She lay in her warm cozy bed and strained her ears to hear what she knew was a noise that had brought her out of a very pleasant dream involving a baking contest in which she was the star baker. There it was again. She looked at the clock. It was the middle of a very dark night and her brain registered cold when her feet touched the floor as she walked with purpose toward the noise, turning on every light outside of her house, and peering out the window.

She listened intently. The sound seemed to be coming from the garage. Could it be rats? They were known to come in when the weather grew cold and wet, but Eleanor didn't have anything in the garage for them to eat. She was positive the garbage can was outside but maybe she should check. Rats or mice in the garage could mean nests inside her car or chewed electrical wires. Eleanor hated rats. She grabbed a baseball bat that she kept in a closet in the laundry room and turned on the garage light. At first the light blinded her but once her eyes adjusted she was able to see what was in the garage. Her silver car sat in its regular spot and next to it sat Mattie May's black Lincoln Town car. No vermin scampered away and no boogie man lurked in the corners. The garbage can was not inside. Perhaps it was just the wind knocking something against the door. Eleanor turned out the light and checked the locks on the doors before returning to that warm spot under her down comforter. The longer she lay in bed the more she worried about the strange noise. Did she check the garage door that led outside to be sure it was locked? Did she want to get up again? Absolutely not, but she knew she wouldn't sleep unless she was sure that door was locked. Once more she rolled out of bed, but this time she slipped on her robe and slippers before heading to the garage with her bat. She turned on the lights in the garage and bravely strode to the door. Just to prove to herself how very brave she was, she unlocked the door and stepped outside into the night. Was that a branch she saw swinging in the wind or a shadow moving away down the lane? Her imagination was working overtime. Eleanor went back inside and locked the door behind her. She didn't notice the marks on the door where someone had tried to pry their way inside. She would find that in the morning along with a pillowcase caught on a shrub that someone left as they hurried away into the night.

When Angus frowned it looked like two furry caterpillars descending over his eyes and he was frowning when Eleanor showed him the marks on the door of her garage.

"It looks like someone wanted to rob you," he said when she brought out the pillowcase. "I think you need a security camera outside and an alarm system. I can get one and install it for you."

Eleanor was tired. She hadn't slept and now she was worried as well.

"Of course, I could sleep over with my faithful guard dog if it would make you feel—at least until the security system is working," Angus offered generously.

"Hmmmm." Eleanor processed the idea. It wouldn't be the first time Angus had spent the night. "Can I get a system here or would I have to get it in the valley?"

"I can pick one up when I go over there next week," he said.

"Maybe Cleo can spend a couple of nights with me. Maybe the entire coffee group can come over for a pajama party!" Eleanor knew the security system would get installed faster if Angus wasn't the one enjoying her company and her cooking. "I'm sure at least two of their husbands are away hunting something."

Angus nodded, "Well, maybe I should spend tonight with you just in case they come back."

"I'll call Cleo and see if she's free," Eleanor added.

Eleanor woke the next morning to a wet nose pressing against her cheek. At first she thought it was Angus who had starred in a vivid dream that she could only describe as R rated but upon opening her eyes discovered Scout staring longingly at her with big brown eyes and a long pink tongue that was very difficult to avoid.

"Scout, get off," she scolded. The sound of her voice only increased his enthusiasm demonstrated by energetic wriggling and jumping first off the bed and then back on combined with intermittent licking.

Eleanor rolled out of her warm nest and went looking for Angus followed by the excited dog. She heard the shower running and followed her nose to the kitchen for coffee. Feathers was perched by the window watching the surf roll in below a cloudy sky. He seemed at ease with his new friend in the house and Eleanor had to admit she slept better than she had in a long time. She was reluctant to think it was because she felt protected and safe but had to admit there was comfort in having someone else in the house.

She would make a delicious omelet for breakfast and stuff it with ham, tomatoes, and cheese. By the time Angus appeared clean-shaven and smelling like Old Spice Eleanor had completed her morning routine, dressed, and plated a breakfast feast.

"Good morning, Sleeping Beauty," Angus greeted, "Did you sleep well?"

"I did until I was awakened by the black prince here," Eleanor said indicating Scout who sat patiently waiting for her to drop a morsel of something.

They sat down to eat like an old married couple—at least that was what Eleanor thought and then realized being with Angus was like wearing a favorite pair of shoes that fit perfectly and felt soft and easy. She wondered if she would feel this way always if they married or if life would grow mundane and the little joys become duties. Eleanor didn't like change.

"I'm going into the station this morning to see if there's anything new regarding the bones," Angus said.

"Do you want to leave Scout here? I could take him for a walk," Eleanor offered.

Angus lowered his brows in thought. He feared that the loyal dog he wished for might be forging a new alliance with the woman he loved. "I'll take him with me. I don't want to confuse him about who his owner is." He watched silently as Eleanor fed him a bite of egg from her plate. "Don't be silly, Angus. I can take him for a walk and if he goes with you, he'll spend the day cooped up in your truck. This way you can go to the Y to work out and pick him up later."

After Angus left, Eleanor settled in with the crossword puzzle and a second cup of coffee. Feathers landed on the back of the sofa and intelligently hummed and hawed over the clues that Eleanor read out loud while Scout lay at her feet and slept. She looked out the window at the gray day and the gray ocean and smiled. Eleanor was happy.

When the coffee group arrived that evening, they each brought something to contribute to Eleanor's leek-crusted beef tenderloin dinner. Josephine brought escarole salad with celery and pine nuts, Dede brought crème fraiche salmon spread and crackers, Pearl made Yukon gold and sweet potatoes, and Anna and Cleo brought chocolate caramel pecan tart. Scout greeted everyone with his usual tail wagging and wet kisses.

Eleanor opened a bottle of cabernet and suddenly it was a party.

"This is fabulous," raved Cleo as she popped a cracker in her mouth.

"Everything looks so festive and perfect, and it's all for us," laughed Pearl.

"Right, how often do we eat like this when it is just us women?" asked Josephine.

"No one has to drive home either, so we can open another bottle of wine," Eleanor said.

"We can open a couple bottles of wine," Dede said.

"Oh, I'm sorry Dede, I forgot you like white." Eleanor opened a bottle of chardonnay and poured a glass for her dear friend. They drank and toasted to their remarkable friendship and then the questions began.

"Tell us what's happened so far," begged Dede.

"Angus called to say the rib bone was from a human fetus," Eleanor said. "They are still waiting for information about the jawbone and the warrant to search the grounds. Sometimes these things take time especially when it's a cold case."

"What could that mean?" asked Cleo. "I was certain they had found Charity Strong."

"The jawbone could still belong to Charity," Josephine said. "This only makes the case more puzzling."

"Do you think Charity had a miscarriage?" asked Pearl.

"Maybe, but we don't know exactly where Scout found that rib bone. It may not have come from the Strong property. It probably didn't. If it's as old as we think it could be from someone who doesn't live here anymore or maybe never did," Eleanor said.

"Could it be possible that a serial murderer used a nearby area to dump his bodies?" asked Cleo.

"I still think Faith is involved," stated Eleanor. "The bones didn't start turning up until she arrived, and don't forget she had a shovel that day and then Angus found a bone in his car—probably from Scout."

"Yes, they didn't start turning up until Scout arrived either," said Dede looking at the dog. "And he doesn't need a shovel."

This gave Eleanor an absolutely outrageous idea. "Let's finish dinner and take Scout out for a walk up to the Strong's house. Maybe he'll dig up something for us. I'm sure he doesn't need a warrant any more than he needs a shovel."

"That's genius!" exclaimed Cleo.

"You don't think it could be dangerous do you?" asked Pearl.

"How could it be dangerous? If anyone catches us we just say we were out walking the dog when he ran off and we followed him." Dede had it all figured out having owned a dog herself.

"Perfect, but what if Angus comes for Scout while we're out?" worried Josephine.

"He stayed in town to play poker with his buddies," Eleanor reassured them. "He won't be back until late."

With that, the coffee group put on their coats and armed with flashlights left the house in search of evidence with the help of Scout, alias Sherlock Bones.

By the time they reached the end of the road, they were all out of breath. "Wait for me," said Cleo, "I didn't wear the proper shoes for investigating."

They rounded the corner and the dark silhouette of the Strong's house loomed large on the horizon.

"Are you sure there's no one in there?" asked Pearl.

"It looks pretty dark," said Eleanor. "Faith and Hope are at Mattie's house. I'm letting Scout loose."

Scout ran toward the house sniffing along the way as the group of women followed. First he went to an empty flower bed near the house but soon lost interest and veered off toward a freshly dug bed farther away.

"This must be where Faith relocated her mother's roses," said Eleanor. The beam from her flashlight revealed the thorny stalks that once held flowers and leaves, but now looked ragged and untended.

"Look, there's a light moving around inside the house," whispered Dede.

"Oh no, someone's in there!" exclaimed Pearl and she turned to run away, but Eleanor grabbed her arm.

"There's someone in there with a flashlight. Someone's snooping where they shouldn't be," Eleanor said.

"Maybe it's the ghost of Charity Strong!" said Cleo.

"What should we do?" asked Josephine.

"Let's find out who it is," Dede said fearlessly.

"I wonder how they got inside," said Eleanor. "Keep your flashlight beams low. Let's try to see through those big windows."

The amateur snoops quietly closed in on the house. They could see two beams of light flickering around what must have been a massive living room. Suddenly, Scout was barking ferociously and running toward the house. Just as suddenly the lights inside went out and after what seemed forever two figures dropped from a small window and scurried toward the rose bed. The intrepid Scout ran after them but before they could escape the tall one in the lead tripped and fell. The ladies were able to reach them before they got up. Eleanor aimed her light on the one laying on the ground and gasped.

"Elise, what are you doing here?"

"I could ask you the same question, Gramma." Elise picked herself up, brushed the dirt off her pants, and fumbled around for her flashlight. What she found instead was a shallow grave filled with the long-dead bones of a baby.

Elise sat in Eleanor's kitchen sipping hot chocolate with her friend Adrianne while her gramma and her friends sipped glasses of Angus' Crown Royal. It had given them all such a start they needed something to calm their nerves.

"Start at the beginning and tell me why you broke into the Strong's house," Eleanor said softly.

"I heard you talking about the house when we were at dinner the other night. My life is so boring. I just wanted to be as fearless and interesting as Mom and Aunt Erin were when they were young. Snooping around an abandoned house that might be haunted sounded exciting," Elise explained.

"We're not in trouble, are we?" asked Adrianne. "If my parents hear about this, they won't let me have the car anymore."

"You're not going to tell Mom, are you?" Elise seemed horrified at the idea.

"Where does your mom think you are?" asked Eleanor.

"Adrianne and I are studying at the library," Elise said. "We did go there for a short time but then we drove out here and parked the car on the other side of the road. We walked in through the trees."

"You know breaking and entering is a crime, don't you?" asked Dede in her official Mayor's voice.

"We didn't break anything, honest!" exclaimed Adrianne.

"We didn't steal anything either. We were just curious about what was inside," admitted Elise.

"Did you see any ghosts?" asked Cleo.

Elise smiled. "No nothing. There wasn't much inside at all, and the rooms were gutted with some of the walls missing."

"If you and Adrianne promise to keep quiet about the break-in, we won't tell the police," Eleanor said.

"You mean you won't tell our parents or Angus," Elise interpreted.

"Exactly, but we *will* have to tell Angus about the bones Scout dug up. We just won't tell about your involvement," Eleanor explained. "Who knows? If you hadn't tripped in that grave, we may not have discovered the bones. When this case is solved and you are older, you can tell your kids about your adventure and how interesting you were."

"It's a deal." Elise and Adrianne both agreed to the terms, finished their hot chocolate, and drove home leaving the coffee ladies to come up with a story that would explain how they stumbled upon the skeleton of an infant buried in a fresh grave among some dying rose bushes.

"I say we just tell Angus the truth," said Josephine. "We didn't do anything wrong."

"It may have been trespassing," corrected Dede.

"We can simply tell him that Scout escaped and we pursued him to the Strong's house where we found the grave," said Eleanor.

"I like that," said Cleo. "It's always best to stick to as much of the truth as possible when telling a lie."

"Let's get our stories straight then. Who will we say fell into the grave?" asked Pearl.

"Which one of us is the clumsiest?" asked Dede, knowing just who everyone would choose.

"We all know it's you, Dede, but we don't want you mentioned in the newspaper if this story gets out," said Josephine.

"I can see the headlines now, 'Mayor Stumbles into Mysterious Grave'," Dede said.

"It will have to be me," said Eleanor. "It was my idea and I'm responsible for Scout getting loose, so I'll take the fall."

"Did you hurt yourself?" asked Cleo.

"No, not at all. I'm very resilient," she laughed and refilled everyone's glasses.

By the time Angus arrived to take Scout home, the ladies were well into a game of Cards Against Humanity. Josephine refused to participate in the vulgar game and had fallen asleep on the sofa, but the rest of them were in hysterics over the information they did not know and could never repeat.

"Come in, Angus, and have a drink with us," Eleanor said.

Angus looked at the almost empty bottle of Crown Royal and raised his eyebrows in surprise. "I wouldn't want to be left out of the fun."

He sipped his whiskey and listened carefully as the ladies retold their story about the night's excitement.

"How do you know it's an infant's bones?" he asked.

"I saw the skull," said Josephine, "But none of us touched anything."

"Scout must have dug them up before we could catch up to him," Eleanor said. "The soil was loose and looked freshly dug."

Angus looked at Scout who lay quietly near the fireplace. Eleanor had cleaned his feet before letting him back in the house. For some reason a little voice inside his head told him he wasn't hearing the whole story. "What is it you aren't telling me?" he asked.

Eleanor knew Angus had an excellent baloney detector. He could sniff out a lie better than anyone she knew, even a lie of omission. "I'm sorry, Angus. It was my fault that Scout got outside. I opened the door to get some fresh air and he rushed out. He really does have a nose for bones. Do you think he could have found that rib on the Strong's property? It doesn't seem like he had time to get up there and back to where we were walking that day."

"You said the grave was shallow. It's possible someone moved it and inadvertently dropped one of the bones." Angus was thoughtful. "I'll call Andy McGraw. He may want to take a look tonight before someone else contaminates the scene. This could be what pushes the judge to issue a warrant to search the property." Angus finished his drink, stood and took his bone-digging dog home.

"I don't think Angus was happy with us," said Dede.

"Why does that man always make us feel like criminals when we are just trying to help solve the case?" asked Cleo.

"He thinks we are meddling," said Pearl.

"We *are* meddling," said Josephine. "We are first-class meddlers."

"Yes, and we dug up some very interesting clues with our meddling," defended Eleanor and smiled at her clever wordplay.

"What do you think an infant buried in a shallow grave means?" asked Dede.

"I don't even want to guess," said Josephine.

"I bet Faith Strong knows something about that baby," Cleo said. "Two and two add up to four and a wild teenager and a dead baby adds up to trouble."

The following morning the coffee group discussed the case of the mysterious bones while they ate breakfast at Eleanor's.

"Angus will probably be at the Strong property today with Officer McGraw. Our story gives them probable cause to investigate the infant's grave," said Eleanor.

"Faith will know that and be on guard now," said Cleo.

"They won't know what relation those bones are to Faith without DNA testing," said Josephine.

"We could get her DNA," suggested Dede. "That would speed up the process."

"How do we do that?" asked Pearl.

"We could make a visit to her house and get a piece of her hair," suggested Dede.

"Brilliant," said Eleanor, "but we can't risk taking it from a hairbrush. We need to know for certain that it's from Faith. Hope would probably give us a sample if we asked her but Faith is a different animal altogether."

"We could invite them over for lunch, or coffee, or something," Pearl said.

"I'm sure Faith wouldn't come. We need to get into their house," Eleanor said, "and we need to do it before they find out the grave has been discovered, otherwise they will be suspicious."

There was a long period of silence while each of them pondered a clever way to get inside.

"I have the key," Eleanor said. "Maybe they aren't home."

"How would we know that?" asked Dede.

"Let's take a walk this morning and find out," Pearl suggested. "We could bring them some of these delicious cinnamon rolls."

"That would be a very neighborly thing to do," said Josephine.

"I'm sure Hope would agree, but Faith would think it was sinful in its excessive sweetness," Eleanor argued.

"Are we talking about the act or the cinnamon rolls?" asked Cleo.

"Probably both," Josephine added.

"I think Eleanor and I should go over," said Dede. "We could say I wanted to meet them because I heard about Faith's church and I want to welcome her to our ecumenical meeting this Saturday."

"Great, we can bring the cinnamon rolls too and if they aren't home, I'll take the key and we'll go in and snoop for DNA," Eleanor said.

"What are we supposed to do?" asked Cleo.

"Do you know what kind of car they drive? We could be lookouts," suggested Pearl.

"I can't say that I do." Eleanor had never seen them with a car. She just assumed they had one in the garage since they put Mattie's town car outside. "Wait, I think it might be on the rental agreement."

Eleanor hurried to her office and returned with a file folder. "Here it is." She read the description of a car that must have belonged to Reverend Strong before he died. "It's an older Toyota 4Runner."

"What color is it?" asked Cleo.

"It says platinum," Eleanor reported.
"Is that silver?" asked Pearl.

"Sort of a silvery gold," said Cleo, "And a boxy sort of SUV. I know because my neighbor drives one."

"Okay then, Dede and I will go over with the cinnamon rolls and get in the house if they are home." Eleanor said. "If they are not home, we will use the key to get inside. Cleo and Pearl will keep watch from my house for the 4Runner. Josephine will station herself outside Faith's house and alert Cleo and Pearl if they are home or not, and call the cell phone if they see their car returning. Does everyone know what to do? Does everyone have their cell phones?"

Cleo saluted and the others nodded. Eleanor wrapped up a couple of cinnamon rolls and left with Dede and Josephine. When they reached the house, Josephine hid in the shrubs while Eleanor and Dede made their way to the front door.

After several loud raps on the door, Eleanor unlocked the door and Dede signaled to Josephine that they were going inside.

"It's been a while since I was in Mattie's house. I see you rented it fully furnished. It hasn't changed much." Dede went immediately to the refrigerator to check out its contents. "Wow, it's almost empty. I bet they're at the grocery store."

Eleanor wasted no time but strode quickly to the bedroom she had witnessed Faith come out of the last time she visited. She wasn't surprised to see how sparse it looked. The full bed that once was there had been replaced with a single cot and thin wool blanket. It looked like a cell a nun might inhabit. There was no mirror over the chest of drawers and only a few items of clothing hung in the closet. A simple wooden chair beside the bed acted as a night stand and held a Bible and a used tissue. Eleanor carefully put the tissue in a plastic bag, being careful not to touch it.

The walls were bare and Eleanor didn't see any sign of toiletries in the room. She checked the limp pillow for strands of hair and had a strange feeling she had seen the embroidery on the pillowcase before. It was the only decoration in the otherwise stark room. She added one long strand of hair to her bag and put it in her pocket. Her heart was beating so loudly she thought Dede might hear it from the other bedroom.

Dede appeared in the doorway with a mass of hair in her hand. "From the look of this room, I'm sure it's Faith's, so this hair must belong to Hope. Her room is a lot nicer than this one."

"We need to get out of here," Eleanor said. "I don't want to get caught by Faith snooping through her things. I'm sure she'd put a curse on me, damn me to hell, or file a suit against me."

"Do you think we have enough to get the DNA we need?" asked Dede as she looked in Faith's closet.

"I don't want to stay here any longer than necessary." Eleanor's palms were sweating.

"I bet Faith never wears a hat. What do you think she keeps in this hatbox?' said Dede, pulling it from the top shelf just as they heard the front door open.

Dede quickly shoved the hatbox back on the shelf and Eleanor and Dede both scrambled to hide behind the door.

"What are you two doing?" asked the figure whose head peered around the door.

"Josephine!" Dede cried. "You just about gave me a heart attack.

"Come on, we have to leave immediately. There's no cell service here and no way to know if and when they're coming back," Josephine warned.

"I don't think we have enough evidence," Dede said, "Maybe there's something in the kitchen trash we can use." She returned to the kitchen with Eleanor and Josephine close behind her. Just as Dede opened the cupboard under the sink, Eleanor spotted the platinum SUV pull up in front of the house.

"Duck," Eleanor hissed. "They're back! I don't know if they saw us so stay low."

"We have to get out of here," Josephine said. "Is there a back way out?"

"Follow me," said Eleanor, "but stay down."

Eleanor led the three elderly snoops as they crawled down the hall, hoping there was a back door somewhere.

"We left the cinnamon rolls in the kitchen," whispered Dede, as she turned back to retrieve them.

Eleanor and Josephine continued on to a laundry room where they waited breathlessly for Dede's return. Eleanor spied a windowed door that led out to a small yard with a clothesline bordered by shrubs. She and Josephine made their way to it and as quietly as possible, Eleanor turned the knob just as Dede came around the corner. They heard the front door open and voices coming from the front of the house and as quick as molasses they scurried out with pulses racing and hid behind the backyard shrubbery. It wasn't long before a dark figure appeared in the laundry room window and looked out over their hiding spot. They pushed back into the brush in an attempt to avoid the piercing eyes of Faith Strong. It seemed like an eternity while they waited without speaking, barely breathing, until the ominous shape retreated.

There was a collected sigh.

"I forgot to lock the front door," said Eleanor.

"Don't worry," said Dede, clutching the cinnamon rolls so tightly they were merely a mass of dough, "I remembered and locked it in the nick of time."

"Thank goodness, you have a cool head," said Josephine. "How do we get out of here?"

"Follow me," Eleanor ordered, "I think I know a back way to my house through the woods."

After one last glance at the house, to make sure no one was watching, they began their trek through damp grass and whipping branches.

"At least it isn't raining," said Josephine minutes before the first raindrop fell.

When they finally reached Eleanor's house, they were wet and covered in forest debris. They kicked off their shoes and picked most of the moss and twigs out of their hair before opening the door.

"Where have you been?" asked Pearl. "We were so worried, we almost called Angus."

"Thank goodness, you didn't do that," said Eleanor. "Our investigation was a success."

Dede held up her handful of hair as if it were a trophy.

"Ewww," said Cleo when she saw what she called the nasty nest of hair. "I hope they can use this to help solve the case. Do you think it will matter that they aren't officially positive whose hair it is?"

"I don't know," Eleanor said. "I'm sure Angus will believe me when I tell him where we found it."

"If they test it and find there is a biological relationship it will help identify the bones," Josephine reasoned.

"Something tells me Angus won't like the way we got the hair," Pearl worried.

"I'm sure of it," agreed Eleanor. "The tissue might have traces of Faith's DNA, and I got this strand from her pillow. I'm fairly certain she doesn't share her bed with anyone else."

"What other things should we investigate?" asked Cleo. "Didn't we have a list of things we needed to learn?"

"Yes, but I have an appointment this afternoon and I need a bath," Josephine said.

"I'll go over to Megan Field's later and see what she can tell me about the mean girls and Faith when they were in high school," Eleanor said. "By the way, Taylor remembers her from high school. He told me she had a reputation as a wild girl: partying, drinking, and lots of boyfriends."

"We can be pretty sure that's true since so many corroborated it," Dede said. "I wonder if anyone knew about the baby. I'll visit Tonya Jones and see what she has to say. If there was a pregnancy, I'm sure she would have blabbed it all over town if she knew, but maybe she can shed some light on other things—like who the father may have been. Her brother is Donnie Gold. Didn't Cary say he remembered Donnie as one of Faith's boyfriends, Pearl?"

"Oh, I forgot Tonya was a Gold," Pearl said. "Donnie was older and surely out of high school before Faith was there. I wonder what he was doing hanging out with a girl that young."

"I can guess," said Dede.

"I can talk to Vivian Thorn," said Josephine. "I'm seeing her this afternoon, but then again maybe not."

"I heard she and her husband are getting a divorce," said Eleanor. "If you're doing mediation between those two you better let me handle that one. I may need another adjustment anyway. My neck seems to be out of line."

After the ladies left, Eleanor walked the lane near Mattie's house, but saw the local PUD truck blocking the lane. They were trimming the hemlock tree and chipping the broken branches from the latest storm. Eleanor was relieved to know those dangling branches wouldn't fall on her but the noise from the chipper and the activity of the workers in their hard hats and yellow vests caused her to reconsider her route. She turned and headed up the hill toward the Strong property to satisfy an enormous case of curiosity. A gust of wind blew through the trees bringing a loose branch down behind her. Startled but not injured, Eleanor spun around and saw members from the PUD crew rushing to her. "Are you okay?" one hollered over the grinding of the chipper. She signaled to them with a wave that she was not injured and noticed Faith standing behind the men, her gaze cold and solemn. Eleanor continued on her way feeling somehow invincible instead of fearful.

When she reached the Strong house, she was surprised to find no police cars but instead a work truck parked outside. The shallow grave they had discovered the night before was undisturbed and hardly noticeable. Looking quickly down into the hole Scout had dug, Eleanor could see the tiny skull partially revealed. Obviously neither Angus nor Officer McGraw had been there yet. She walked to the house and called out as she stepped inside, "Hello, is anybody here?"

"In here," came a man's deep voice.

Eleanor followed the voice to a large open room where a middle-aged man wearing a heavy tool belt stood in thought. "I'm just trying to visualize this place as a church," he said. "I've done most of the demolition to open it up but it's just hard to imagine why Faith wants this remodel. There was nothing wrong with this house the way it was."

"I'm Eleanor Penrose," she said. "I live just down the street and was curious about the remodel too."

"How do you do?" the man reached out his hand to shake hers. "I'm Jude Thorn. Faith hired me as contractor and carpenter." Eleanor tried to imagine what he must have looked like when he was younger. He was small in stature, almost entirely gray haired with his face lined from years of squinting into the sun, giving him the appearance of an older man.

"I just recently met Faith and have to admit, I've never been in this house before. It certainly has a magnificent view." Eleanor stood in front of the large windows that looked out over the ocean and provided an almost 360-degree view that stretched beyond the three arch rocks and as far south as Camp Cheerful and the lighthouse at Cape Lookout.

"I don't think I could pay attention to anything but the view if I were a church-going man, which I'm not, so I guess it doesn't matter." Jude took off his cap and scratched his balding head. "The only thing that matters is what Faith wants and she's determined to make this a church."

"You must be a friend of hers," Eleanor said, "From what I understand most contractors around here are booked months and sometimes years in advance."

Jude turned and looked at Eleanor for the first time. "You could say I owe her—call it atonement for sins of the past. When she was in high school, I wasn't very nice to her. Back then she was a carpenter's dream but now she's different. I don't know what happened to her. Maybe time hit her with the ugly stick. Who knows? She got religion and it took the spit out of her. I can't say I'm an expert on women—at least not on their minds, but if Faith wants a church, I'll build her one. Maybe she can pray me into heaven. Sure as hell can't hurt."

"I'll leave you to it." Eleanor didn't want to be here if Angus showed up. She had already done enough amateur investigating for the time being. "It was nice meeting you Jude Thorn."

Eleanor opened her computer to her Facebook page. She didn't often look at it and seldom checked the friend requests. Sybil said she received several from men she didn't know. Eleanor was surprised to see a few odd requests and clicked on the first picture. A dark-haired man in army camo filled the screen. He knelt beside a dog somewhere in the desert. There was no information other than the photo and a description of his military rank. Fake she thought. Surely Mavis wouldn't fall for a guy with no history.

She clicked on the next one and found a similar description only this man was obviously in Russia. The signs were unreadable to Eleanor who did not speak the language but did recognize the army uniform. They must think women love a man in uniform. She quickly deleted the requests and worried that Mavis might have gotten herself into a scam. She Googled private investigators in Seattle, Washington and quickly found Parker and Patrick Private Investigators next to a large thumb print. It seemed they hadn't wasted any time forming their mutual agency, but then Delia had been a detective already so adding Angus' son Michael Patrick to the ad wasn't a big endeavor. Eleanor wondered if he had a license or if he was just a detective in training at this point. She dialed the number. Of course, they were out of their office and couldn't be reached but would get back to her as soon as possible. She left her name, number, and a short description of her problem and hung up. Doing a thorough background check on Captain Fox was the least she could do for a Do Nothing friend.

Megan Fields had just come home from work at the Waterton City Bank. Eleanor knew she would be tired so she brought a tuna noodle casserole and a bottle of white wine hoping to lull Megan into talking about the past.

"How thoughtful of you," Megan cooed, "Please come in, Mrs. Penrose. I've had quite a day. Let's just open this wine right now." Megan led the way into the bright yellow kitchen with the wine and Eleanor followed with the casserole. "This is such a treat! I was wondering what to fix for dinner and now I can just relax."

"Where's little Willy?" Eleanor looked around and saw Megan's older daughter glued to the television.

"I just fed him and put him in his crib. I think he's going through a growth spurt because he's been so sleepy lately." Megan handed a glass to Eleanor and they sat at the kitchen table. "Turn the television down, sweetheart," she ordered, "Mrs. Penrose and I want to talk."

Eleanor sipped her wine quietly. She knew that a pregnant pause could lead to information.

"You won't believe what a crazy day it's been. Do you know Mr. Thistlewhite?" Megan asked.

"Oh yes, he's a lawyer in Waterton and a pillar of the community. I think almost everyone knows him. He wrote up my will and if you need a lawyer I would certainly recommend him."

Megan laughed. "He came into the bank today and I asked him for his ID. He was very offended and said, 'Do you know who I am, young lady?' I said, 'No, do you know who I am?' Of course he didn't but he introduced himself and then I felt so very foolish. I've been away from Waterton for so long I've forgotten what it's like to live in a small town. Anyway, I told him I would never forget him. I hope he doesn't report me to the manager."

Eleanor smiled and sipped more wine. Megan's husband was in the military and was recently deployed so she had moved home to be close to her family. Being a single working mother was a challenge and Eleanor was a good listener.

"Then Mrs. Gomez came in with a large jar filled with pennies and began counting them out one penny at a time,"

Megan continued. "I tried to explain to her that there was a machine for that but she either didn't understand or just didn't want to do it that way. Pretty soon a long line of people formed behind her and I just didn't know how to stop her without being rude. Fortunately, one of my coworkers saw my distress and got the manager who took her into a private corner and handled it. I thought they were all having a good laugh at my expense."

"It must be difficult starting a new job with two children and being on your own. It must be such a blessing having your family near," Eleanor said.

"I absolutely couldn't manage without them." Megan filled her glass again.

"You must have friends here," Eleanor said. "Wasn't Faith Strong one of them? You know she and her sister just returned after a long time away too." Eleanor watched the expression on Megan's face change from light to dark as if she smelled something unpleasant.

"Faith was in my sister's class in school. She wasn't really a friend," Megan said.

"She and her sister Hope are renting a cottage from me. I just wondered if you remembered her," Eleanor said.

"Oh, I remember her all right. My sister, Martha was her friend for a while, but it didn't last. Martha claimed Reverend Strong gave her the creeps. He yelled at Faith and accused Martha of leading her down the path of 'wanton ways'. Martha never went back and after that she didn't like Faith—probably because she was pretty and popular with the guys. Martha hung out with some older girls who made Faith miserable. Faith had a reputation for being easy. I'm not sure what they really did to her, probably spread stories or exaggerated the truth and emailed gossip about her. I remember one of them was Sally Lutz. Her email address was slutz and I always thought that was hilarious considering the names they called Faith. I don't blame her for leaving here. She must have been horribly unhappy sandwiched between an ultra-religious father and a clique of judgmental jealous girls. Even after she came back from wherever they sent incorrigible girls, she couldn't repair her reputation. Those girls moved on, died in Martha's case, got married, and forgot about Faith. They were all in love with Dr. Baxter back then. He was new in town and really gorgeous, but he was older and not interested in any of them. Is he still in Waterton?"

"Yes, he's my chiropractor and still a handsome man," Eleanor said. "Was Vivian Thorn one of your sister's friends?"

"There was a Vivian but her name was Reynolds. She must have married that horrid Jude Thorn. As young as I was then, I knew to stay away from that bad boy. He was an older guy and cute, but his reputation for sleeping around was well known. His goal in life was putting more notches on his bedpost than Donnie Gold and bragging about his conquests. I bet there are several little Thorns sprouting up all over the county," Megan said.

Eleanor almost laughed at the image that appeared in her mind. Thorns were the worst kind of weed—prickly and hard to remove. She tried envisioning the middle-aged man she saw earlier as the ladies' man Megan described and wondered what the young girls found so attractive. Maybe time had hit him with the ugly stick.

"I'm sorry about your sister's death," Eleanor said.

"Yes, I'm sorry too but we weren't close. Martha wasn't only mean to Faith. She was just inherently mean and I know because she tortured me for years. She criticized me; the way I looked, how I dressed and how I talked, who I called my friends, and she spread vicious lies about people, especially Faith and even Faith's mother—actually anyone she perceived as a rival. I cried when she died, but my life was happier without her in it. I suppose she might have grown kinder as she grew older, but she never got that chance, so I always think of her as my mean big sister," Megan confided. "Even her accident was caused by her own rage. She was showing off for her so-called friends and passed on a blind corner after tailgating a slow driver. A milk truck was coming. A head-on collision would have killed them all, but she was the only one to die. The police said she drove off the road and hit a tree. She took the brunt of the impact, as though she was a hero or something. It may have been the kindest thing she ever did. I think the survivors changed after the accident."

"Who was in the car with her?" Eleanor asked.

"Vivian, Tonya, Jude, and Donnie," Megan yawned. "I didn't hear much about them after that, so I thought they might have changed, but maybe they didn't. They've certainly had enough time to straighten out their lives—get therapy or whatever. It was a long time ago."

"I can see you're tired. I'll go. Kiss little Willy for me." Eleanor let herself out.

Angus hadn't been invited for dinner, but showed up just as Eleanor sat down to eat the extra tuna noodle casserole she had left out for herself.

"Hi Darlin'," he said as he drew her into his arms and kissed her tuna-flavored lips. "Yum, you taste delicious."

"You must be hungry. Where's Bones, I mean Scout?" Eleanor opened the door and Scout dashed inside with his muddy dog feet.

"No, Scout!" Angus chased after him and Feathers joined in the chaos flying after the two calling, "No Scout! No Scout! Go boy, go boy!"

Angus finally caught the naughty beast, put him in the garage, and cleaned up the mess while Eleanor dished up another plate of tuna noodle casserole.

"Sorry, Ellie." Angus washed his hands and joined Eleanor at the table. He knew she liked things neat and tidy. Her house was immaculate and filled with beautiful things. It wasn't any wonder she had a pet that could be caged instead of a wild animal that ran amok through her lovely home soiling the plush carpets and scratching the polished hardwood floors. He knew he brought disorder and ugliness into her life through his past line of work, but he didn't want his dog to be the straw that caused Eleanor to throw them both out and forced Angus to eat his own cooking.

Eleanor suppressed a smile. She knew Angus would feel guilty and she could use this to her advantage when she revealed the messy hair nest of DNA evidence she planned to give him after dinner.

"Did you help Officer McGraw collect the baby bones?" Eleanor probed.

"Yes, although it took a while. We were able to get the warrant to search the grounds where there was fresh digging, but we didn't turn up anything new. Officer McGraw bagged the baby bones and sent them to a lab in Portland for testing. It's unlikely we'll know who it is without DNA to match, but we can get a court order if it comes to that. I'm hoping Faith or Hope will want to cooperate with us since it might bring closure to the disappearance of their mother." Angus filled his mouth with the last bite of creamy pasta.

"I might have something to help you with that," Eleanor said.

Angus looked at her skeptically from under his bushy brows and frowned.

"Ellie, what have you done?"

Before she could answer, a deafening clamor came from the garage in the form of riotous barking. They both rose from their chairs and hustled to the source of the disturbance. Scout was barking at Mattie May's car as if it were a robber threatening to enter the house.

"Scout, stop," Angus commanded without result. The black dog circled the car and continued to bark and sniff at the trunk. Eleanor and Angus' eyes met as understanding dawned. "Get the keys, Ellie."

Eleanor hurried back with the keys and reluctantly handed them to Angus who unlocked the trunk of Mattie's vintage Lincoln Town car. Both of them knew what they would find but neither was prepared for the reality of the petite bones adorned with moldy rags that once dressed a living woman and now lay carefully nestled in the trunk.

"It has to be Charity Strong," Eleanor said. "Faith must have dug her up and used Mattie's car to move her, possibly dropping some bones during the process."

"Probably," said Angus, "but where's her head?"

"It didn't take long after the discovery of the bones in Mattie's car to identify them as the remains of Charity Strong. The jawbone found earlier and dental records cinched it. When questioned, Faith refused to reveal any information other than that she found them when she moved the roses." Eleanor told her friends when they met for coffee.

"Oh, for heaven's sake, why did she move them?" asked Cleo.

"She said she wanted to protect them from the contractor when they began work and planned to give her a proper Christian burial in her church later along with her father," Eleanor said.

"I don't believe it," Dede said. "Now we don't know how she died. Without the head valuable evidence is missing."

"Faith said she didn't know anything about the missing head, but I think she's lying," Eleanor said. "I think she dropped the jawbone when she carried the skull in the house. I'm sure I saw her going in the front door the day before that big storm when Angus and I were walking. Mattie's car was parked out front and I went over later to bring it to my house out of the weather. She just didn't have time to get all the bones out of the trunk."

"Maybe it was Faith who tried breaking into your garage. She was after the bones," Pearl said.

"Wow, we've pretty much solved the case!" exclaimed Josephine. "All we need now is who killed her, how, and why."

The other ladies gave Josephine their over-the-glasses "teacher stare."

"You know sarcasm is the lowest form of humor," said Cleo.

"Well what other information have you got?" Josephine asked.

"Angus found a bone in his truck," Eleanor added. "He thinks Scout must have dropped it there after the first time we saw Faith with the shovel. It must have rolled under the seat. It too belongs to Charity and makes it clear that she was digging up the bones that day."

"I visited Tonya Jones," said Dede. "Boy, is she a piece of work and mean as all get out! She almost threw me off her porch when I told her I was the mayor and just wanted her opinion of the new road project. She hates everything about the city and the road project, including the mayor. If I gave her a million dollars she would complain about the shade of green on the bills. Then when I told her Faith Strong was in town and planning to build a church she went white as a sheet and totally shut her mouth. I didn't find out a thing."

"That is interesting in itself," said Josephine as if she knew something no one else could discern.

"What?" asked Pearl, "What does that mean?"

"I think it means she feels guilty about Faith and doesn't want to face her," said Josephine.

"So far everyone we've talked to tells the same story. Faith was behaving badly, partying and having sex with every man in town while these mean girls tortured her but no one says how," Eleanor sighed. "Megan Fields said it was Tonya, Vivian, a girl named Sally, and her sister Martha who were all older than Faith. I don't understand why they would bother with her. She couldn't have posed a threat to them."

"Maybe she did," said Pearl. "Remember there were some of the older boys involved with her too. Jude Thorn and Donnie Gold were bad boys who were popular with those girls."

"I talked to Jude," Eleanor said. "He's the contractor working on Faith's church. He said he owed her for things he did to her when she was in high school. He also said she was a carpenter's dream, but I have no idea what that means."

"I've never heard that phrase before," said Dede. Cleo shook her head and Josephine remained silent.

"I'll Google it," Pearl pulled out her phone and began to laugh. "A carpenter's dream is flat as a board and easy to nail."

When Eleanor pulled into the Lumbar Yard she noticed a platinum 4Runner parked next to Dr. Baxter's white pickup truck and wondered if it could be Faith's. Her suspicions were answered when she met Hope in the doorway on her way out.

"Oh Hello, Mrs. Penrose," she said as if startled by Eleanor's presence outside the village of Sand Beach.

Eleanor didn't have time to answer as Hope rushed out, got in her car, and drove away.

"Good afternoon, Vivian," Eleanor greeted. "I was hoping you could squeeze me in to see Dr. Baxter today. My neck is bothering me."

Vivian's eyes were wide open but it was obvious her mind was elsewhere. She looked through Eleanor as if she were made of mist. "Vivian, is the doctor in today?" Eleanor repeated.

"Oh, I'm sorry Mrs. Penrose, did you say something?" Vivian's frozen gaze dropped away.

"Is it possible to see Dr. Baxter today?" Eleanor said.

"Oh no, he left for the day. I can get you in later this week," she said.

"I just saw Hope Strong leaving," Eleanor said, "Did you know she and her sister are building a church in Sand Beach?"

"No, but I did hear her mother's bones were discovered. I can't believe she's been dead this whole time. Believe me it was a shock to see her here. She didn't have an appointment and was with the doctor when I came back from lunch. It's unbelievable!"

"What's unbelievable? Are you talking about Hope? Surely even young people need the services of a chiropractor," Eleanor said.

"When she came out, I could have sworn it was her mother. She is the spitting image of Charity Strong."

Eleanor left with an appointment for another day and an intense desire to know how Dr. Baxter had left when his truck was in the parking lot.

Eleanor sat at her desk and rubbed the rich mahogany wood with her fingers. The glow from the gas fireplace reflected on the panels that surrounded her and created a pleasant work environment. She really felt like snuggling up on the couch with a good book and maybe a nap, but had been ignoring her writing and knew that writers needed to practice their craft or be prepared to lose it.

She picked up her pen and doodled. Hours had passed and Eleanor had not written one word. Her mind seemed disconnected, there was a kink in her neck, and she wasn't thinking clearly. Feathers flew in to inspect things. "It was a dark and stormy night," he offered after viewing the wet weather from his window perch. Eleanor put down her pen.

"Maybe I just need a cup of tea," she said. Feathers ignored her and flew to see who was ringing the doorbell.

"Intruders!" he warned.

Dede entered carrying a lovely coffee cake. "Hi, I hope you don't mind, but I had a brilliant idea and just had to share it with you."

Eleanor was intrigued, "Should I make tea or coffee?"

"Later, right now we need to go over to Faith's house and see what's in that hatbox. If my suspicions are correct, we'll find the skull of Charity Strong," Dede said.

"Don't the police have a warrant to search her place? She might be home, Dede," Eleanor protested. The last time they were in the house, Eleanor had suffered extreme anxiety and she didn't want a repeat.

"The warrant may only be for the grounds not the inside of the house, besides I saw both Faith and Hope entering the Bijou to catch the matinee. *The Ten Commandments* is experiencing a revival. They'll be tied up for hours, but we should go now." Dede deposited the coffee cake in the kitchen and Eleanor hurriedly grabbed her raincoat and the key to the rental house.

"The two sisters are neat and tidy," said Dede upon entering Mattie May's sweet cottage. Eleanor strode immediately to Faith's bedroom.

"It's easy to keep things in order when your belongings are limited," Eleanor said as she opened the closet and searched the upper shelf for the hatbox. "It's not here, Dede."

Dede moved a small wooden chair to the closet, climbed up on it and reached back into the darkest recesses of the closet's shelf. "Nope, it's not here. Faith must have thought the police would be searching her house for it. It must be incriminating in some way."

"Incriminating for whom? Both her parents are dead. Do you think she knows who killed her mother and is protecting them?" Eleanor asked.

"My bet is her father did it and she doesn't want to tarnish his stellar reputation," Dede speculated.

"If the baby wasn't his he may have killed it too," Eleanor said. "At least the baby skeleton is intact, but I don't know if they can determine how it died by its bones alone."

"They can tell if it was his or not," Dede said, "and that could give the police motive for both murders."

"Where do you think she could have hidden the head?" Eleanor muttered. "She must have moved it out of the house."

"That's what I would have done," Dede said as she began to search in the hall closet.

Eleanor left the bedroom and went out to the garage. The door was locked but Eleanor's key unlocked it easily. Dede found an overwhelmed Eleanor inside the small garage staring at a multitude of boxes stacked against all the walls up to the ceiling. There was only a narrow trail that allowed one person to walk through the maze of stuff. "There's no way we can search through all this, no matter how long the movie is," Eleanor sighed. "I doubt the skull is even in here. Faith must have moved it somewhere hoping the police wouldn't find it. "

"This must be everything she moved out of the house and didn't give away," Dede said opening one box that was filled with Christmas ornaments.

"I don't have the energy to even start," Eleanor said. "The enormity of the task has drained me."

"Me too," Dede said. "Let's go back inside and see if we can find anything else."

Dede closed the box and Eleanor locked the door behind them. "We don't want Faith to have an inkling that we were here, so be sure to move that chair in the bedroom back where it was," Eleanor cautioned.

While Dede returned to the bedroom, Eleanor wandered into the cozy living room. She remembered sitting with Mattie May in this very room, drinking tea and chatting. It was easy to keep Mattie in her thoughts when so many of her things remained just as she had left them. Amazing that Mattie would leave her this house upon her death. Eleanor missed the matriarch of the Do Nothings. When she left them she took a wealth of knowledge and wisdom with her. Secretly, Eleanor held on to the ridiculous hope that Mattie had somehow escaped with her lover and was living out her life in something like the witness protection program. Deep in thought, Eleanor almost tripped on the box beside the overstuffed chair.

"Did you bring that box in here?" asked Dede entering the room.

"No, it looks like someone was sorting through it. If this is how they intend to inspect each box, it will take years." Eleanor sat down and reached into the box that held books and some envelopes tied with blue rickrack. "These are journals."

Dede pulled out one of the books and began to read it. "This is Charity's diary and it's very boring. It sounds to me like Prissy was a prude."

'Went to church today and sat next to Prissy. She is such a good friend to me, always truthful but in a kind way. I know she would never mean to hurt my feelings but she whispered that my dress was inappropriate for church. I didn't see anything wrong with it and it's one of my favorites. My husband complimented me on it just this morning and said it was lovely. I'm sure he would have told me if the neckline was too revealing or the hem too short. Nevertheless, I will donate it to Goodwill. I can't afford to be the object of gossip in this congregation.'

"Either that or jealous of the way Charity looked in that dress," Eleanor said. "Gladys said many of the women resented her beauty. We can't read all these, but we should tell Angus what we found. The real detective work is sorting through this evidence to find clues to solve a cold case. Let's go."

Back at her house, Eleanor made a fresh pot of coffee and Dede cut the coffee cake. "I don't think I have the patience to be a real detective," Eleanor admitted. "It must take hours of tedious reading and sorting through useless data to come up with one meaningful clue."

"I know, and then if you aren't paying attention, you might miss the clue. I'm glad I'm the mayor and not an investigator," Dede said.

"Unfortunately, I can't seem to get any writing done now," Eleanor admitted. "Come into my office. I want to show you something." Dede obediently followed.

Eleanor's office was warm and comfortable and a perfect location for her work, yet one wall was completely devoted to the cold case. On a whiteboard were the names and pictures of possible suspects taped next to the victim. Under each name was the possible motive for killing Charity Strong. She had even posted pictures she had taken with her phone of the grave sites. It looked very professional and Dede was impressed. She studied it carefully.

"You don't think I'm obsessed, do you?" asked Eleanor.

"No, I think you are very thorough and organized," Dede said. "I especially like this timeline you've created. It helps to put things in perspective since all this happened so long ago. Where did you get these pictures?"

"I copied them from the yearbooks Pearl brought. It's what I've been working on instead of my writing," Eleanor admitted.

"Have you shown it to Angus?" Dede asked.

"Not yet."

"He has a different kind of mind and may see things we missed," Dede said.

"I think the coffee's ready." Eleanor and Dede left the office to enjoy a tasty treat, but were interrupted by knocking at the door.

"Angus, your timing is perfect. We were just going to have some coffee cake," Eleanor said.

"Would you like to join us?" invited Dede.

"Another time," Angus said. "I need you to watch Scout, Ellie. Something's come up at the Strong house and I don't know how long they'll need me."

"What's happened?" asked Eleanor.

"Jude Thorn's been shot."

Sand Beach is a small village so it didn't take long for word to spread about the death of Jude Thorn. People speculated about which of the many women he'd wronged who could have done it or whose husband might have shot him, but the possibilities were so many there were no concrete suspects. His exploits were legendary throughout the county. The fact that he and Vivian were divorcing made her the prime suspect. Some citizens even suggested one of his many wild oats might have done him in. Eleanor suspected it was connected to Charity Strong's bones.

"I talked to the man just a few days ago. It seemed as though he had worked it out with Faith, so I don't think she could have killed him," Eleanor told her coffee group the next morning at an unscheduled meeting.

"No, I don't think Faith did it either unless she did him in before the matinee," said Dede. "What would her motive be?"

"Perhaps she has unresolved issues that have been stirred up by her father's death and her return home," Josephine said.

"She certainly is at the heart of everything," Pearl said. "At least Faith and Charity are central figures."

"Well, I can remove Jude from my list of suspects in the cold case," Eleanor said.

"Did you actually suspect that he killed Charity and her baby?" asked Cleo, "I didn't think of that possibility but it's brilliant."

"Are you implying that Charity was having an affair with a boy. Not only is that statutory rape but it's adultery, both very unchristian and even illegal," said Dede.

"You know what Josephine always says about everyone having a dark side. Maybe Charity wasn't as pure as people believed," Cleo argued.

"Not everyone described her as pure. Gladys told me many women were jealous of her because she was beautiful. Several girls spread rumors about her being with other men. Even her good friend Prissy accused her of dressing provocatively, so maybe they weren't lies." Eleanor shared the diary entry that involved Prissy's criticism.

"Remember that line from *Anne of Green Gables?* 'Which would you rather be if you had the choice—divinely beautiful or dazzlingly clever or angelically good?' I always thought I would like to be divinely beautiful but now I see the downside to that," Cleo said thoughtfully.

"No women friends and men who are blinded to the beauty of your soul by your physical attributes," Eleanor said. "That sounds like a very lonely life."

"Maybe she killed herself because it was more than she could bear," suggested Josephine.

"I'm sure she didn't bury herself," said Cleo.

"If we found her skull, we might know how she died," Dede said.

The vision of Faith standing next to the PUD's chipping machine flooded Eleanor's memory and she wondered if Faith had disposed of the skull while the crew was distracted by the falling branch. "I'm beginning to think we may never know," Eleanor lamented.

"I wouldn't remove Jude Thorn from your list yet, Eleanor," said Pearl. "These are two separate murders. He could have killed Charity and now someone may be exacting their revenge on him."

"It all comes back to Faith," said Dede. "She had a motive. Jude's murder happened after she moved back and the bones were found. We know she lied about the missing skull, so she's hiding something."

"Right, but his death will delay the building of her church. If Faith wanted to kill him she would have waited until the church was finished," Eleanor reasoned.

"Emotions could have overridden her logic," Josephine said calmly. "Or she may never have intended to build a church at all but used the idea to lure him there so she could kill him."

"What if Jude got her pregnant and she lost the baby so her parents buried it to keep it a secret?" Cleo speculated. "She might harbor a great deal of anger over that."

"But why kill him now?" asked Pearl.

"Shame?" said Josephine.

"We don't know anything. There are too many suspects and not enough facts," sighed Eleanor.

"Does Angus know anything?" asked Cleo.

"I don't know. I haven't seen much of him lately. As a matter of fact, I have to get back home to walk the dog."

Eleanor hurried out of the Boat House and swung by the Lumbar Yard to keep her appointment with Dr. Baxter. When she entered his office she saw no one in the waiting room and no one behind the receptionist's desk. She wondered if Dr. Baxter was in and peeked out the window to see if his truck was in the lot. His white pickup truck sat next to her own car. She really needed to work on her observation skills.

There were no other cars parked outside, but Eleanor could hear the muffled sound of someone sobbing. She opened the door and closed it with a bang. It wasn't long before Dr. Baxter emerged, "Hello, Mrs. Penrose. I didn't see that you had an appointment today. Are you all right?"

"I made the appointment with Vivian," Eleanor said as she noticed the redness of the doctor's eyes. She wondered if Dr. Baxter had a relationship with Vivian and her husband outside of work. Perhaps he was crying over Jude's death.

"Well, that explains it. Vivian hasn't been herself lately and is off today. She probably forgot to put you in the book," he fumbled around with some papers on her desk and Eleanor noticed a piece of blue rickrack. She had seen that same blue rickrack before.

"My neck is giving me a little trouble. I think I may need another adjustment," she explained. "I seem to be experiencing everything in a fog."

Dr. Baxter led the way into his examining room and typed something into his computer and washed his hands. He was unusually quiet and somber. Eleanor noticed several envelopes on his stool and took the time to observe the skeleton that hung in the corner of the room. It was very clean and white, not at all like the bones she had discovered in her garage. She wondered if a beautiful person also had beautiful bones.

"Can you tell by someone's bones if they are divinely beautiful?" she asked as she lay on the table.

"No, you have to see into their soul to discover real beauty," he said. Eleanor heard her neck crack and realized a sudden clearness of thought. She drove home and added Dr. Baxter to her list of suspects before she took Scout out for a walk.

Eleanor opened a bottle of pinot and danced through the kitchen in her stockinged feet. She felt good. It was amazing how good she felt. She didn't even know how bad she was feeling until she had Dr. Baxter realign her neck. It had happened slowly and insidiously. Her neck muscles connected to her shoulder muscles, connected to her back muscles had pulled little by little until they caused such discomfort that she couldn't think straight. It was like a frog that is boiled in a pot when the water is warmed so slowly he doesn't notice until it is too late.

She felt an affection borne out of gratitude for Dr. Baxter, but that didn't keep her from adding him to her list of suspects. He had letters from Charity Strong's box. Eleanor was positive Hope had found them in the box in Mattie's living room. There were other letters in that box tied up with blue rickrack that matched what Eleanor had seen on the receptionist's desk in his office. Hope was delivering them to him when Eleanor saw her there. The same day Vivian was shocked by Hope's resemblance to her mother. Eleanor wondered if Dr. Baxter had been in love with Charity. Maybe the letters were love letters he had written to her. She wondered if Hope had read them before returning them. Whatever happened had obviously upset him so much that he couldn't work that day and today he was sobbing and Eleanor knew strong feelings often resulted in equally strong actions.

Eleanor greeted Angus with open arms and an offering of Crown Royal. Scout's welcome was much more vigorous and involved sloppy kisses and a happy dance Eleanor could not emulate.

"It's good to be loved," Angus smiled, dimpling his handsome cheeks, and took a long sip of his drink. "What are you cooking?"

"Stuffed salmon with Mediterranean sauce, new potatoes, and broccoli," Eleanor answered.

"Where did you get the salmon? Have you been fishing?" Angus teased although he wouldn't be surprised if her answer was yes. He liked to think he was the only man who put food on Eleanor's table.

"I bought it," she admitted.

"Shame on you, naughty girl," Angus approached her in a menacing way. "Naughty girls need spanking."

"Intruders, intruders," squawked Feathers as he flew to the door and Scout began to bark.

"Saved by the bell," said Angus.

"I forgot to tell you, I invited Amy and Taylor for dinner. The children are at a fun night at school." Eleanor opened the door and greeted the couple who presented her with a bottle of Viognier, which would pair perfectly with the salmon.

"Come in. Amy would you open the wine while I take care of the sauce, please." Eleanor went to the kitchen while Angus hung up coats and tried in vain to stop an unruly dog from jumping up on the guests.

"Scout, down," he ordered in his stern master voice but Scout continued his happy dance that included leaps and licks.

"Bones, down," Eleanor's voice came from the kitchen doorway and produced an obedient response quickly rewarded with a treat.

"Eleanor, what have you done to my dog?" Angus cried indignantly. "I knew if I left him here you would take over. Have you changed his name too?"

"Yes," Eleanor answered and returned to her sauce with Angus following close behind.

Amy and Taylor watched with amused smiles on their faces. They had never witnessed an argument between the couple before and wondered how it would play out. Taylor took advantage of the moment to pour a glass of Crown Royal from Angus' bottle.

"I was only gone for the day." Angus was amazed. "I suppose you seduced him with delicious gourmet doggy treats and now he loves you more than he loves me. That is lower than low, Eleanor. I can't believe you could stab me in the back this way."

"Angus, you are overreacting," Eleanor spoke calmly. "I did nothing subversive. Your dog just responds to his original name, Bones, and he likes these little liver bits. I'm sure he will react to you in the same way if you call him by the name he knows."

Angus' bushy brows descended but he couldn't come up with a reasonable response, so he simply gave his dog a rough petting. "Bones, sit," he commanded and his dog sat meekly at his feet. "Where do you keep the liver bits?"

Dinner was a delight. Eleanor had forgotten how fun and entertaining Amy and Taylor could be when their children weren't around to demand all the adult attention. There were no knock-knock jokes or arguments over who would sit where or be first to go in a game of Birds and Binoculars. Eleanor did miss the knock-knock jokes, but adult conversation did not have to be carefully monitored and that was refreshing.

"I heard Jude Thorn was shot," Taylor said. "Are you part of the investigation?"

"Did you know him?" asked Angus.

"Not well, but I did know of him," Taylor said. "He was a master carpenter."

"You don't know who would want to kill him do you?" Angus asked.

"Probably lots of people wished him dead, but I never heard any complaints about his craftsmanship—only his sexual exploits, and that was mostly in the past. Hopefully he matured over the years," Taylor said. "Do you have any suspects?"

"Nope." Angus obviously didn't want to talk about the case with Taylor who seemed to have little new information to offer.

"What about the cold case? Are you still working on that?" asked Amy.

Angus watched the color drain from Eleanor's face. Eleanor suddenly realized that Elise could be implicated in the murder investigation. She and her friend Adrianne were in the Strong house and surely had left their fingerprints there. How could she keep her promise not to tell when so much was a stake?

"Are you all right, Ellie?" Angus asked.

"Yes, I just forgot about the dessert," she left the table and Angus followed sensing something was amiss.

"What's wrong?" His voice was full of concern.

"I promised not to tell, but Elise and her friend were in the Strong house the night Bones dug up the baby bones. They thought it would be exciting to snoop around. Now it's the scene of a murder investigation and their fingerprints are probably all over." Eleanor's worry was evident.

"She's just like her Gramma, a meddling busy body. It must be genetic. Maybe she should learn early in life to leave the snooping to professionals. I could have Officer McGraw bring her in for questioning and nip this genetic flaw in the bud." Angus was enjoying the opportunity to observe Eleanor's discomfort, but he wasn't prepared for her mother bear reaction.

"Don't you dare! Angus McBride, if you do I swear I will never speak to you again and that's a promise," she hissed. "I have a very special relationship with that child and if you do that she will never confide in me again. I can't tell Amy either. You have to help me." Angus had never seen Eleanor so upset about anything before, or so worried. He thought she might cry and that was something he couldn't suffer.

"Don't worry, Ellie, I'll take care of it." he caught her in an embrace and held her until he felt her sigh. "You know I was only kidding. Elise's prints aren't on file are they?" Eleanor pushed him away and grabbed the tray that held the dishes of decadent chocolate mousse and returned to the table.

Amy and Taylor looked at each other knowingly. They had often fled to the kitchen to discuss private matters themselves.

"I'm worried about Elise," Eleanor began as she balanced the chocolate confection on her spoon. "I've been hearing a lot about how Faith Strong was bullied by those mean girls at school. There are so many more ways teens can torment each other today."

"Don't worry about Elise, Mom. Taylor and I have discussed this already. Elise will never be bullied anywhere by anyone. Of our three children the one most likely to be a serial killer is Elise." Amy and Taylor laughed hysterically.

Angus was afraid to laugh. "What a horrible thing to say." Eleanor put her spoon down. "You can't really believe such nonsense."

"Well, she does terrorize Addie and Wesley," Taylor said. "Have you seen her scary clown eyes?"

Eleanor had to admit she had seen them and they were very disturbing. "You don't think she could be one of those mean girls do you?"

"Of course not, Mom, you know Elise. She's very naïve and sweet unless she's dealing with Addie and Wesley," Amy explained. "But she has confidence and that makes it possible for her to stand her ground and better than that, she's a protector of the underdog. She would never stand by and watch someone bully anyone else."

"We're very proud of Elise," Taylor said, "and because of the excellent parenting she's received, she's someone you can be proud of too, Eleanor."

"Now back to that cold case. What's happened?" Amy persisted.

"Is the murder of Jude Thorn connected to the bones?" Taylor asked.

Angus spoke up before Eleanor could muddy the waters with her unsubstantiated theories. "It's way too early to tell," he said.

"I'd put my money on Faith," said Taylor. "She had good reason to knock him off."

"Poor Faith, it seems she can't escape the rumor mill. They just grind her up and spit her out. I don't think you should be making accusations, Taylor. She's had enough of that in her life," Amy scolded. Eleanor wondered if Amy was consciously protecting the underdog.

"I'm just saying she seems like the obvious choice," said Taylor.

"Maybe too obvious; 'There is nothing as deceptive as an obvious fact.'" Angus quoted Sir Arthur Canon Doyle.

After Amy and Taylor left, Angus and Eleanor cleaned up the kitchen together. "I know you don't like Faith, but you don't believe she killed Jude do you?" Eleanor said.

"I find it hard to believe someone who is building a church would shoot a man in the back when he's standing on what she would consider holy ground," Angus said.

"Maybe building a church isn't her real goal. She might be misguided and think it's her calling to cleanse the world of sinners like Jude," Eleanor speculated.

"Maybe," he said thoughtfully, "I think she's all bluster and bluff. She's been through a lot of heartache in her life. Inside, she's still a sad and lonely little girl looking for someone to accept her and love her."

Eleanor studied Angus and wondered if he saw a kindred spirit in Faith Strong. After all she had seen his demon—maybe she recognized it because it resembled her own. Eleanor put her arms around him and melted into his warmth. Whatever demon Angus had, she knew he was a good man. It made her love him all the more when she saw evidence of his kindness and his willingness to see the good in someone as cold as Faith Strong. "She's only shown you her bad side. What's changed?" she asked.

"The DNA tests from the bones and hair came back. Charity Strong wasn't Hope's mother. She was her grandmother. Faith isn't Hope's sister. She's her mother."

Eleanor opened her eyes but could not erase the dream . . .
A skeleton dressed in a sexy gossamer gown stepped out of the grave and began to gyrate in a provocative way. Suddenly, her head fell off and rolled back into her grave. She danced on unaware until she realized something was wrong, then stepped back into her grave and stooped to pick up her head but came out with a baby instead.

She didn't even try to make sense of it. Obviously it was a remnant of her daily dose of death and mystery. Eleanor lay in bed thinking about the information she knew and how she could use it to solve this case. Something about the return of

Faith and Hope, the discovery of what was left of Charity, had stirred up someone and caused the murder of Jude Thorn. Angus said he was shot in the back—a cowardly act. She didn't know the exact time of Jude's death, but Hope had been at Dr. Baxter's office in the morning, and with Faith at the matinee that afternoon. Vivian was also at work that day but had gone home early. Angus hadn't said if the murder weapon had been found or if he had a suspect other than Faith, who was the obvious one. If she hadn't committed the crime, she might know who did. She was hiding something or protecting someone. Eleanor got out of bed and added another suspect to her list.

A warrant had been issued to search the house Faith and Hope were renting. Nothing had been found in the Strong house and now Eleanor suspected the police were looking for a weapon. Faith offered nothing to help either herself or the police in the investigation.

"It's a delicate situation," Angus explained as he and Eleanor sat on her couch gazing into the fire. "No one wants to traumatize Hope by telling her that Faith is her mother and Faith isn't giving up any information. She isn't willing to tell Hope the truth. My guess is she's afraid Hope will lose respect for her if she knows about her past."

"Do you think Jude is Hope's father?" asked Eleanor.

"I don't know," Angus replied. "She had a reputation for sleeping around and DNA testing isn't always conclusive. My hunch is it wasn't any of those boys, but there are more tests that can be done. Meanwhile, we keep searching for a weapon. There must be a hundred boxes stored in Mattie's garage and that's going to take time too. Until we get a break in this case, we can't arrest anyone."

"I understand that Jude had a reputation too," Eleanor said. "There must be several people who wanted him dead including Vivian, his estranged wife."

Angus put his arm around Eleanor and drew her close. "What do you know about his wife?"

"I can't prove it, but I just know she's in love with Dr. Baxter, the chiropractor. I suspect he was in love with Charity Strong before she disappeared." Eleanor rested her head on Angus' shoulder and felt him tighten his embrace.

"Tell me more," he whispered.

"Well, as I was going into Dr. Baxter's office, Hope was coming out and Vivian, the receptionist, said Hope was the spitting image of Charity Strong. She seemed frazzled and then said Hope was with Dr. Baxter when she came back from lunch but that he was out of the office for the rest of the day. I made an appointment for the following day and when I returned Vivian wasn't at work. Dr. Baxter was in his office sobbing and I noticed letters tied with blue rickrack on the receptionist's desk. I'm pretty sure they were letters from Dr. Baxter to Charity and Hope had returned them after finding them among her things."

"Wait, wait." Angus sat up and looked at Eleanor beneath his lowered brows. "That's quite a leap, Ellie. What makes you think these letters were from Dr. Baxter to Charity? What the hell has blue rickrack got to do with it? What is rickrack anyway?"

Eleanor took a deep breath. "Rickrack is a kind of zigzag ribbon. I saw the same blue rickrack tied around letters in a box in Faith's living room." Half way through her explanation she realized she would have to tell Angus about Dede's suspicions and their attempt to find the skull.

"Go on." Angus tilted his head and clenched his jaw. Eleanor wondered if he was stifling his urge to lecture her about snooping.

"That's it," she said.

"Was this the same time you broke into Faith's house to get her DNA or another time?" he asked.

"Well, the first time, Dede saw a hatbox in the closet but we didn't open it because Josephine came in and told us we had to leave because there wasn't any cell service and there was no way we could tell if Faith was coming back. After we found the bones in the trunk of Mattie's car, Dede suspected the skull might be in the hatbox but when we went back, the hatbox was gone. We looked in the garage, saw the hundreds of boxes, and then discovered one in the living room that contained journals and letters tied with blue rickrack." Eleanor took a breath and looked cautiously at Angus who was biting his lip.

"Okay, what makes you think Vivian Thorn is in love with Dr. Baxter?" he asked.

"I saw the way she looked at him," Eleanor said.

Angus stroked his mustache. He wondered if people knew he loved Eleanor by the way he looked at her. Was she looking at him that way? Maybe he had missed it. It was impossible for Eleanor to know what Angus was thinking. Perhaps the trained professional had solved the case.

Mavis Bench was in a state of eager excitement. She had showered, styled her wavy white hair, and even applied mascara to her thinning lashes. Usually calm and sensible Mavis, who prided herself on her ability to see things clearly through a scientific and logical perspective, was as giddy as a school girl getting ready for her first date. She had spent the last hour selecting the perfect outfit to complement her aging figure. Standing in front of the mirror she decided she looked as good as she ever would and left her house to meet Sybil for coffee at Suzanna's.

She was surprised to find Eleanor sitting at their usual table with Sybil.

"Mavis, you look different. Did you do something new with your hair?" asked Eleanor.

"No, yes, well maybe," she stammered as she sat down.

"You look absolutely radiant!" Sybil exclaimed. "Are you wearing makeup?"

Mavis rolled her eyes. Couldn't a person try something new without everyone making such a fuss? "Yes, I'm wearing makeup and I have a new outfit and I used hair spray. Now I need coffee."

Sybil poured a cup of coffee from the table's carafe while exchanging a look with Eleanor. "Are you meeting a man? Do you have a date with Captain Fox?" she asked.

Mavis couldn't lie. "Yes, he's coming today and I have to admit I'm terribly nervous."

"How exciting." Eleanor was afraid of saying the wrong thing. She didn't want to comment on her appearance. A woman shouldn't have to wear makeup to impress a man and Eleanor thought Mavis always looked attractive with or without hair spray. "When is he arriving?"

"He said he would be here this afternoon."

"Can we meet him or are you keeping him a secret?" asked Sybil.

"Oh, I'd love it if you could meet him. I was planning to cook him a wonderful meal, but really I think I'd rather bring him here for dinner. It's been forever since I entertained a man. I could use some support."

"Why don't we make a party of it?" suggested Eleanor. "We can all meet here for dinner and then if he turns out to be a dud, you can send him on his way."

Mavis was caught off guard. It was obvious she wasn't planning to meet a dud but, of course, Eleanor *was* right. Even though she felt like she knew this man, she didn't. "Yes, I think that would be delightful."

By the time Eleanor and Angus arrived at Suzanna's with Sybil later that evening, Mavis and her man were seated near the window drinking martinis and giggling. Eleanor was surprised to see how familiar they had become in such a short time. They were obviously unaware that the new arrivals were watching as they sat close together constantly touching and gazing into each other's eyes, but as they approached the man stood and held out his hand.

"So glad you could make it!" His voice was deep and his manner cheerful. "I'm Phineas Fox."

"Angus McBride and this is Eleanor and Sybil." Angus introduced them as they found seats at the table.

"What's your pleasure? The drinks are on me," Phineas offered generously as he raised his hand to signal the waitress.

Eleanor tried to be open-minded but the idea that he was trying to get Mavis drunk crept into her thoughts. "I'd love a martini." Angus ordered Crown Royal and Sybil asked for a glass of the white house wine. As they waited for their drinks Eleanor studied the man with the eyes of a protective mother.

Phineas Fox held his full head of white hair with dignity. He wasn't what Eleanor would consider a handsome man and stood a good half-foot shorter than Angus, but emanated a certain aura of charm and power. His brown eyes twinkled when he laughed and he laughed often. By the time their drinks arrived Eleanor had decided she liked Phineas, against her own good judgment. It was all too apparent that Mavis was smitten. Sybil, on the other hand, had taken it upon herself to interrogate the man with ruthless honesty. "So Mr. Fox, what are your intentions with our friend Mavis?"

"I intend to woo her in style, sweep her off her pretty little feet, and take her home to San Diego to be one of my favorite wives," he laughed. "Then after I've ravished her, we will travel the world so I can show her all the places I've been and introduce her to the most interesting people I've ever encountered." He met Sybil's suspicious eyes head on and flashed the most charismatic smile.

Sybil simply sighed and sipped her wine. "Oh, Foxy Loxy," Mavis cooed as she stroked his arm affectionately.

"How many wives do you have, Foxy Loxy?" asked Eleanor flashing her own enchanting smile.

He laughed in such an infectious way they all joined in and the inquisition of Phineas Fox came to a temporary end. After a delicious meal of green salad, surf and turf, and delicately seasoned rosemary potatoes, they ordered the marionberry cobbler for dessert. Phineas insisted on picking up the tab, and then invited Angus to accompany him outside for a cigar.

"So what do you think of my surprising find?" Mavis asked. Her eyes sparkled with intense curiosity.

"I like him," Eleanor confessed.

"Yes, he seems very charming," Sybil said, "but what do you really know about him?"

"I'm old, but I'm no fool, Sybil." Mavis leaned in. "I intend to find out all about him before I commit to anything."

Eleanor was sure Mavis would use her scientific method of coming to a conclusion to sort out the man and his honest intentions. She, however, was not giving up on the team of Parker and Patrick Private Investigators she'd hired to do a background check on Mr. Foxy Loxy.

When Angus brought Eleanor home, they were greeted by two excited animals. Feathers flew to Eleanor's shoulder and pressed his bird face to hers in a fowl hug and then kissed her with a loud smack.

"Is that a new trick?" Angus asked as he caressed the dog that danced around him happily.

Eleanor just smiled until her wide eyes took in the large pile in the kitchen that could only be a present from the dog.

"Oh, no!" she rushed to the bathroom to fetch toilet paper while Angus watched in amusement. He knew how much Eleanor valued cleanliness and was somehow pleased by her overreaction to the dog's mess. It was all the more entertaining because he stood by idly watching. Eleanor could not believe his audacity and threw the roll of toilet paper at him with all the force of a quarterback.

"I don't know what you're so upset about, Ellie," he said calmly walking to the pile. "It's just a little doggy doo." And with that he picked it up in his hand and threw it at her.

Eleanor's scream startled Feathers who flew at Angus in a fit of parrot rage and caused the dog to commence barking wildly. It was chaos and pandemonium until Eleanor realized the doggy doo in question was merely made of rubber. The sheer relief sent her into peals of hysterical laughter as she sunk to the floor where the dog licked her all over. Angus freed himself from the crazed parrot and gave Eleanor a hand up.

"I can't believe you did that," she said between laughs. "When did you put that there?"

"Just before we left for dinner." Angus stroked her back until she gained control and was quite pleased with his little prank. "I'll take Bones out for a bit now if you think you've recovered."

"Oh, please do that. I'm having a nightcap. Shall I make one for you?" she asked wiping tears of mirth from her eyes.

"Absolutely, but Ellie don't even think of putting that in my Crown Royal," he warned.

The weekly meeting of the coffee group commenced with a review of everything they thought they knew about the case of Charity Strong's bones, and the murder of Jude Thorn.

"You say you saw the same blue rickrack in Dr. Baxter's office as in the box of Charity's letters and journals," Dede pondered.

"That does sound like an important clue," Cleo concurred. "Could there be another explanation besides a love connection between them? He might be the lover everyone says she had."

"Maybe, but it's possible it was only a one way kind of crush. She was older than he was and it appears that Hope was returning the letters to him," Josephine reasoned. "We can't be sure *she* loved him."

"But she kept them," said Pearl. "That indicates some emotion."

"That could indicate nothing more than vanity," said Dede.

"He was obviously moved by those letters and the return of Charity in the form of Hope who must look a great deal like her grandmother. Could it still be so painful after all these years if it was merely a crush?" asked Eleanor.

"Maybe Dr. Baxter was blackmailing Charity and then killed her because she wouldn't pay anymore. Hope found the letters and now she's blackmailing him and that's why he's crying," Cleo speculated.

"What do you think he had on her?" asked Dede.

"Who knows? Maybe he knew who her lover was and was threatening to tell everyone what a lustful creature she was," Cleo said.

"It's unlikely Charity would tie up blackmail letters with blue rickrack," countered Josephine.

"Wait a minute. Did you call Charity Hope's grandmother? Wasn't Charity her mother?" asked Pearl.

"Oh, I forgot to tell you, the DNA tests came back and revealed that Faith is Hope's mother. I'm not sure if that's public knowledge," Eleanor whispered.

"Well, that definitely answers the question about a baby," said Cleo, "Now we know for sure that Faith was sexually active, and most likely sent away because of her scandalous condition."

"Yes, but what about the baby that was buried? Is there a DNA test from it?" asked Josephine. "And who was the father of Faith's child?"

"Maybe it was Dr. Baxter and that was his blackmail," Cleo continued.

"That would make him guilty of statutory rape," said Pearl.

"If they find that Jude Thorn was the father, that might be a motive for Faith to kill him," Dede said.

"If Hope found out somehow, maybe she killed him," Eleanor said. "I'm not sure Hope knows who her mother and father really are yet."

"I wonder who killed Charity and how this is connected to Jude's murder. I don't believe it's just a coincidence," Pearl said.

"What is the connection between Charity and Jude Thorn?" asked Josephine.

"What or who?" asked Eleanor.

"I'm sure the answers are somewhere in those boxes that were stored in Faith's garage," Dede said.

"The police are working through them but as far as I know they haven't found a weapon or the hatbox that we saw in Faith's closet," Eleanor explained.

"That's a lot of stuff to go through," Dede said. "I wonder how much stuff Faith gave away."

"Her father lived in that house for decades. I bet he kept a lot of Charity's things, plus all the other memorabilia of a lifetime," Pearl said.

"Wait a minute," Cleo said. "What would you do if you had to clean out your family home in a hurry and couldn't decide what to keep?"

"Put it in boxes and store it just like Faith did," Eleanor said. "Are you thinking she didn't give anything away?"

"The garage was full. What if there was more stuff that didn't fit in the garage?" asked Cleo.

"She has a storage unit!" exclaimed Pearl. "She moved the incriminating stuff to it."

"How can we be sure?" asked Josephine. "And even if she does, how would we find it?"

"She had to get someone to help move it," suggested Cleo.

"If she rented a U-Haul she and Hope could have done it by themselves," Pearl said.

"They are young and strong, but I bet they needed help lifting some of the heavier pieces. There wasn't any furniture in the garage. I bet Jude Thorn helped them. He said he had to atone for things he'd done to Faith in the past. What if he got her pregnant and felt guilty?" Eleanor said.

"So you think she killed him when she was finished using him to help her move?" asked Pearl.

"She may have killed him to tie up the loose ends, and to keep her secret safe," Josephine said.

"It seems too obvious . . . not to mention stupid to kill him inside her home." Eleanor sighed.

"All this is mere speculation," Josephine said. "We still need solid proof."

"If we could find a key to the storage unit, we could find the evidence we need," Dede said.

"We'll have to get back inside Faith's house and look for a key. We need a plan to get the two of them away for a significant amount of time so we can do a complete search," Pearl said.

"Isn't there a better way than breaking into that house, one that doesn't involve heart-pounding anxiety?" asked Eleanor, whose palms were getting sweaty just thinking about it.

"I know," said Cleo. "We send a cryptic note to Faith telling her we found the gun she used to kill Jude, then do a stakeout and watch for Faith to visit her unit to check on it."

"How does that get us in the unit to snoop around?" Eleanor asked.

"Not only is that dangerous," Josephine said, "but it totally depends on Faith being the killer. Jude had other enemies and we don't know if Faith has the gun. It would make more sense to tell her we know what's in the hatbox. We know she dug up the bones."

"That only tells us which unit she's rented but still doesn't get us inside," Dede said.

"Don't private investigators trick people into letting them inside places they're not allowed? Maybe we could convince the storage unit managers to let us into Faith's," Cleo suggested.

"Okay, how? How do we convince them?" Pearl asked.

"We send the mayor to the storage facility and she tells them Faith is making a donation to her church from her storage unit," Cleo said.

"The storage manager would want proof and would probably stand there while I looked for whatever I have no idea is in there," Dede dismissed the entire idea with the wave of her hand. She could already envision the headline: "Mayor Indicted for Fraud in Storage Theft."

"I guess we search for the key in Faith's house," Eleanor sighed but felt an unexpected thrill. "It's obviously the best way."

"We'll need to get them out of the house," Dede said thoughtfully. "I could still invite them to an ecumenical meeting of our community churches."

"The rest of us will meet at Eleanor's and then search the house for the key," Josephine said. "Does anyone know what kind of lock is used or what the key might look like?"

"It's just a padlock, with the kind of key that fits a padlock," said Dede. "I'll find an example somewhere."

"We should make a mold of the key so we can get a copy made," Cleo suggested.

"Does that really work?" asked Eleanor.

"Let's just take the key," suggested Josephine. "We're already committing breaking and entering. We might as well add stealing to the list."

"When is the meeting?" asked Pearl.

"Monday night," answered Dede.

Eleanor lay in bed that night but couldn't sleep. Her mind was buzzing with thoughts of the upcoming break-in. Something wasn't right. If the storage unit was locked with a simple padlock how would they ever know which unit belonged to Faith? There wouldn't be a number on it telling them which one it was, so having the key meant nothing. They didn't know for sure if Faith even had a storage unit.

They had to use Cleo's dangerous plan that sent Faith to the storage unit so they could follow her there. Eleanor's mind kept her thinking and planning well into the night. How could they get Faith to visit the storage unit before Monday? In the morning, she called the ladies to tell them of her plan.

That evening the members of the coffee group met at Dede's house dressed in black. Josephine made a telephone call to Faith pretending to be the manager of the storage facility. She claimed someone had broken in to Faith's unit and she needed to come in to make sure nothing had been taken. Cleo brought a variety of mustaches and insisted they wear them along with stocking caps and glasses. Eleanor rented an inconspicuous black van and they all piled in to stakeout the only storage facility in town, Lock N Roll.

Eleanor parked the van behind a hedge near the entrance to the facility and the waiting began.

"Do we have to wear these ridiculous mustaches?" asked Josephine whose nose was sensitive and began to itch.

"I think you look so very attractive with that one," Pearl said. "You remind me of Magnum PI."

"It's exactly like his," Dede agreed.

Suddenly Cleo began to giggle about the absurdity of five senior women dressed in black disguised as men pretending to be private detectives. Once she started she could not stop and soon Dede and Pearl began to laugh as well. When Cleo snorted, it was all Josephine and Eleanor could do to keep from joining in the hilarity. The laughter went on for quite some time until Pearl choked out the disturbing phrase that brought them all back to reality, "I think I've peed my pants!" But it was only a pause and then the giggling and snorting began all over again.

"If we are going to solve this case, the least I expect is a minimum of silliness." Eleanor finally managed to gain control and the laughing faded away, erupted again, and then finally ceased altogether.

"I forgot how horrible stakeouts could be," grumbled Pearl through her droopy mustache. At least they had refrained from bringing treats and beverages—a lesson they learned from a previous experience.

"What are we going to do once Faith arrives?" asked Cleo.

"What if she never comes?" asked Dede. "Are you sure she has a storage unit?"

"She told me she would come right away," Josephine reassured. "If she didn't have a unit, I'm sure she would have said so."

"Patience ladies," Eleanor said, "It takes a while to drive into Waterton from Sand Beach. When she comes we'll have to follow her to her unit and get the number so we can find the evidence."

"Do you think all of us need to follow her?" asked Pearl. "It might be less obvious if only two or three go."

"Good thinking," Dede said, "Pearl and I will stay in the van."

"The three of us will keep to the shadows," Eleanor said.

"I didn't think to wear sneakers," said Cleo. "Maybe I should stay in the van."

Josephine checked her shoes. "I'm sure you and I can pull this off Eleanor. It's probably best that only two of us go anyway."

"We'll keep a lookout for police or other suspicious characters and call if there's a problem," Dede said.

"Set your phone to vibrate, Eleanor. You wouldn't want Faith to hear your phone ringing," Cleo cautioned.

"Oh, someone's pulling into the entrance," warned Pearl. "Do you have a flashlight?"

Eleanor nodded in the darkness, turned off the overhead light, and slipped silently out of the car. Josephine followed her lead. They moved toward the hedge and disappeared as the others slunk down in their seats.

It was a very dark night but there were a few overhead lights mounted on the storage buildings. Eleanor watched Faith get out of her car and move quickly toward one of the buildings. They waited until she rounded the corner before following her. Their bodies cast long shadows near the lights until they reached the safety of the building where they pressed themselves close. Eleanor suppressed the desire to react when she spotted a spider crawling nearby. They could see Faith fumbling with her keys. Josephine made a brave move forward and ducked between two buildings. Eleanor followed behind and peeked out of the narrow passage to see Faith stop and mutter to herself. She was obviously annoyed and confused to find her lock intact. She unlocked the door, pulled it up with a loud clanging noise that split the still night, and went inside.

Eleanor and Josephine could see the beam from her flashlight move over the contents as she looked quickly inside and then closed it once more. They pressed their bodies tight against the side of the passage and watched the dark shape that was Faith walk by muttering. When she had turned the corner they walked slowly toward her unit and Josephine jotted down the number. It didn't take long for Eleanor's phone to vibrate.

"She's gone," Pearl whispered into the phone.

"It's time to get to work," Eleanor said. "Bring your flashlights and meet us at unit 204. Don't forget to put on your gloves."

Eleanor pulled out her special key ring and inserted a key in the padlock of unit 204. She had spent the better part of the morning shopping for padlocks and keys, and filing three keys to make them smooth as if they were worn. Tonight she was lucky and the second key she tried opened the lock. Josephine helped her pull up the door and they were in. The others arrived soon after and they pulled the door down behind them.

"It's really creepy in here," Cleo said as she ran her light over the contents. A variety of items filled the unit. Most of the big furniture pieces were on the bottom or along one side with several boxes stacked against the other wall.

"How did you learn to pick the lock?" asked Dede who still couldn't believe they had gotten inside.

"When I was on the grand jury last year, there was a case that involved car clouting. The thieves had a huge ring of various keys they had filed smooth and they used them to unlock almost any car. Most of the victims didn't even know their cars had been broken into until they missed something. By then the thieves were far away," Eleanor said.

"I'm glad you remembered that," said Cleo. "As soon as Faith contacts the real manager about her unit, she's going to know that someone knows about it. We wouldn't have time to break in and get her key."

"Besides that, she keeps the key on her key ring with her car keys," Josephine said. "We never would have found it in her house."

"If she knows the storage unit isn't a secret anymore, she might move the evidence again," Cleo said.

"I hope our meddling doesn't mess up the investigation for the police," worried Josephine.

"I'm sure they'll be grateful for our help," said Eleanor. "Heaven knows they need it."

"Jackpot!" exclaimed Dede. Here's that box filled with letters and journals. It's different from the packing boxes."

"There's a hatbox," said Pearl lifting it from a stack of boxes. "Is it the one you saw in her closet? Should I open it?"

"Yes," said Dede.

The ladies all gathered around the box and watched with dread as Pearl lifted the lid. Suddenly, she slammed the lid back on the box, the ladies doused their lights, and scattered behind the sofa stacked with boxes. Someone was outside. The clinking of the lock against the door rattled more than their nerves. What if Faith had come back and found the lock open. Worse yet, what if someone locked them inside the storage unit. Eleanor's mind raced along with her beating heart. Why hadn't she taken the lock inside with her? When none of them could stand it any longer, Cleo whispered. "Maybe it was the wind."

"I don't hear anything," Josephine said.

"Let's get out of here," urged Dede.

The ladies knew they only had one opportunity to grab the evidence they needed, but they could only carry so much and didn't want Faith to notice that anything was missing. That's why they only took two boxes from the storage unit, the one with the journal and another that was labeled "Faith's Keeping Box". They all breathed a collective sigh of relief when the storage door opened.

"It must have been the wind," repeated Cleo.

"Before we go, we need to open this hatbox," Dede insisted. She was sure it contained the skull but when they lifted the lid, instead they found a white hat surrounded by layers of tulle.

"Don't forget to take off your mustache," warned Eleanor as they pulled up to Dede's house. "It might be difficult to explain to Mark. Let's meet at my house Monday afternoon to look through the boxes."

Eleanor was in a hurry to get home. She needed to return her rental car and pick up a few things at the grocery store for a dinner party she was hosting. Focusing on her list made her almost miss the two women chatting in the produce section. One of the women was Vivian Thorn and the other was someone Eleanor didn't recognize. Eleanor stood behind a pillar studying the organic vegetables while rubbernecking on their conversation.

"I saw her with my own eyes," Vivian said.

"The timing was perfect," the other one hissed and tucked a strand of platinum blond hair in her scarf. "It will only work in our favor."

"There were letters. We don't know what's in them," Vivian said. "What if she knows something? I'm afraid this is all going to come out."

"Stop worrying. We have him where we want him. Don't you dare chicken out now! Do your part and just keep your mouth shut," ordered the other woman who looked around and spotted Eleanor who slowly turned her face away. "I've got to go. It was great seeing you." The two women walked away in separate directions. Vivian didn't acknowledge Eleanor or maybe she just didn't see her behind the pillar.

Eleanor finished shopping and drove home but couldn't shake the feeling that Vivian and her friend knew a dark secret that may have been at the marrow of this case. When she finished unloading her groceries Eleanor studied the crime wall in her office. Yes, Vivian had to be on the list of suspects that killed her husband, Jude Thorn—along with Faith, Hope, and Dr. Baxter but now there was this other woman. Eleanor needed to find out who she was. It took all of her discipline not to look in the box that she put in her office. Maybe she should bring in the other box, too. Instead, she went to the kitchen and poured a glass of red wine. Her feet led her back to the office where she picked up the journal of Charity Strong.

Eleanor rose early. There was a great deal to do. She had invited Mavis and Captain Fox to a dinner party this evening along with Angus and Sybil. While on her morning walk along the beach, she noticed a rental car parked at Angus' house and wondered if she would have to add more company for dinner. She hurried home, gathered the morning paper, showered, and then happily snuggled by the fire in her robe to complete the crossword puzzle. Half way through the telephone rang.

"Good morning, Ellie." Angus sounded happy.

"What's up?" she asked, knowing it must be about dinner plans.

"Michael and Delia showed up late last night and plan to stay a couple of days. Is there enough food to feed them tonight or should I bring a pizza?"

"The more the merrier," she said. "I'll look forward to seeing them."

"Super, I'm taking them on a hike to Cape Lookout today," Angus said. "That should be a workout for Bones. They say a tired dog is a good dog."

"Stay dry," Eleanor said for lack of anything better. She worried how the evening would turn out with two private investigators, a homicide detective, one amateur snoop, and the subject of a suspicious internet hook-up all sitting around the table. Maybe she should invite Faith and Hope too.

Her thoughts turned to what she discovered in Charity Strong's journal last night. Most of it had been ho-hum, everyday boring ramblings of a dutiful wife and mother, but there was that one interesting tidbit that Eleanor needed to discuss with Josephine. She would have Googled it but she really didn't have the time. Fish chowder was on the menu along with seafood slaw, crusty bread, and lemon meringue pie. Perfect dining for what appeared to be another rainy day on the Oregon coast.

Eleanor listened to music from the sixties while she worked in her kitchen. She slid around in her slippers and sang along to the tunes she loved the most—at least the ones she knew the words to which included most of the Beatle's hits and some by the Rolling Stones. She started with the pie and put the chowder ingredients in the Crock-Pot while the lemon curd cooled. After cleaning up she decided to take advantage of a break in the weather to deliver a little surprise to Angus in the form of rubber dog poo. She walked to his house, unlocked the door, and hid the offensive prank near his bed where he would discover it late at night when he might be susceptible to thinking it was real. She returned to her house, set the table with her fine China and crystal glassware, arranged flowers, and rewarded herself with a lovely nap by the fire. By six, Eleanor was dressed, rested, and ready for her guests. Angus was precisely on time and arrived with a lovely bouquet of lilies and a bottle of white wine. He gave Eleanor a long, passionate kiss that tickled her nose and sent tingles down her spine.

"Wow," was all she could say. "Where's your trusty friend?"

"I left Bones home. He was all tuckered out," Angus smiled. Eleanor thought she noticed his dimples looked more like long creases that just got deeper with his smile but never really left his face.

"Perfect," she said.

"Does that mean you'd rather I left him home *every* time?" Angus asked as he continued to hold her close and nuzzled her neck.

"Feathers would miss him I'm afraid," she said, but she was really thinking how perfect for Angus to find the doggy doo on his return home.

Delia and Michael arrived shortly along with Mavis and Foxy Loxy, who flirted with all the women, including Sybil, who came by herself. Angus offered drinks while Eleanor put the finishing touches on her dinner, eventually bringing a beautifully crafted white soup tureen shaped like a pumpkin to the table along with the seafood salad and crusty bread.

"Absolutely delicious, Ellie," Phineas raved. It seems all the ladies of Sand Beach have mastered the culinary arts. Mavis made a fabulous feast for me this morning and I must say I've never eaten such perfectly fried bacon in my life."

At this point, Angus decided he did not like the Foxy Phineas. No one called Eleanor Ellie except him. Not only that, but the cad was bragging about breakfasting with Mavis, which led everyone at the table to believe he had spent the night with her. Even if it wasn't true, everyone would believe it now. He lowered his brows in disapproval.

Eleanor could tell Angus was upset by the way he clenched his jaw and she too was disturbed by the blush that deepened Mavis' powdered cheeks. As hostess she changed the subject quickly before Phineas could do any more damage. "So how did you entertain yourself today, Captain Fox?"

"I found the company of Mavis more than entertaining," he continued. "Of course, she showed me the sights of the area. Even in the rain, I find the Oregon coast very impressive and extremely beautiful. We saw the Cape Mears Lighthouse, a huge octopus tree, the site of a city on the spit that was washed into the ocean, and then we visited the creamery and ate the richest chocolate ice cream. It was 'udderly' delicious."

"When are you leaving?" asked Angus with no attempt to hide his dislike.

"I'd like to stay a few more days, but only if Mavis is in agreement." Phineas smiled sweetly at Mavis and patted her arm. He was unaware of any ill feelings. "What is it that you do Michael?" He asked when Mavis made no comment.

"Delia and I are private investigators," Michael said coolly. Eleanor saw a young leaner version of Angus sitting across the table, his hair still dark with a matching mustache and dimples. It was no wonder Delia was drawn to him.

"How exciting!" Sybil exclaimed. "Are you currently on a case?"

"We just came back from Alaska and are finishing up some work with a client in the area," Delia said as she reached out and touched Michael's arm in a proprietary way.

Eleanor saw Angus chew his lip but he did not make eye contact with her. She didn't know for sure but suspected Angus had hired them to check on Faith and Hope's history in Alaska. This must be his way of discovering if Charity Strong had connections there. By now, almost everyone knew Charity was dead. She wondered what other facts they had learned.

"Were you in Juneau by any chance?" she asked looking directly at Angus who continued to stare off in the distance.

"Yes, we were. It's really very dark there this time of year," Michael added. "I wouldn't recommend traveling there. It's just as beautiful here and not nearly as isolated."

"Were you able to take advantage of the sour toe?" asked Phineas.

"The sour toe, what in heaven's name is that?" asked Mavis.

"It's a drink that consists of whiskey and the special flavoring of an amputated pinky toe," Phineas said. "It's really very distinctive, but if you swallow the toe, it will cost you five hundred dollars. They only have one toe so it has to be left in the glass for reuse."

"That's absolutely disgusting!" Sybil said. "I suppose you drank it."

"You only live once, Sybil. It's best to give everything a try." Phineas winked knowingly at her and she too blushed.

"Unfortunately, we were on a case and didn't take time to catch the local color," Delia smiled charmingly.

"Maybe next time," Michael said, trying not to appear to be a stick in the mud.

"Does your case involve the local murder?" asked Sybil.

"Sorry Sybil, our cases are confidential." Delia gave Michael a look that could have been a warning. Eleanor wondered what their relationship had become. Was it possible to have an affair with someone and then stop but remain friends and coworkers? Eleanor didn't think so.

"Has there been a murder?" asked Phineas with interest.

"Yes, a shooting in a nearby house," Mavis said. "I totally forgot about it or I would have told you, Foxy."

"Sand Beach doesn't seem a likely place for a capital crime," Phineas pondered. "It's so peaceful and serene here."

"Don't let the calm ocean surface deceive you," Eleanor said. "You must know how dangerous the underlying currents of the Pacific can be living in San Diego."

"Nature has a different kind of ruthlessness than the kind committed by men," Angus said.

"Has the killer been apprehended?" Phineas asked.

"No," said Angus.

"So there is a murderer still at large in this small town?" Phineas seemed concerned. "Aren't you afraid the killer will strike again?"

"I don't believe the community is in danger of that," Angus said with authority.

"Curiosity will conquer fear even more than bravery will." Eleanor quoted James Stephens thinking of her recent snoop adventure.

"Avoiding danger is no safer in the long run than outright exposure. The fearful are caught as often as the bold." Sybil quoted Helen Keller as she thought about hiding inside her home until the killer was apprehended.

"There are three things all wise men fear: the sea in storm, a night with no moon, and the anger of a gentle man." Michael quoted Patrick Rothfuss as he considered what he knew about the charismatic Captain Fox.

Phineas looked dumbfounded by all the quoting. He stood and began a recitation of his own:

"'Out of the night that covers me
Black as the pit from pole to pole,
I thank whatever gods may be
For my unconquerable soul.

In the fell clutch of circumstance,
I have not winced nor cried aloud.
Under the bludgeonings of chance
My head is bloody, but unbowed.

Beyond this place of wrath and tears
Looms but the Horror of the shade,

And yet the menace of the years
Finds, and shall find me, unafraid.

It matters not how strait the gate,
How charged with punishments the scroll,
I am the master of my fate:
I am the captain of my soul.'"

Mavis clapped wildly and Phineas bowed dramatically. "Well, done," Mavis cried," I so love Henley's *Invictus.*"

"Would anyone like to step out on the deck for a smoke? I have some Cuban cigars," Phineas asked. Angus and Michael took the man up on his offer and left the ladies to clear the table.

"I'm afraid there's no moon tonight," Angus said as they walked away.

"Yes, and there are a couple of angry gentlemen," said Michael.

All and all the evening was a great success and everyone was pleasantly surprised when Phineas returned with the men somewhat subdued and took to the Bosendorfer to play a medley of ragtime tunes. Even Delia and Michael danced and Angus showed off his skills as he spun each lady around the room in turns. Mavis suddenly pleaded exhaustion and begged Foxy to take her home. There was some serious winking between the men, which Eleanor felt extremely inappropriate, but their departure led to a mass exodus that left her alone with Angus who helped her clean up in the kitchen.

"That was fun," Angus stated as he wiped the pie pan. "My only complaint is that they ate the entire pie. Now the only thing sweet enough to eat is you." He advanced upon her with a maniacal gleam in his eye. Eleanor tried to avoid his advances first by using her dishcloth to protect her honor, but that only wet his appetite as well as his shirt, and then by retreating to her office where she attempted to lock him out. Unfortunately, he was able to get his foot in the door and gain entrance to her inner sanctum, but suddenly lost interest when his eye fell upon the crime chart Eleanor had posted on her wall.

"Eleanor you've outdone yourself," he exclaimed as he studied the well laid out facts of Charity Strong's case. "I'm impressed."

Eleanor suddenly regretted entering the office and hoped that Angus' professional eye didn't see the box of evidence the coffee ladies had taken from the storage unit. In an attempt to distract him she asked, "So, what did you learn from Michael and Delia's investigation?"

Angus looked to Eleanor and away from the crime chart. "It seems Charity's mother lives in Juneau. That's where they sent Faith when she was pregnant with Hope and that's where the girls went when they left here. They thought their grandmother would know where Charity was but, of course, she didn't. They lived with the grandmother all those years. First she took care of them and later they cared for her. She's still there waiting for them to come back."

"That's it?" Eleanor seemed a little disappointed.

"Yes, I don't want to talk about murder tonight. Aren't you curious about what I'm thinking?"

"Of course," Eleanor said.

"Let's go to bed and I'll show you."

In the morning, Eleanor could not get rid of Angus. He drank coffee, ate a huge breakfast, and then lounged on the sofa and read the paper.

"Don't you have to feed Bones?" she asked.

"Michael can do that," he said.

"Don't you want to spend time with Michael while he's here?" she continued.

"Are you trying to get rid of me?"

"No, but the coffee group is coming over for lunch."

"Why? Are they planning to look through that box of stuff you took from the storage unit?" Angus did not look up from his paper.

"You saw that? How did you know it was from the storage unit?" Eleanor was almost speechless.

"When will you learn, Ellie? I'm a trained professional. I'm trained to detect things. I've had Faith under surveillance for some time. I followed her to the storage unit and saw you and your amateur detectives in your disguises. I watched you break in and steal evidence from an ongoing murder case."

He didn't mention the fact that he had messed with the padlock to give them a fright they well deserved or that he had watched Faith return to the storage unit shortly after they left and saw her leave with a hatbox and a Bible.

"I could have arrested you on the spot and taken the evidence into custody. As a matter of fact, I might still take the box." Angus got up from the sofa and strode to the office, picked up the box, and left Eleanor's house. He didn't even kiss her goodbye. Little did he know that Eleanor had taken a journal out of the box and the second box was still in her car. Angus hadn't discovered shit—at least not yet.

The coffee group ladies arrived with lunch. It was a salad extravaganza with Josephine's cauliflower and broccoli festival, Cleo's seven-layer salad, Pearl's jubilee mold, Eleanor's marinated three-bean salad, and the long-awaited candle salad that Dede's mother used to make. Because of the nature of this famous salad Dede had to prepare it on site while the other ladies watched in shock and awe.

"I'm telling you the truth when I say this recipe was in the church cookbook," Dede affirmed as she drove the banana through the pineapple ring into the cottage cheese with lettuce base and added whipped cream and a cherry on top.

"It looks good enough to eat even though a little phallic," laughed Josephine.

"I find it highly offensive," teased Eleanor.

"Mine has Peyronie's disease," complained Cleo looking critically at her banana.

"What's that?" asked Pearl.

"Haven't you seen those commercials on television where the man is holding all those bent vegetables?" asked Dede.

"I don't watch commercials," Pearl explained. "That's why I have a DVD."

"If that's a disease, you should go to the doctor," said Cleo.

"Let's eat," said Eleanor. "There's a lot to discuss."

"So have you inspected the boxes?" asked Josephine as they sat at the table.

"There's been a setback," Eleanor began. "On the night of our stakeout Faith was under surveillance by a certain retired homicide detective who followed her to the storage facility and observed all of our actions."

"Angus!" Dede exclaimed.

"Yes," Eleanor said. "Evidently our disguises did nothing to conceal our identities. Angus has confiscated the evidence and threatened to arrest us for interfering in a murder investigation."

"He wouldn't dare!" Josephine was outraged. "Can he even do that?"

"We got that evidence fair and square," Pearl complained. "He wouldn't arrest us, would he?"

"Worse," Eleanor sighed dramatically, "he called us amateur detectives."

"Poppycock," said Cleo. "That plan was absolutely genius. You put that plan together, Eleanor and now he's reaped the rewards. If we hadn't called Faith she may have waited weeks to visit the storage unit and Angus might still be on a stakeout. We took all the risks and now he has the spoils."

"That was probably his plan all along. The man is diabolical," Josephine said. "He let us break the law and now he has the evidence to piece together what happened and solve the case."

"He didn't get everything," Eleanor confessed. "I took a journal out of one box because I was reading it, and he didn't take the box I left in the car. He must know we took two boxes since he's a trained professional and doesn't miss a thing. I'm sure he'll be back for it later."

"We better get to it then," said Dede stuffing some banana in her mouth.

"Did you discover anything in the journal?" asked Cleo.

"It was mostly boring, but there was one really interesting bit of information. Reverend Strong and Charity were seeing a counselor about a problem he had called Madonna–Whore

Complex. I thought you could shed some light on that Josephine." Eleanor waited for Josephine to respond.

"I guess it's not surprising that a religious man like the reverend would suffer from that. He most likely viewed the world in black and white, good and evil, saints and sinners." Josephine adjusted the glasses she wore only to conceal the bags under her eyes. "The Madonna–Whore Complex is when a man can't desire the woman he loves but can't love the women he desires. He compartmentalizes women into two categories, those who are depraved and sexual and those who are respected and asexual. Sadly, organized religions have used these power structures to repress women's sexuality throughout time. We still demonize female promiscuity, practice slut-shaming, and have a dismissive rape culture. These are all products of the Madonna–Whore Complex and manifestations of the fear men have of women's power. That must have been a very frustrated marriage."

"What did Charity say about it in her journal?" asked Dede. "Did the counseling help?"

"I don't think so. She talks about not being appealing to him for a while and then the counseling but that's at the end. Mostly she blames herself for not being worthy somehow. There didn't seem to be much time for him to respond to therapy. I think there were other issues at play. I can't imagine a super religious man opening up to a stranger about his sex life," Eleanor said.

"They must have had sex," said Pearl. "They produced Faith and Hope."

"It's not uncommon for a man with this disorder to have sex with his wife until she has a child. Then he puts her on a pedestal and she becomes sacred to him," Josephine added.

"You forgot that Hope was Faith's child, Pearl," Eleanor reminded.

"Okay, but whose baby was buried in the shallow grave?" asked Cleo.

"I don't know," admitted Eleanor.

"Do you suppose the reverend had a mistress or two?" asked Cleo.

"Knowing about this problem makes it easier to believe Charity might have had a lover too. Who could blame her? Maybe she got pregnant and the reverend killed it and buried it," Pearl speculated.

"Maybe she was pregnant. She was supposed to be pregnant with Hope so she had to at least look the part. The reverend might have had sex with her to avoid the scandal of a sinful daughter, but that would have been difficult to plan." Josephine said.

"If Charity miscarried late in the pregnancy, they could have just buried it without reporting it," Eleanor thought out loud. "We need more information about the infant skeleton."

"I think Angus is holding out on us, Eleanor," Dede remarked.

"The answers could be in that box in my car." Eleanor rose to go to the garage and returned with a brown cardboard packing box.

"I almost forgot," she said. "When I was at the grocery store the night of the stakeout, I saw Vivian Thorn whispering with another woman in the produce section. I kept behind a pillar and could only hear a few sentences. Vivian said something about seeing her, and I think she meant Hope, although she didn't mention any names. The other woman said it would work in their favor and the timing was perfect. Vivian said she was afraid it was all going to come out and the other woman said not to chicken out and to keep her mouth shut. Then they spotted me and left."

"What did this other woman look like?" asked Josephine.

"She looked a lot like Vivian only not as pretty. She wore black eye makeup, red lipstick, and had platinum blond hair." Eleanor tried to remember other details but couldn't.

"Tonya Jones," said Dede without hesitation. "I knew she was hiding something when I visited her before. She turned white as a sheet when I said Faith was back in town."

"What do you think it means?" asked Pearl.

"Let's read Faith's diary and find out," said Cleo, who held a small pink book in her hand. "Oh no, she has terrible penmanship."

"Just read it out loud," said Pearl. "You should be good at deciphering bad penmanship after all those years teaching third grade."

"That's not the best use of our time," Josephine said. "Let's each take a diary and only share the important items. If Faith is anything like other teenage girls, these books will be filled with trivial events and dramatic feelings." Josephine passed out two more diaries and several letters and a sketchbook filled with drawings.

It didn't take long for Josephine to react to the drawings in the sketchbook. "If these pictures are any indication of Faith's mental state, there's no doubt she was the victim of sexual abuse." The ladies gathered around and saw what looked like primitive depictions of male genitalia and stick figures engaged in various sexual acts. Other pages revealed angry scribblings in vibrant red and black.

"Are we sure they are her drawings?" Eleanor asked.

"She didn't put her name or date on them," Josephine said, "but whoever used this sketchbook was very young."

"Why would anyone keep this?" asked Dede.

"Faith may have blocked all this out of her memory. She may not remember what was in the sketchbook or the diaries," Josephine said. "Her parents may never have seen this."

"I read something in Charity's journal that might be important in the context of child abuse." Eleanor left and returned with her book. "Charity dated her entries so this should give us some kind of timeline. This is after Faith comes home from Alaska with the baby:

'I can't believe the difference in my girl. She is so good and obedient. Having this event in her life has caused her to give up her sinful ways and come back to Jesus. Her father and I are so pleased at how things have worked out. Our prayers have not been in vain. He still spends hours praying with her in her room, but she does so willingly now. He must be right to keep me out of it. He says I am too soft and some of his strategies would make me cry. Fourteen is so young to be a mother, but this is the consequence of her sin. Gone are the angry tantrums, dyed hair, make up and provocative outfits. My dear husband is so good and pure. He rarely touches me although there are times when I long for it. I fear I have passed my wanton desires on to my daughter, and I pray for forgiveness.

"This was before the counseling," Eleanor said.

"What do you suppose he was really doing in her room for hours?" asked Dede.

"It sounds as if he created the Madonna and the Whore in his own home," said Pearl.

"This just makes me sad," said Eleanor. "I have an entirely new view of Faith now."

"It still doesn't explain who killed Charity or why," said Cleo.

I hate him	I hate him	I hate him	I hate him
I hate him	I hate him	I hate him	I hate him
I hate him	I hate him	I hate him	I hate him
I hate him	I hate him	I hate him	I hate him
I hate him	I hate him	I hate him	

"Gee, I wonder who she hates?" asked Pearl.

"Can we find out if Hope is the reverend's daughter?" asked Dede.

"If Charity found out about the abuse maybe she confronted him and he killed her," said Pearl.

"I just had a thought," said Eleanor. "I think Angus doesn't care if we work Charity's murder because it's a cold case. He's letting us solve it so he can work on the recent killing of Jude Thorn without our interference."

"These cases have to be connected, Eleanor," said Josephine. "We just have to be persistent."

"Couldn't we be persistent after some ice cream?" asked Cleo.

The ladies continued to read through the chronicles of what was turning out to be a very disturbing case.

They held me down and tore at my clothes ... the others just watched. I would have let him but not both of them and not while they watched. I can't go to school. I can't go anywhere. I can't see them. I'd rather be dead.

Pearl skipped through the journal and continued to read,

Mom said I don't have to go to school anymore if I'm sick. I wonder how long I'll feel sick. I have to throw up every morning. I don't think it's because of what happened in the woods. Maybe it's the flu, but Mom says I don't have a fever. She looks at me as if she knows what happened. I could never tell her. I could never tell anyone.

"What are the dates?" asked Eleanor.

"I'm not sure. She doesn't write the dates every time, but it's the last entry in this diary," Pearl said.

"Someone raped her and she's obviously pregnant," Josephine said. "Charity would have to be blind and stupid not to notice her child was experiencing morning sickness."

"She probably thought it was because Faith was promiscuous. Do you think she even considered that it could be her husband's child?" asked Dede. "I never would have suspected him of such a thing. It suddenly makes sense to me why the reverend would marry a younger woman who was so much like a child. He was a pedophile."

"We don't know that for sure," Cleo said.

"If Jude Thorn is Hope's father, he might be the rapist or maybe her boyfriend. He said he hadn't been nice to her, was atoning for it, and she was a carpenter's dream," Eleanor reminded them. "That means he was intimate with her."

"Jude and Donnie could be the rapists, and the ones who watched might be the mean girls," Pearl said.

"That would obviously be a motive for murder," Cleo said. "If those girls were the ones who watched they may be next if Faith has a hit list."

"But the reverend could also be the father since neither child molesters nor rapists use birth control," Josephine said.

"Oh, when I go back in her diary, I see that she talks about her father coming into her room for what she calls 'prayer therapy'. I wonder if that's code for incest," Pearl said.

"He might have been 'the-rapist'," said Dede. "It's too bad she doesn't mention anyone by name."

"She probably blamed herself for all of it," Josephine said. "I wonder if she's a cutter."

"That poor child suffered everywhere she went. At school, she was tortured by mean girls. Older lustful boys raped her, and she couldn't even find refuge in her own home." Eleanor sighed.

"Do you think the infant buried in the shallow grave could have been hers too?" asked Cleo.

Eleanor said. "I'll try to find out if Angus knows anything about the infant's DNA or the time of Jude's death. Faith may have an alibi if he was killed during the matinee."

"I wonder what Angus found in *his* box," said Josephine, "Or if he'll share information."

"I suspect he's going to turn it over to the police along with this box and the other things in the storage facility. You know, just to keep us out of trouble," Dede said. "But I don't know if it's enough to arrest Faith for the murder of Jude Thorn."

"Who knows? The murder weapon could be in there too," Eleanor said.

"That would solve one case anyway," Pearl said. "Is there anything we missed in the box?"

"There is absolutely no dessert in the box," said Cleo digging through some loose papers.

Shortly after her guests drove away, someone else knocked on Eleanor's door. Feathers flew from his perch and complained angrily, "Lock the door, Ellie. Lock the door!" He was tired of company and needed attention.

Delia Parker stood on the porch looking very professional in a pair of black slacks and a red wool coat. Eleanor didn't remember her looking so attractive the other night at dinner but she was focused on Phineas Fox and hadn't paid much attention to her. With her brown hair highlighted and her face made up, she looked pretty.

"Hi, Eleanor, I waited until your company left to come over. I hope it's a good time to talk about the background check you wanted on Phineas Fox," Delia said. "Angus and Michael have gone hiking with Bones."

"Please come in Delia. Would you like tea or coffee?" Eleanor asked, taking her coat.

"No thank you," Delia said as she followed Eleanor into the large living area and sat down on the sofa facing Eleanor. She opened a file folder.

"So what have you got?" asked Eleanor.

"You were right to be suspicious. There's no such person as Captain Phineas Fox registered in naval records. His real name is Elmer Pettigrew, a retired railroad conductor who lives in Portland." Delia laid a file folder on the table. "He's 58 years old and is married to the mustard heiress, Alana Colman, who owns a house in the west hills. He also owns a house in northeast Portland."

"How did you find out his real name?" Eleanor asked.

"When we danced at your house the other night, I picked his pocket," Delia confessed. "He doesn't have a record, but that doesn't mean he isn't up to no good. It just means he hasn't been caught."

"What does he want from Mavis?" Eleanor asked.

"That I can't tell you," Delia said, "but I can keep working on it if you want."

"I'd better tell Mavis before she gets more involved with him," Eleanor said.

"I wouldn't just yet if you want to keep your friend. He might already be scared off and you had nothing to do with it. Michael and Angus talked to him out on the deck when they were smoking his cigars," Delia said. "It seems they took a dislike to him from the get-go."

"Really, what did they say to him?"

"They made it clear that they cared for Mavis and he would be smart to get out of town unless his intentions were honest," Delia said. "I'm sure they said it in other words, but you get the gist."

"Did they even know he wasn't who he said he was?"

"No, but they both seem to have a nose for sniffing out scumbags," Delia said. "It's a gift."

"Delia, what if he convinces her to meet him somewhere else? I'd like you to continue to find out more about this fraud. If he's up to no good, he may be hurting other women who don't have protectors like Angus and Michael. Poor Mavis, she was so happy." Eleanor sighed.

"It's tough today, finding a good man." Delia's sigh mirrored Eleanor's.

"Aren't things good with Michael?" Eleanor pried.

"Not really, I don't like being the one in a relationship who cares more about him than he cares about me," Delia confided.

"Are you sure that's true?"

"I never thought I would be that woman," Delia said. "You know the one who puts up with his fooling around on the side and comes running every time there's a booty call, but here I am, and I hate it. I guess it's true when they say, 'if he cheats *with* you, he'll cheat *on* you.'"

"What is the status of your relationship that you feel he's cheating on you?" Eleanor asked.

"I know, we're not married, or even in an exclusive relationship, so technically he's not cheating. I just want to be his one and only, and I'm not."

"Have you been following him? How do you know you're not his one and only?" Eleanor knew how much love could hurt. She had watched Walter love Alice not so long ago.

"I'm a private investigator. I know all the signs and all the tricks—besides, Michael never claimed to love me and he doesn't hide the fact that he's attracted to other women. He's says he's playing the field now and weighing his options."

"And you love him?" Eleanor asked.

"Completely, I know it's mad, but I can't stop it. Working with him is how I keep him in my life. I think if he wasn't interning with me, he'd be gone. I'm sorry to plague you with my problems, Eleanor. It's very unprofessional of me."

"Maybe given time, he'll see what a wonderful thing he has in you. It isn't everyday a man can find a friend and coworker who loves him completely."

"I was thinking if I learned to cook, it might help. What are you doing for dinner?" Delia smiled but she wasn't kidding.

*

"The secret to a good steak is the cut of meat," Eleanor said as she watched Delia chop the red potatoes in Angus' kitchen. "Always buy the best ingredients you can afford."

"What is the best cut of meat?" Delia asked.

"We're grilling tenderloin tonight. I guess you could overcook and ruin it, so just use this meat thermometer and remember to let it rest for at least ten minutes before serving it. Would you like some wine?"

"I'm not sure I can drink and cook at the same time," Delia said.

"I'll grate the cheese. I wonder where Angus keeps the grater." Eleanor searched in every drawer until she found it. When the cheese was grated Eleanor watched Delia chopping onions as tears mixed with black mascara ran down her cheeks, giving her a clownish look. "I'll see about finding some wine." Eleanor made her way into Angus' bedroom. The doggy doo-doo was no longer where she'd left it, but the box of evidence from the storage unit sat by the side of his bed. Charity Strong had kept a history of her life. The box held several journals, letters tied with blue rickrack, and loose papers. Eleanor sat on the bed and picked one at random. An envelope stuck in its pages caught her eye. Inside was a thin gold ring wrapped in tissue. On that page in the journal Charity had written

"I cannot be married to this man!"

Eleanor heard voices from the living room and quickly stuffed the journal back into the box, knocking it over. In her haste, she didn't notice that the letters tied with rickrack fell out and slipped under the bed as she hurried to right the box and rushed to find a bottle of wine. When she returned upstairs, Angus was wiping Bones' paws and Michael had wandered into the kitchen.

"What's going on?" asked Angus. He didn't seem particularly pleased to see her.

Eleanor raised the wine bottle. "Delia's cooking and invited me to dinner."

"Really?" Angus' face registered concern mixed with wonder.

"Are you afraid, Angus?" came Delia's voice from the kitchen.

"I am," teased Michael who returned with two beers looking dapper in a shirt and tie.

"I just hope you plan on cleaning up after yourself," Angus replied as he took a beer from Michael. "Red wine . . . what's she cooking in there, Ellie?"

"Meat and potatoes," she answered. "Why are you being so mean?"

"Ellie, you don't know," he whispered, "but Delia can't cook. She has a culinary disability."

Eleanor took the wine to the kitchen to oversee the rest of the dinner preparations. When the potatoes were in the oven and the steaks were on the grill, she poured the wine and watched Delia chop the vegetables for the salad. "Trust me Delia. This is a foolproof meal."

"That's done," said Delia wiping her hands on a kitchen towel and picking up her wine.

As she was walking out of the kitchen, Eleanor spoke, "Delia, where are you going?"

Delia paused a moment, "I thought I'd join Michael for a drink . . . no?"

Eleanor shook her head. "The steaks need watching. If you leave the kitchen they might burn and that would be such a waste. Not to mention, you could set Angus' kitchen on fire. When the steaks are nice and brown, take their temperature. At about 130 degrees you can take them off the grill to rest. Angus likes his rare to medium rare. How does Michael prefer his steak?"

Delia sighed, "I don't know. I'll go ask him."

"I'll ask him, you stay in the kitchen. It's important that those two know who's cooking this dinner. You might want to wash your face." Eleanor left with her wine and a better understanding of Delia's failure as a food magician.

The four of them sat around Angus' table and ate what Eleanor thought was an excellent meal.

"I have to say this steak is pretty good, Delia." Michael said.

"I agree and the potatoes are tasty too," Angus said. "If I hadn't seen you in the kitchen, I wouldn't have believed it."

"Thank you, I think," Delia flushed with pride at the compliments.

"So where did you hike dressed like that?" Eleanor asked Michael.

"Who said anything about hiking," asked Michael who had loosened his tie. "We were working the case."

"What case is that?" asked Eleanor, noticing the looks passed between Angus and Michael.

"They're helping with the murder case," Angus admitted.

"You mean we're working the case together," said Delia who evidently didn't receive the eye messages.

A long pause ensued while everyone except Eleanor stuffed their mouths and chewed intently.

"We might as well tell her," said Angus, "she's going to figure it out anyway."

"Yes, please tell me," Eleanor said.

"I'm working with these two private investigators to help solve the murder of Charity Strong," Angus admitted.

"Really? Who hired you?"

"Can't tell you that," said Michael.

"What does this mean, Angus?" Eleanor was puzzled. "Are you consulting with the Waterton police?"

"I'm trying something new," he explained. "Someone asked about investigating her disappearance after Faith moved back here with Hope and I suggested Delia and Michael who were starting this new enterprise. They asked me to join them and I said I'd give it a try. It's local and I think it's connected to the Jude Thorn murder, so I'm investigating one case and consulting on another hoping to solve them both."

"Is it ethical?" Eleanor asked.

"I'm retired," Angus said as if that was an answer.

"I want in," Eleanor said. "I know things that can help in the case."

"What? What do you know?" Michael asked.

"I know that Charity Strong had an unhappy marriage to a man who had a Madonna–Whore Complex. I know Faith Strong was molested, possibly by her father, and most certainly by Jude Thorn, was pregnant and is passing this child off as her sister, Hope. Faith dug up her mother's body and moved it hiding the head to prevent the authorities from determining the cause of her death. I believe Dr. Baxter was in love with Charity and may have written her love letters which Hope found and returned to him. Vivian Thorn knows about these letters and now she is worried that somehow a terrible secret that she shares with Tonya Jones is going to come out." Eleanor paused to take a breath.

"Okay," Michael interjected. "You know some things, but you're not an investigator and we do have a responsibility to keep our client and other facts confidential."

"Do you know who the infant buried in the shallow grave belonged to?" Eleanor asked.

"Yes," answered Delia, "but we can't tell you."

"I can tell you that the night you broke into Faith's storage unit, she came back and took a hatbox and a Bible. Do you know what was in the hatbox or why she would take the Bible?" Angus asked.

"She must have figured out that someone found her secret storage unit and returned to remove the most incriminating evidence." Eleanor furrowed her brow in puzzlement. "Was that Faith messing with the lock? She must have known we were inside. Why didn't she confront us or lock us inside? It doesn't make sense."

"Ellie," Angus said, "I was the one who rattled the lock. I thought if I scared you and your posse, you'd stay out of the case. If Faith killed Jude she could be dangerous. She wouldn't have just rattled the lock."

"There was a hat in the hatbox," Eleanor said and rose to clear the table. She knew it was killing Delia that Michael and Angus had worked the case while she was home cooking dinner. Eleanor also wanted desperately to know what they'd learned. Maybe if she was very quiet and stayed in the kitchen she could overhear something. She rattled some pots and pans.

"So what did you learn?" Delia spoke quietly and peered over her shoulder.

Eleanor could only hear parts of the conversation. Michael and Angus had talked to Prissy about church finances. Evidently Michael convinced her he was a forensic auditor auditing accounts that went back to Reverend Strong's ministry. There were substantial discrepancies. Embezzlement of funds was mentioned. Charity's disappearance was proof that she was guilty, but after her body turned up Prissy knew it had to be the reverend. She heard the words blackmail, mistresses, prostitutes, and her own name. She rattled more dishes. Finally finishing the dirty work, Eleanor coughed loudly and came out of the kitchen.

"I'm going home now," she said.

"I'll walk you." Angus stood and got his coat.

"No need, Angus." Eleanor was a little miffed and hurried out the door.

"Wait Ellie." Angus didn't want her walking home alone in the dark. He rushed after her.

Eleanor walked briskly but Angus had a long stride and easily caught up to her.

"I know you're mad, Ellie, and I don't blame you. It must feel really unfair giving out information and not getting anything in return except kitchen duty," Angus empathized. "I'm sure Delia couldn't have produced that delicious dinner without your help." Eleanor kept walking.

"Ellie, I'm sorry about leaving you out, but confidentiality is a big part of the private investigator's job," Angus continued. "You probably feel like you're being used, but I'd never use you. I think you and your friends have really helped get some important information that could solve the case."

Eleanor stopped and turned to Angus. It was too dark to see her expression, but he knew it wasn't a look filled with love and affection.

"I am not a baby, Angus. I don't need you to scare me away from Faith Strong, to protect me, or to walk me home," she said firmly and began to move quickly away, but Angus followed closely behind. He knew it was useless talking to her while she was angry, but he wanted to see her home safely. He watched her unlock her door, step inside and turn on the lights before he circled back home. Loving a strong woman was the pits.

Eleanor needed a long walk to clear her head. She hadn't slept well and the night had been long. The fall weather wasn't conducive to outdoor activities but undaunted she dressed in her rain gear and headed for the beach. She plodded down the hill past Angus' house and glared at it as though it was guilty of some personal infraction. Of course it was too early for anyone to be up and about. The windows were dark and revealed nothing.

A fine mist had her face wet in no time as she squinted against the slight wind that blew from the west. The waves were large but the tide was out so there was ample beach for walking. Eleanor moved briskly and by the time she reached her usual halfway mark, the wind had stopped, and a small clearing appeared showing a deceptive patch of blue sky.

She turned for home and with each step felt her anger fall away little by little. It wasn't Angus' fault that private investigators had a code of ethics. She should be glad to learn that Delia and Michael valued confidentiality. After all, she had hired them too and wouldn't want them to tell just anyone the details of Mavis' scam. She imagined a group of their friends laughing about the exploits of a con artist taking advantage of an old woman and how easily duped lonely women could be just because a man winked at them or glanced their way. That would never do. She decided to stop in at Suzanna's to see how Mavis was doing. Sure enough, Sybil and Mavis sat at their usual table with a coffee carafe in the center.

"Oh, Eleanor, you are soaking wet and must be freezing," said Mavis.

Eleanor stripped off her raincoat and sat at the table while Sybil poured her a cup of hot coffee.

"There is nothing better than warm after cold," cooed Eleanor as she wrapped her hands around the steaming cup.

"Or love after a long dry spell," Mavis winked. "Thank you so much for that evening, Eleanor. It was such fun."

"How is Phineas?"

"Well, he had to leave that very night to go back to San Diego. Some family emergency he said. That, of course, was disappointing as your delightful party had put me in the mood for romance, if you know what I mean." Mavis was still floating on the cloud of deception. "But he calls every night and has invited me to San Diego when things settle down there, of course. He's much too thoughtful to immerse me in his family drama."

"He was charming," Eleanor admitted.

"Have you seen Faith Strong lately?" asked Sybil, who was more than ready to change the subject.

"No, why do you ask?"

"It just occurred to me that I haven't seen either of them around at all. I was just wondering if they moved away," Sybil said.

"I'm sure she would have told me, since she's renting from me. Plus, I think she's a person of interest in Jude Thorn's murder and probably can't leave town." Eleanor found herself gossiping.

"I didn't realize that," Mavis said. "Why would she be a person of interest?"

"Possibly because he was shot in her house," Eleanor reminded her.

"That's right, but what about the bones?" asked Sybil. "Do we know anything more about who might have killed Faith's mother?"

"I don't know anything." Eleanor did know that all she had was speculation and there was no solving a murder new or old without proof.

It was raining again when Eleanor met her friends at the Boat House. "I have new shoes," said Cleo sticking her foot out for all to see.

"I love the red," said Josephine.

"Are they comfortable?" asked Pearl. "I need some red shoes, but only if they feel good."

"Please no talking about bunions, plantar fasciitis, or Mortenson's neuroma," ordered Cleo who had no patience for health issues. "The shoes feel great and when I click the heels together there's magic."

"Have any of you been getting friend requests from strange men on Facebook?" asked Eleanor."

"Yes, once in a while, but I just delete them," Josephine said.

"How strange do they have to be exactly?" asked Cleo, "and why are you asking?"

"Are you being stalked, Eleanor?" asked Dede.

"That hardly seems fair since you already have a hunky man," said Pearl.

"Mavis Bench friended a man on Facebook and she's quite smitten with him. He's very charming but as it turns out he's not who he says he is," Eleanor said.

"Oh, tell us more. This is very interesting," said Cleo.

"He came to Sand Beach to meet Mavis, and I had them over for dinner. He claims to be a retired navy captain named Phineas Fox who lives in San Diego, but it turns out his real name is Elmer Pettigrew and he lives in Portland," Eleanor said.

"Eleanor, I'm impressed with your mad detecting skills. How did you get all that information?" asked Dede.

"I hired a private investigator," she admitted.

"Do you know what he's doing with Mavis?" asked Josephine.

"No, but I have his address," Eleanor said.

"What are you suggesting?" asked Pearl.

"Be still, my heart!" exclaimed Cleo. "I can't believe there is another mystery afoot."

"I don't know. The PI is following up on him, but it couldn't hurt to check out his lair," said Eleanor.

"Do you think he's dangerous?" asked Pearl.

"No, but we might find out what he's up to if we follow him around for a while," Eleanor suggested.

"I'm in if it includes shopping and lunch," said Cleo.

"I could use a trip to the big city," said Dede.

"What are you doing today?" asked Eleanor. That was all it took and the ladies finished their breakfasts and piled into Eleanor's car.

"Any breakthroughs on the murder cases?" asked Josephine as they drove down the highway. Eleanor translated this to mean: Did you get any new information from Angus?

"I haven't seen Angus for a couple of days." Eleanor didn't want to explain or try to justify her bad behavior on the night of Delia's dinner.

"Did he come back for the box?" asked Dede.

"No, he hasn't come back, but I did learn some interesting things when I was at his house. I looked in the box he took and found an envelope with a thin gold band stuck in a journal and written on the page she wrote: *I cannot be married to this man. I* think it was Charity's wedding ring and may mean she planned to leave him. Then there were mostly words and phrases I heard from rubbernecking on the investigator's confidential conversations. I suppose we could piece them together but they aren't facts," Eleanor said.

"Well what did you learn?" asked Cleo impatiently.

"Someone has hired private investigators to look into Charity Strong's murder but I don't know who it is," Eleanor explained. "There was some hint of blackmail, mistresses, and prostitutes involving Reverend Strong, and embezzlement of funds from his church that was blamed on Charity, at least until they found out she didn't run off with another man."

"Oh, that makes Reverend Strong look even guiltier," Pearl said. "He must have taken church money to pay for his dirty deeds."

"Yes, it looks like he had a very black soul," Dede said. "I can't believe he fooled us into thinking he was a pious man."

"Clearly Delia and Michael are the private investigators," Josephine stated. "Are they working for Angus?"

"No, he's working *with* them," Eleanor said. "He's trying out the private investigator thing. You know the night of the stakeout, Angus said he was the one messing around with the padlock. He wanted to scare us away because he thinks Faith might be dangerous. Then he said she came back after we left and took the hatbox and a Bible."

"Why would she come back?" asked Pearl.

"She came back to get the evidence that she was afraid the police would find once her secret storage unit was discovered," said Dede. "She probably put two and two together on her way home."

"You know what that means . . . ," said Cleo. "The hatbox did have the skull in it."

"Maybe, we didn't take the hat out of the box, so it's possible the skull was under it," said Pearl.

"We weren't very thorough," Eleanor said. "We didn't check out the hatbox or notice Angus was following Faith."

"Well we were frightened and distracted," Pearl said defensively. "While we waited in the car, Cleo and I were having an intense debate about the difference between turquoise and aqua."

"Don't forget the discussion about whether dogs can think," Dede reminded.

"Why the Bible?" asked Josephine.

"She probably just carries a Bible everywhere. Angus may not know for sure that she took it from the unit," said Cleo. "You know how some religious people can be."

"Angus would know if she had it when she went in. He notices things like that," Eleanor said.

"I wonder how many she owns," said Dede. "There was one on the chair in her room the first time we were there, but it was gone the next time."

"Maybe there's something in it like a confession," suggested Cleo.

"Whatever it is, we know Faith is going to hide it somewhere else. It's too bad Angus didn't follow her to find out," Josephine said.

"Maybe he did," Eleanor said.

When they arrived at the address Eleanor remembered from Delia's report, they found a modest pink house in a cul-de-sac east of the city and did a quick drive through before parking a distance away where they could still watch the shiny blue Lexus parked in the driveway.

"Maybe we should ask his neighbors about him," suggested Dede.

"What would we tell them?" asked Josephine.

"We could say he's been selected to win an award of some kind and we want to know what they have to say about him as a neighbor," suggested Dede.

"Maybe they'd let me use their bathroom," said Pearl.

"We don't have anything official, not even paper," said Eleanor.

"Just use your phone and record their comments," said Josephine.

"Perfect," said Dede and she got out of the car.

"I'll go too," said Cleo.

There was no one home at the first house. The ladies in the car watched as Cleo and Dede knocked on two more doors and talked with the neighbors. It wasn't long before they saw Elmer (*aka* Phineas Fox) come out and drive away.

"Are we going to follow him?" asked Pearl, "I have to use the rest room."

"While they're talking with the neighbors, let's snoop around his house," suggested Eleanor.

"You are getting very bold, Eleanor," Josephine commented. "Pearl, you be the lookout and stay in the car."

Eleanor and Josephine walked down the sidewalk as if they owned it, stopped at the gate that opened into the backyard of the pink house, and entered. The well-manicured lawn was surrounded by a fence that provided privacy from the neighbors and had a large willow tree and a koi pond near the center. Eleanor went quickly to the patio that held an outdoor grill, patio chairs, and several smaller items covered and stored for winter. She slid the patio door open without a hitch and stepped inside with Josephine right behind.

"What are we looking for?" asked Josephine.

"I haven't a clue," admitted Eleanor as she began to look in every room. "I hope he doesn't have a wife in here somewhere."

"The office seems the best place to start," Josephine suggested. The office was a third bedroom with a desk and computer.

"He probably has a password to get into his computer," Eleanor said as she turned it on.

"I don't know, he didn't lock his back door when he left," Josephine said as she rifled through some papers on the desktop. "Shhh, I hear something. Someone is in the house."

They quickly hid behind the door.

"Pssst, where are you guys?" a voice whispered from the hall.

"It's Pearl," said Eleanor. "What are you doing? You're supposed to be the lookout."

"I had to go to the bathroom." Pearl disappeared behind the door across the hall.

Eleanor returned to the computer and typed "Phineas Fox'" in the password box. "I got in!" she exclaimed. Josephine rushed to look over her shoulder. Eleanor tried his Facebook account but had no luck. She clicked on his photos and heard Josephine gasp as several pictures of older women in compromising positions popped up.

"This guy is a pervert!" Eleanor said. "He's into geriatric porn. This is like a train wreck, but I can't seem to look away."

"No, it's worse than that," Josephine said holding up a tan envelope full of cash. "I think he's into blackmail."

"Maybe there is a list of names to go with these pictures. If we could talk to some of these women, we could find out his scam and maybe they would press charges," Eleanor said as she began a search through his files.

"Stop right there," came a voice from the doorway. Eleanor's heart skipped a beat and it wasn't in a good way. Josephine and Eleanor turned toward the voice that was attached to Michael Patrick who stood next to Delia Parker. Neither of them saw the tall figure that came up behind Michael poised to hit him on the head with a can of air freshener.

"Pearl, nooooo," yelled Eleanor. Pearl stood frozen as Michael spun around and grabbed her by the wrist.

"Who the hell are these people?" he asked.

"I'm pretty sure this is Eleanor's coffee group." Delia remembered them from an earlier episode that involved gummy bears and tequila, chocolate lava cakes, and lots of giggling.

"The meddling amateur detectives that Angus is always talking about?" he asked.

"That would be the ones," Delia said. "Eleanor, why did you hire us if you intended to investigate on your own?"

"Never mind that," Eleanor ordered. "Look what we found." Michael and Delia checked out the senior detective's find.

"It looks like he courts these women, photographs them, then uses the photos to blackmail them," Delia said.

"He's got quite a list of victims," Michael noted. "There must be at least twenty."

"Can we go now?" asked Pearl. "I can't take any more excitement for one day."

"Yes, you ladies need to get out of here. We'll take over from here, Eleanor," Delia said sitting down at the computer. "I don't know how you got in here or how you gained access to his computer, but I'm impressed."

"We can give you a detailed account tonight when we get back," Michael said.

"Good news," said Pearl who led the way out the patio door and back to the car where Dede and Cleo were waiting. "I've never been so glad to leave someone's house."

"Where were you?" asked Dede.

"Let's go get lunch," Cleo urged.

On their way to Bless Your Heart Burgers they filled each other in on their experiences.

Dede and Cleo discovered that everyone in the neighborhood thought Elmer Pettigrew was the best neighbor they knew. Although he was away much of the time, he hosted barbecues every summer and charmed all the ladies with his stories of travel and adventure from his time in the foreign legion. He was always willing to help out, loan tools, and offer his expertise as well as sponsor their children's school fundraisers. He certainly deserved to be neighbor of the year.

"I can't believe his neighbors bought those lies, Foreign Legion, indeed!" said Eleanor.

"I've really worked up an appetite," said Cleo.

"Me too," said Dede. "It must have been all that walking."

"I just want a stiff drink," said Pearl, who was still traumatized.

They sat at the rustic tables on metal stools and ate their gourmet burgers and French fries.

"I don't think I'm cut out for this line of work," said Eleanor. "My heart just can't take it."

"I know what you mean," said Josephine as she bit into her classic burger and dipped her French fry into the special sauce. It appeared no one was who they seemed.

When Eleanor entered her house, the first thing she spotted was the pile of fake poop on the laundry room floor. Even though she knew it was fake she felt a jolt of despair followed by a welcome sense of relief. Angus had been here. She quickly checked in the office to see if the box of evidence was still where she left it. Nothing seemed out of place. She went to the kitchen and poured herself a stiff drink from Angus' Crown Royal and sipped it as she stroked the sleek feathers of her pet.

"I wish you could tell me what happened here today," she said as she looked into his beady yellow eyes.

Feathers took the fifth and stared back, reminding Eleanor of Faith Strong for some reason. Was she silent to protect someone or was she simply protecting herself? The answer might have been on the other end of the ringing phone if only she could piece together the clues.

"Ellie, it's Angus, I need to see you right away. Donnie Gold's been murdered. They found his body in the densifier at the recycling center this afternoon."

"It's looking more and more like Faith is the killer," Eleanor said as Angus sat with her on the sofa looking into the flickering flames of the fire he built while Bones lay at his feet. "First Jude Thorn and now Donnie Gold, the two we think raped her. It sounds like revenge to me."

"There isn't enough evidence to bring her in. Everything is circumstantial," he said. "Now if we could just find the gun that killed them. We'd have her."

"I thought he was in the densifier," Eleanor said. "What is that anyway?"

"Think of it as a giant trash compactor," Angus said.

"That sounds messy. How would someone like Faith get a grown man into a trash compactor?" Eleanor's nose wrinkled in distaste.

"Perhaps there's more than one person involved. Maybe it's not Faith, but a man. The autopsy will tell us if he was dead before he went in, which I assume is the case. At least I hope it was for his sake. If he was shot we can match the bullet with the one that killed Jude and then we'll know if it is the same killer. His death may not be related to this case at all, but I'm fairly certain it is."

"You mean if it was the same gun, don't you?" Eleanor asked.

"If it's the same gun, it's likely the same person," Angus said. "There are too many events linking these crimes for them not to be related to Faith Strong. It started when she arrived in Sand Beach, so even if she's not committing them, she may be the catalyst that caused them to occur."

"Angus, why was it so important to see me? You could have just told me this over the phone," Eleanor said.

"I wanted to see you," he said. "I needed to tell you face to face that I think you have to stay away from Faith and Hope because they could be dangerous, especially if you go snooping around their house. I'm only telling you this for your own safety and I don't want to lose you . . . because I love you." Angus put his arms around Eleanor and gently pulled her into his embrace pressing his face into her hair and nuzzling her ear. "And I'm hungry."

Eleanor pushed him away and went to the kitchen to find something for dinner, but she was smiling. Angus followed her. "Who do you think it is, Ellie?"

"Maybe it's Vivian Thorn," she said as she defrosted a package of pulled pork in the microwave. "She was divorcing Jude. She was around when Faith was raped and probably witnessed it along with Tonya Jones. I know for a fact that she's concerned about Faith coming back here. Maybe it's put her over the edge."

"Dr. Baxter claims she was working during the time Jude was killed, so she has an alibi. Why would she kill Donnie Gold?" Angus topped off his glass of Crown Royal.

"Well, what if it's Tonya Jones then? She might be afraid that those two guys would tell about her part in the rape. Maybe she plans to kill them all."

"Donnie Gold is her brother. I doubt either of them would rat the other out," Angus said.

"I know . . . Tonya killed Donnie because of an inheritance. She took advantage of the killings to get him out of the way so she could collect all his money." Eleanor chopped cabbage for coleslaw while her mind considered the possibilities.

"Donnie's wife would inherit his money," Angus said, opening a bag of potato chips.

"What about her parents. Did they have money?" Eleanor finished the coleslaw, stirred the bourbon barbecue sauce, and took out some Kaiser rolls.

"That might be worth a look," Angus said as he went to answer the door along with Feather's who flew around singing, "Look who's here, look."

Delia and Michael came inside, hung up their coats, and helped themselves to Angus' potato chips.

Evidently the gift of arriving in time to eat was hereditary, Eleanor thought as she took out more rolls and dished up an impromptu meal.

"We thought you might like to hear what we found out today," Michael said before he took a big bite of his sandwich. Delia watched the sauce run down his arm and then dabbed his face gently as if he were a child. The tender scene made Eleanor slightly uncomfortable. Michael seemed more than annoyed but stared ahead and ignored Delia's efforts at intimacy.

"So . . . ?" She prompted.

"So we didn't know you had company and don't want to compromise your confidential agreement with us," Delia said widening her eyes as a clue to Michael that this was not the time to discuss Eleanor's case.

Angus and Eleanor looked at each other until Eleanor said, "I don't mind if Angus knows I hired you to do a background check on Phineas Fox."

"Michael already told me, anyway," Angus tattled.

"It isn't exactly personal," Eleanor said when she saw the look Delia gave her intern. Michael didn't seem at all chastised.

"We compiled a list of the women he's been in contact with," Michael continued, "and followed up with two of them who were in small towns just outside of Waterton. Both of them were reluctant to reveal the nature of their relationship with the 'Scammander' but when convinced they could be saving other women a fate like theirs they cooperated."

"Their stories were similar in that both friended him on Facebook and had a one-night stand with him. He photographed them without their knowledge and later asked for money to keep the photos off the internet. Each woman paid him five thousand dollars. He hasn't asked for more but they were both afraid that he would be back," Delia reported.

"That scoundrel!" Angus exclaimed. "I knew he was up to no good. Ellie do you know if he's had his way with Mavis?"

"Mavis wouldn't tell me if he had. She'd be embarrassed, but I know he left the night of the dinner party and he's still calling her so probably not," Eleanor concluded.

"He needs to get his investment back," Angus said. "He spent a pretty penny on us at Suzanna's that first night."

"What do you want us to do next?" asked Delia. "We could contact more of his victims or give you the list if you want to act on your own."

"What did you tell these women to get them to talk?" asked Eleanor.

"I told them I was from the Center for Venereal Diseases and that he had given me their names because he was infected and urged them to get tested," Delia said. "After that they spilled their guts and asked for help hanging him."

"Thank you for your services. I think I'll take the list," Eleanor said. "I may have to give some thought to how to approach Mavis with this information."

Angus knew what was coming next, but he had no way to stop it. It was part of being involved with a determined woman who knew her own mind.

"There's been another death," Angus informed Delia and Michael, but that was the end of that discussion at least until everyone went back to Angus' house and left Eleanor with the dirty dishes . . . again.

It was an emergency meeting of the coffee group held at Dede's house.

"I have important new information," said Dede as she brought coffee to the ladies gathered around her dining room table. "Prissy Sullivan opened up to me and told me about the financial mess their church has suffered under the direction of Reverend Strong. I'm sure she thinks it will be all over the community now that the church is being audited. She said she felt terrible because the rift she had with Charity was all about money because she believed Charity was taking hundreds of dollars from the church coffers every month. When Prissy confronted Charity she denied it so Prissy went to Reverend Strong and he told her Charity had a gambling problem but he would handle it. Some of the money was returned, but there continued to be a shortfall every month. Then, Charity disappeared and the money drain ended, so Prissy believed that she was responsible. Now she feels regret, and was eager to confess her error."

"Still not proof that he killed her," said Eleanor.

"No, but I have another idea," said Dede. "I'm sure the hatbox and Bible hold the answers to finding key evidence. Where would you hide them after you took them from the storage unit?"

"I don't know," said Cleo. "Maybe back in the closet. After all, the police searched her house once already didn't they?"

"I sure don't want to go back there," Eleanor said. "Angus warned me that Faith may be dangerous."

"If she's guilty she's definitely dangerous," said Pearl. "She may be killing everyone who did her wrong and that could be us if she finds us in her house."

"I think she hid the evidence in her old house. No one is paying attention to the old crime scene and the focus has shifted to Donnie Gold. Who would question a Bible in a potential church?" Dede said.

"They might question a hatbox," said Cleo.

"But they wouldn't look in a place they've already searched," mused Josephine. "She may have buried the skull back in the rose bed."

"So you're suggesting that we go back to the Strong house and search for the Bible and the skull?" asked Eleanor.

"I don't like it," said Pearl. "Actually, I hate it. The whole idea of searching a deserted house for a Bible sounds horrifying not to mention digging. Do we have to do it at night?"

"Yes, we have to do it at night," said Cleo. "We're less likely to be seen in the dark."

"We're also less likely to see in the dark," Pearl grumbled.

"Before we plan this investigation I have another problem that needs addressing." Eleanor filled them in on the list of victims Delia and Michael brought her. "What do you think of this idea? We lure Captain Foxy Loxy to a motel and take some photos of him in compromising positions?"

"Why would he care?" asked Josephine. "He's a man and most of them have no shame."

"He has a wife with a great deal of money," Eleanor said.

"So why does he blackmail women for money?" asked Pearl.

"She must hold the purse strings," offered Josephine.

"What if we lured him there with Mavis as the bait and then all his other victims show up?" Dede proposed. "We could also invite his wife."

"I love it, but we have to act fast before Mavis runs off to meet him somewhere. It won't be pleasant, but I will inform Mavis. I'm going to need help contacting these other women."

Everyone was in and "Operation Foxy Loxy" was on.

Telling Mavis wasn't as unpleasant as Eleanor anticipated. Mavis knew her Foxy Loxy was younger and his interest in her was suspect so she wasn't surprised to learn of his scam. Her pride was hurt but her bank account was safe and for that she was grateful. Her only concern was keeping her humiliation to as few people as possible. The ladies of the coffee group were happy to help by staying home and out of the action. When Eleanor explained her plan, Mavis was eager to teach the charming Foxy Loxy what hens could do when threatened.

Before the day Operation Foxy Loxy was to go into effect, Mavis had texted Phineas inviting him to her room at the Heathman Hotel in downtown Portland after what she claimed was a social committee meeting she was attending on behalf of octogenarians. Mavis didn't believe in lying and Phineas Fox was more than eager to get what he was after—even better to get it while spending the night in the best the city had to offer in the way of hospitality. Phineas made the most of it, ordering the finest bottle of wine, a shuckers dozen oysters, grilled Broccolini, and Columbia River sturgeon steak.

"Please order whatever you like, darling," he chirped. "This is going to be a night to remember." He held Mavis' hand and raised it to his lips.

"Yes, it will definitely be that," Mavis said ordering only a mixed green salad. "I had a rather large lunch."

While Mavis and her paramour were wining and dining in the hotel's restaurant, Eleanor and seven other women, including Phineas' wife, Alana Colman, gathered in a suite upstairs across the hall from Mavis' room.

"I've ordered three bottles of the finest champagne to toast our grand venture," said Alana. "This is the most fun I've had in a long time."

"Who knew revenge could be such fun?" hooted another.

"I have enjoyed the company in this room more than I ever enjoyed Phineas," someone admitted.

"I think we should make this a yearly event," suggested one of the victims.

"I hope you know Elmer will be paying each of you back plus interest. I'll be taking it out of his allowance. No doubt the man has committed a crime of passion. He has a passion for money but believe me when I say the man will suffer, so have no regrets about not filing a police report. I'll be sure justice is served." Alana Colman was a woman of steely substance and she meant business.

Mavis accidentally on purpose tried to get into the wrong room, as a signal that they were back.

"Oopsie, I guess I've had a bit too much wine," she said loudly.

Eleanor peeked through the peephole and watched them enter the room across the hall, then gave them a few minutes to get comfortable before she led the women outside, used the key card Mavis had given her, and watched as the wronged sisterhood barged through the door just in time to catch Phineas with his pants down.

"What's the meaning of this? You are in the wrong room. Get out of here immediately," he ordered as he unsuccessfully tried to cover his wilting manhood. So concerned with his own embarrassment, he didn't realize who had actually barged into room interrupting his plan.

Mavis lay sprawled on the bed and watched the drama unfold gleefully. The wild-eyed worried look on his face when he recognized his harem was extremely satisfying but when he saw his wife, he did the only thing a man like him could do: he fell to the floor pretending to be dead. Foxy Loxy was trapped in the henhouse without escape and there was a great deal of pecking to be done.

"Strip the bastard!" ordered a lady in red. The mob of angry women disrobed him as he lay limp until he was totally exposed.

"Someone take a picture to post on the internet," suggested another.

"Let's drag the cad into the hall and let everyone witness his disgrace," yelled one of the women.

"We wouldn't want anyone to be subjected to this poor specimen of a man," said his wife, "Let's put his sorry ass in the bathtub and leave him for the maids to find."

Phineas made no move to resist—the only reaction noticeable was the tight squeezing of his eyelids. Several women worked together to drag him into the bathroom and dump him into the tub. Eleanor stood by enjoying the show but did not participate. This was not her battle, but Mavis joined in the action with gusto. She tied a white handkerchief to his mast and smiled when she saw him twitch. Captain Fox had surrendered and was officially sunk.

"Remove anything he can possibly use to cover himself, including towels, bedding and that plush robe in the closet," Alana ordered. "I want him exposed for what he is . . . an odious and insensitive coward."

Two women moved a chest in front of the bathroom door and the rowdy mob cheered as they left the room to celebrate their revenge.

The following morning Eleanor and Mavis left their room at the Heathman and enjoyed a shopping spree, then returned to Sand Beach with refreshed wardrobes and entertaining stories to share with their friends.

"I can't thank you enough, Eleanor," Mavis said as Eleanor stopped in front of her house. "I guess not everyone is as lucky in love as Mattie was. For some reason I still can't believe she's gone and I miss her every day."

"Lifelong friends can't be replaced, Mavis. That's one of the saddest things about growing old: the people who knew you when you were young and are the keepers of your stories die and their memories die with them," Eleanor said.

"Sometimes I pretend she's still with us just living somewhere else. Our Do Nothing group has dwindled to two, first Eva and then Mattie. What will happen if Sybil goes and I'm left alone?" Mavis lamented.

"Live one day at a time, Mavis. Otherwise you'll miss out on the good stuff while you're worrying about what *might* happen," Eleanor advised. "It causes anxiety for me when I think too far ahead."

"You're right, I'll have to plan some outings so I can wear my new outfits." Mavis got out of the car with her shopping bags and blew a kiss to Eleanor as she drove away.

Eleanor had left Feathers in his cage alone. He was more than excited to see her and did a happy dance while chastising her for leaving him. "Bad girl, Ellie, bad, bad."

"Who are you to judge?" Eleanor freed him and cleaned out his cage while he flew around stretching his wings, scolding her as he flew. She gave him fresh water and filled his food dish. Spotting the fake dog poop in the laundry room prompted her to change her shoes and make a quick trip to Angus' house to hide it. There were no cars at his place so it seemed like the perfect time. Then she would come home, pour a glass of wine and relax, after all it had been a busy two days. As she walked down the hill, she planned where she could put the prank to best effect. When she unlocked the door, she was surprised by Bones who greeted her with almost as much enthusiasm as Feathers. There was lots of happy dancing, licking and wiggling, and then Eleanor saw it—a massive pile of the real thing in the middle of the living room floor. "Oh no, Bones, what have you done?" She toyed with the idea of cleaning it up and thought better of it. "Let's get you outside," she said, then grabbed his leash and took him for a short walk up and around by the Strong house.

"Where's your daddy?" she asked Bones, but he was only interested in running and marking his territory with what must have been a day's accumulation of marking solution. "I feel for you, Bones, but I'm not cleaning up that mess."

When Eleanor opened the door to Angus' house the odor hit her like a powerful blow. She couldn't in good conscience leave it there, so she rolled up her sleeves, held her breath, and cleaned it up. "I guess the jokes on me," she said to Bones as she scrubbed the floor. When she was done she put her prank poop on the spot and went into Angus' bedroom in search of the box of evidence. It was exactly where it had been the last time she was there. Eleanor picked up one of Charity Strong's journals, sat on the bed, and began to read.

"Someone's been sleeping in my bed, and there she is," Angus' voice growled waking Eleanor from a deep sleep. She sat up like a rocket. Eleanor realized she had dozed off in Angus' bed.

"Oh dear, how embarrassing!" she muttered orienting herself. "I'm so sorry."

"Don't be, if it were up to me you'd be in my bed every night," Angus said. It was obvious that Eleanor had been reading Charity's journal but he didn't mention that.

"What time is it?" she asked.

"Time for dinner if you have the stomach for Delia's cooking," Angus offered.

"No thank you." Eleanor shook her head as if to wake up from a dream she didn't like. "I really should be getting home.

"Come on, Ellie, Delia's cooking isn't that bad." Angus took her hand and pulled her to her feet.

He led her up the stairs and into the dining room where Delia was setting the table. "Eleanor, I didn't know you were here," Delia said.

Angus didn't explain. He simply pulled a chair out for Eleanor and seated her at the table, and then brought another place setting. Delia put a large pizza box in the center with a plastic tub of salad greens and poured two glasses of zinfandel. "Cheers," she said.

Eleanor nibbled on a piece of Canadian bacon and pineapple pizza. "Where's Michael?" she asked.

There was an uncomfortable silence until Delia reluctantly answered, "He's working a case."

Angus' eyebrows spoke volumes and Eleanor read his message clearly. It was definitely time to change the subject. "Let me tell you how the nefarious Captain Phineas Fox got his comeuppance."

By the time she was finished with her tale of trickery, betrayal, and revenge, Delia's smile had returned.

"I really do need to go home, all this plotting and avenging has taken the sap out of me." Eleanor rose from the table and wobbled into Angus' arms as he stood to catch her.

"I'll drive you home," Angus said with authority. Not even Eleanor would argue with those eyes that looked at her pale face with a concern he could not hide.

When they reached her house, Angus held her arm and guided her inside. "Really Angus, you needn't fuss I'm just overtired," Eleanor said.

"Maybe or maybe you're coming down with something." Angus led her to the sofa and made her sit. "Stay here," he ordered. "I'll draw you a bath."

Eleanor was all too happy to obey. She wasn't herself and had to admit to a sort of dizzy light-headed feeling. Maybe it was something she ate, but she couldn't remember what she ate for lunch. That must be it. She and Mavis hadn't eaten lunch. She had slept badly and they had left the hotel late to spend the day shopping and hadn't eaten breakfast either. It wasn't like Eleanor to forget to eat, but it had been an exciting time. The pizza wasn't what she needed either. Eleanor got up and went to the kitchen where she found a banana. She had heard of old people who didn't eat for one reason or another; eating alone was sad, cooking for one person was difficult, shopping for food was too arduous, the food in the cupboard got stale and moldy, nothing tasted good anymore. Eleanor worried that she had reached old age overnight.

"Come on your highness, your bath is ready." Angus took her hand and led her to the bath, where he disrobed her and scrubbed every inch of her old body, and Eleanor let him do it. Then he wrapped her in a fluffy towel, helped her into her nightgown, and tucked her into bed.

"Are you going to read me a story?" she teased.

"What story do you want to hear?" he asked.

"Tell me what Michael is doing tonight."

Angus sighed. "He's working on the Jude Thorn case."

"Yes, but Delia's upset. Why is that?"

"Michael is sort of on a date with Vivian Thorn," Angus said. "He followed her to the Red Shed and took her to some no-tell motel."

"Really, is that part of a private investigator's job?" she asked.

"He thinks he can get some information from Vivian that way," Angus said. "It's above and beyond the job description."

"I suppose you and Delia were at the Red Shed too," Eleanor said. "It must be very painful for her to watch that kind of behavior."

"It's not my problem," Angus said, shaking his head. "I'm staying out it."

"I suppose Michael won't be home until late if he comes home at all," Eleanor said. "Delia will be at your house all alone."

"It will give her time to think about what she's willing to put up with from Michael." Angus began to nibble Eleanor's neck.

"I need some ice cream," Eleanor said rolling out of bed.

"I'm glad to see you're feeling better," said Angus. "I'll take a shower. You shouldn't be alone tonight and I don't want to be anywhere near Delia when Michael comes home."

Eleanor woke in the morning refreshed but oddly disturbed by a dream that came back to her little by little. She lay in her bed and stretched slowly moving each of her achy limbs. Angus had left a note on the pillow. "Gone fishing," it read. Good, she thought, she could lounge around until it was time to meet her coffee friends. She remembered the dream now but knew if she didn't work at pulling it back, it would fade away like most of her nighttime visions.

Eleanor was in a house with many rooms, but the rooms were bare and the walls consisted of two by fours. It was the Strong house and she was alone. As she walked through each space she planned where she would put her things. The two matching sofas would go on each side of the massive fireplace and two wing chairs would look out over the expansive ocean view. Over the mantle she would hang her favorite painting of water lilies and a print of Gustav Klimt's Kiss would adorn the wall in the bedroom she shared with Angus. In her imagination the dining room was filled with happy people eating and laughing around her large table. Suddenly, Faith appeared in the window looking in like a beggar whose home had been lost through unspeakable misfortune. She held a worn suitcase in her hand and then she was inside, and all the happy people were gone. When she opened the suitcase, Eleanor saw the bones of Charity Strong neatly packed away. Faith lifted a Bible out of the suitcase, and in an instant the house was transformed into a large vacuous room whose windows were filled with stained glass that told hideous stories of life in the Strong house. Eleanor could see the photo of Faith as a high school rebel with black hair and lips, and tattoos in one window, the bones of an infant in another, and a corrupt man with a black soul wearing a cleric's collar smiled benevolently over everything. All of it captured in beautiful colored glass back lit by a full luminous moon. A statue of the Virgin Mary with the face of Charity Strong stood near an altar, and in an eerie strobe light film sequence, stepped down from her pedestal and lay on the altar and turned to bones. One by one the windows were broken by some outside force and the sun rose filling the house with light.

What would the coffee group make of that? Eleanor finished her morning routine and drove to the Boat House. Today she had a great deal to share. There was the entire saga of "Wrath of the Wronged Women"; a story of revenge by Mavis Bench, that Eleanor related in full dramatic detail as well as her creepy dream.

"Did Captain Fox have a heart attack?" asked Dede.

"No," Eleanor reassured them. "Playing dead was just his way of not dealing with the situation."

"How is Mavis dealing with the entire episode?" asked Josephine.

"She treated herself to a number of expensive new outfits since she didn't have to pay any blackmail. I gathered from her spree that she's fairly well off financially," Eleanor said. "She was totally under the influence of shopping endorphins yesterday."

"Yes, but did she buy any fabulous shoes?" Cleo wanted to know.

"I think Mavis has been into orthopedic inserts for some time. However, we did find some very fashionable and comfortable shoes at the Walking Store," Eleanor reported.

"Did you get anything?" asked Pearl. "Are those earrings new?"

"Yes, I bought some new things too," Eleanor admitted and showed off the butterscotch amber earrings dangling from her lobes that complemented the mustard sweater she was wearing.

"Were you wearing any of your purchases in your dream?" Josephine asked. "I'm surprised Foxy Loxy didn't play a part in your nighttime vision."

"I think your dream is about our plan to explore the Strong house in search of the missing Bible," said Cleo. "We're still doing it, aren't we?"

"Yes, we have to do it," Dede demanded. "I'm sure we'll find the skull there too."

"When?" asked Pearl.

"Tomorrow night works for me," said Dede who was always overbooked. They all pulled out their phones to check their calendars and nodded.

"Okay then, tomorrow night it is," said Josephine.

"While you have your calendars out cancel the annual Halloween Party at the Community Center," said Eleanor. "During the last big blow the roof was damaged and it's closed for repairs."

"Oh no," said Cleo, "Pearl and I were planning to dress up as Thing 1 and Thing 2."

"I've decided to have a party at my house so you can still do that," Eleanor said. "What do you think about hiring our local medium, Madame Patruska for the evening?"

"That sounds like fun," Dede said. "I'll bring my Ouija board."

"Maybe we should come dressed as something scarier," said Pearl, "or at least a disguise of some kind."

"We could always wear our mustaches," suggested Cleo.

"I'll insist that everyone come in disguise," said Eleanor. "That will increase the fun factor."

"So we'll keep our disguises a secret, even from each other," said Josephine thinking she would be able to recognize each of her friends even in costume. Surely, they would dress as their shadow selves. They left the Boat House with a sense of renewed purpose.

Eleanor went home and spent the afternoon reading the book selection for book club, napping and planning her Halloween party. That evening Angus appeared with a fall Chinook, and they feasted on roast salmon, fried potatoes, and a salad of harvest greens. While Eleanor tidied up the kitchen, Angus took Bones outside for short walk, and then they cuddled up on the couch sipping a night cap of Hennessy Cognac that Eleanor picked up on her shopping spree. Eleanor felt an overwhelming and inexplicable happiness. She realized she had so much: health, money, good friends, ample food and excellent drink, something to look forward to and someone to love. She leaned into Angus who seemed lost in his own thoughts as he absently wrapped his arm around her pulling her closer.

"What's on your mind?" Eleanor asked.

"Nothing," he answered.

Eleanor knew there were men who actually had nothing on their minds but Angus wasn't one of them.

"Great, then you can help me think of a Halloween costume for my party," she said.

"You can borrow my Zorro costume," he generously offered, "and I can wear your witches' outfit. That way we won't have to buy new ones."

"No one would ever suspect who we were then would they?" Eleanor pondered the possibility. "Do you think Delia and Michael will be around for the party?"

"I'm sure they would extend their stay just for the party," Angus said.

"What's happening with them anyway?" asked Eleanor.

"Michael's been putting in some pretty long hours with Vivian Thorn, so I haven't seen much of him lately and Delia's been studying Charity Strong's journals. She's frustrated since there's no way of proving how she died and no weapon to point to a suspect. It's all speculation."

"What about the murders? Are there any leads there?"

"You mean besides the one Michael is pursuing with Vivian?" Angus looked at Eleanor with a raised brow.

"I gather you think Michael is off track with Vivian? Does he think she's somehow involved in Charity's case?"

"I think Michael is being an idiot. Vivian was Jude's wife even though they were divorcing and now that Donnie Gold is dead, she claims she's afraid Faith Strong is out to kill her next. He's acting like her protector but I suspect she's using him to learn what we know about the case."

"Has she confessed to watching those two molest Faith?" asked Eleanor.

"She's only admitted to being mean to Faith in high school. Just how do you know they raped her?"

"It's in her diary. She details it clearly. Don't you think Faith would have to be unbalanced to kill two people just because they hurt her feelings twenty years ago? If she murdered those men it's because they molested her and maybe impregnated her."

"Well there's no proof of that. The DNA determined that Hope and the fetal skeleton are both Faith's and have the same father but the father isn't Jude Thorn or Donnie Gold," Angus revealed.

"It's the reverend isn't it? He fathered those children with Faith," Eleanor said.

"Most likely." Angus sipped his cognac.

"Angus, you've broken your confidence agreement as a PI," Eleanor said.

"Delia and Michael aren't here and don't have to know everything. I don't want to be a private investigator, at least not with them. I'd rather play house with you." Angus kissed her cheek and Eleanor felt in that moment that there was nothing she would rather do than stay wrapped in his embrace indefinitely.

"What about the consultation with the police? Is there anything new on that end?"

"The police are buried in Faith's piles of evidence but haven't found anything linking her to Jude's murder. She doesn't own a gun. It seems no one saw anything in either case. Faith and Hope are claiming they were both home together when Jude was shot."

"That may not be true. I saw Hope at Dr. Baxter's office that morning, so Faith was home alone. Dede saw them both at the matinee that afternoon," Eleanor said. "Angus, you never told me if you followed Faith after she left the storage unit the night of the stakeout," Eleanor said.

"Of course I followed her, but I'm only consulting. I don't have the authority to search her car or her house. When Officer McGraw got to her place she showed him a Bible she said she got from the storage unit and a hatbox with a hat in it, but there wasn't anything useful there." Angus seemed frustrated. "Now the department is searching even more boxes of stuff from the storage unit. Faith isn't obstructing, she's just being silently uncooperative."

Eleanor woke up next to Angus, and thought how pleasant it was to share her bed. She watched his chest rise and fall with the peaceful rhythm of his breathing and noticed how long and thick his lashes were as his lids fluttered in sleep. Suddenly, a black shape catapulted onto the bed in a fury of wriggles and licks. "Bones!" Eleanor tried in vain to get out of his way while Angus sat up immediately awake.

"Meet my alarm dog," he spoke as he captured the dog in his arms and tried to calm his enthusiasm. Finally, the dog lay still and allowed the two to pet him as they discussed how they would start their day.

"I'll take Bones out and bring back the morning paper," Angus said rolling out of bed on one side.

"I'll put on the coffee," Eleanor offered getting out of the other side. By the time Angus came back with Bones and the paper, Eleanor had cooked up pancakes and sausages with a side of fruit. They sat at the table like an old married couple reading separate sections of the newspaper while they ate. Eleanor noticed everything and loved it. Why was she so resistant to getting married? Angus was perfect for her. He loved her and demanded very little—a decent meal, companionship, and a little romance once in a while. She observed his handsome face and determined that it wouldn't be bad looking at it every morning.

"What are you grinning about?" he asked suddenly.

"What's a five letter word for happiness?" she asked.

"Bliss," he answered without hesitation and resumed his reading.

"Angus, who do you think killed Charity Strong?" asked Eleanor.

Angus looked up from the sports page, "I don't have a clue."

"What about Jude and Donnie?" Eleanor asked.

"Faith, or Hope, or Vivian, or Donnie's wife, or maybe somebody's husband who caught Jude with his wife, or Donnie killed Jude and then someone who found out killed Donnie because they were in love with Jude. Should I continue?"

"You could have just said you didn't know," Eleanor said.

"I should read Faith's journals. You might have overlooked something. I'll take them with me this morning." Angus stood, took his dishes to the kitchen and put them in the dishwasher. "Do you want to grab Chinese tonight?" he asked as he was leaving with the box of evidence.

"I've made plans with friends tonight," Eleanor said. Angus cocked one brow and was out the door.

That was when Eleanor got busy getting ready for tonight's adventure. "Let's see, she said to Feathers. I'll need dark clothing, gloves, a flashlight, lock picks, a shovel . . .

The coffee group arrived shortly after dark wearing what they now called their stakeout uniforms. Now that fall was here they added the stocking hats, but left off the mustaches.

"This isn't really a stakeout," Pearl said. "It's more like breaking and entering."

"It's exactly breaking and entering," Josephine corrected.

"I brought this chocolate cake for the celebration when we find the skull." Dede made the most delicious cakes.

"I brought a fifth of Drambuie," Cleo said. "We may need it to settle our nerves."

"Does Drambuie go with chocolate cake?" asked Pearl. "I don't think I've ever had it before."

"Everything goes with chocolate cake," insisted Dede.

"Let's drive by Faith's house to see if the lights are on there. I don't think they would be at the Strong house after dark, but we should check to see if they're home," Eleanor said.

Josephine drove slowly down the lane and passed the house.

"I see someone moving around inside," Dede said. "Yep, they're both home."

They drove up the hill and partially hid the car behind some bushes in a wide spot a little way from the house. As they turned the bend a full moon rose over the trees illuminating the Strong house.

"This is creepy," said Cleo.

"How are we going to get inside?" asked Pearl.

"I ordered lock picks from Amazon," Eleanor said. "I've been practicing with them ever since they came."

"Do they work?" asked Dede.

"Sometimes," Eleanor said. "While I'm working the lock, why don't a couple of you dig around the rose bed for the skull?"

Eleanor took out her new tools and inserted the picks while Josephine held the flashlight.

"I'll check the windows," said Pearl. "You know just in case one is open."

After what seemed an eternity Eleanor achieved success and she and Josephine entered the house followed by the reluctant diggers who had turned up nothing and Pearl, of course, who had spent the time checking out the extraordinary view of the ocean in the moonlight.

"What are we looking for?" asked Pearl.

"A Bible," said Eleanor. "I don't know if Faith would bother hiding it but we have to assume she did."

"There aren't all that many hiding places, since there's nothing in the house," noted Dede.

"Where would you hide something in a house this big?" asked Josephine.

"Let's split up and each take a different room," suggested Cleo. "Listen for creaky floorboards or hollow sounding walls."

"I'm not going upstairs by myself," said Josephine.

"I'll go with you," said Pearl.

Twenty minutes later they gathered in the large room having found absolutely nothing.

"We should have known it would be difficult to find anything in the dark," said Pearl.

"I just know it's here," insisted Dede. "Did you check the closets in the upstairs bedrooms?"

"Yes," said Josephine, "We were very thorough."

"What about the fireplace?" asked Eleanor.

"I looked in the fireplace already," said Cleo. "But I didn't look up the chimney."

They moved slowly toward the large fireplace carefully sidestepping the body drawn on the wooden floor trying hard to ignore the bloodstains.

Eleanor put her head in the firebox and shone her light into the cavity. "There's no damper," she said.

"Cleo, hold the flashlight," she ordered and then reached up into the smoke chamber. "There's definitely something up there on the smoke shelf." Suddenly Eleanor pulled back with a scream knocking Cleo down, sending her flashlight flying as its beam flickered around the room. A black shadow flew out of the fireplace and flapped overhead while the others screamed and crouched to avoid the menacing beast.

"What just happened?" asked Cleo, getting up and dusting herself off.

"It's a bat!" yelled Dede, covering her head as the flying animal continued to soar and flap amid the chaos.

"Stop screaming," said Pearl. "You're just scaring the poor thing. Maybe it's a sign that we should leave." "Let's be still and maybe it will land somewhere," said Josephine."

"I'm not leaving until we find that skull," said Dede.

Cleo recovered her flashlight and resumed her position on the hearth, shining the beam up the chimney while Eleanor tentatively reached up once more.

"I can feel something, but I can't get my hand around it," Eleanor said. She adjusted her position so she could get both hands on the object. Then slowly Eleanor's hands came out with something in a soot-covered box. The women circled Eleanor with their flashlights aimed at the object she held as she cautiously opened the box revealing a human skull.

"I knew it!" exclaimed Dede.

"There's more up there," Eleanor said, handing the head to Dede. This time Eleanor's hand retrieved something wrapped in a cloth.

"This is so exciting," Cleo said as they watched Eleanor unwrap a plain black Bible.

"We've done it," said Dede. "I just know the answer to Charity Strong's murder will be in that Bible."

"Well, let's open it then," said a deep voice from behind them.

Startled and speechless the amateur detectives froze and then slowly turned their attention away from their discovery to the large looming figure that spoke. "You really shouldn't have left the door unlocked or your shovel on the porch."

"Angus," muttered Eleanor. "Why are you here?"

"The same reason you're here. I figured that Faith would hide her secret items where she thought no one would look and that would be where we had already searched." Angus moved quickly to retrieve the articles but did not study them. "Let's get out of here before we're discovered. You realize this is a crime scene."

The ladies did not hesitate but followed Angus out of the house like groupies following a rock star with Eleanor locking the door behind them. By the time they returned to Eleanor's house Angus was already on the porch with the skull and Bible in hand waiting to be let inside.

"It doesn't take a forensic examiner to see what killed Charity Strong," said Josephine as she studied the hole in the skull.

Angus picked up the skull and ran his finger over the hole that appeared to enter the right side but left no exit. "I'd say a 22-caliber bullet did this."

"Do you think it could have been fired by this?" asked Dede as she held up a small 22-caliber pistol that was hidden inside the carved out Bible.

"It looks like we found the murder weapon," said Cleo.

"Does this mean Faith killed her mother?" asked Pearl.

"It could have been her father," Dede said. "He was obviously morally bankrupt."

"Maybe not any of them," Angus said. "Faith was protecting someone."

"After reading her journals I think I know who killed Charity Strong," Eleanor said.

"Charity Strong," said Josephine. "She must have been so tired of playing the part of the perfect wife and mother when all this sinning was going on right under her nose."

"How long do you think she knew her husband was abusing their daughter?" asked Eleanor.

"Everything I know about her says she was naïve and childlike so maybe she killed herself as soon as she found out," Angus said.

"That's being generous, Angus. She knew but just didn't want to face it. When she was forced to, she took the easy way out instead of fighting for those girls," Josephine said.

"By the time Charity disappeared Faith would have been of age and could have left home. Maybe Charity didn't feel she needed her anymore," Dede said.

"A child who was abused and had a child of her own certainly needed someone and it should have been someone who wasn't her abuser," Josephine said.

"How do we know for sure it wasn't her father who killed Charity?" asked Cleo.

"We don't," Angus said, "but I bet Faith is tired of protecting those who never protected her. Maybe now she'll talk."

"Could this be the same gun that killed Jude Thorn?" asked Dede.

"He was shot with a thirty-eight," Angus said. "So was Donnie Gold."

"What do we do now?" asked Eleanor, whose face was streaked with soot from her search in the chimney.

"I suggest you wash your face, Ellie. I'll take care of this," said Angus and he gathered up the evidence and left.

"Wow, that was anticlimactic," said Eleanor.

"Now what?" asked Pearl.

"It's time for Dede's chocolate cake," said Cleo, "I'll pour the Drambuie."

Eleanor's book club met in Wren's home to discuss *The Goldfinch*. Wren lived alone with her two dogs in Bayside and had a lovely view of the bay from her large window. As the ladies waited for everyone to arrive they chatted amiably about their personal lives and shared the news of the community.

"I heard about a body being found at Sand Beach," said Dolly.

"It was Charity Strong's," said Wren. "She's been missing for at least twenty years."

"Was she murdered?" asked Mercedes.

"I don't think anyone knows for sure how she died," Eleanor said.

"Surely in this day and age they could determine cause of death by her bones," said Kim.

"Well, I heard her head was missing," said Dede.

"That is just so creepy," said Kim. "This area is getting more and more like the city. Just last night the police were at my neighbor's house because she claims someone tried to kill her."

"Who's your neighbor?" asked Cleo.

"Tonya Jones," Kim replied. "She lives close enough for me to see the police lights but I didn't hear any gunshots."

"Were there gunshots?" asked Dolly.

"Her front window was shot out," Kim reported. "I can't believe someone wanted to kill her."

"Didn't someone kill her brother?" asked Wren.

"Yes," said Dede, "Her brother is Donnie Gold. He was shot and stuffed in the densifier at the recycling center."

"See what I mean about our peaceful neighborhoods becoming crime infested?" said Kim.

"Do you think gangs are moving here?" asked Dolly.

"No, it sounds domestic," said Mercedes. "If the victims were a brother and his sister maybe there's a family feud."

"Don't forget that Jude Thorn was also shot and killed," said Josephine.

"That's right!" exclaimed Wren. "They were friends if I remember right. It makes me wonder if someone isn't getting revenge for an old grudge. Wasn't Vivian Thorn part of that group?"

"I wouldn't know about that," said Kim, "but I know lots of people who might want to do Tonya in. She's just mean—complains about people's dogs, music, children in her yard. If there's a person nearby, she has a complaint about them. She even complains about her own mother. I don't think I've ever heard a positive thing come out of her mouth or anyone say a kind word about her."

"Maybe it's Karma at her window," said Josephine. "They say Karma never forgets an address."

Each member had two uninterrupted minutes to express their opinion about the book before they held a discussion. This was meant to give everyone an opportunity to talk as some members had a great deal to say while others never got a chance to speak.

"I found the book distasteful. Those boys and the way they were raised was unbelievably horrible," said Pearl. "If children drank like that I'm sure they would die from alcohol poisoning."

"The kind of life depicted in Las Vegas wasn't to my liking either," said Josephine, "And the lack of parenting could only be called neglect."

"Just look at how they turned out," said Dede. "They grew up to be criminals."

"I didn't enjoy reading the book either," said Cleo, "but I experienced an epiphany concerning the various types of lives people live. From early on I've seen my path clearly before me and I've followed it with little deviation. The universe seemed to gently nudge me on my way to school, teaching, marriage, parenthood, travel, but after reading this book I began to realize that not everyone is on my path. Those boys had something to learn, and they took a different way, and that's all right because the world needs different kinds of people with various beliefs and skills. After all, Boris and Theo grew up and saved the day. When I look at the painting of the goldfinch chained to its perch I see resignation and acceptance of its fate in its eyes. It makes me sad, but we all need to surrender to our place in this life—at least to a certain degree."

"That reminds me of *The Poisonwood Bible*," Eleanor said. "After we read that book, I never felt the same way about missionaries. Even though their intentions are good and they only want to spread Christianity to the world because they believe it is for the greater good, they totally ignore the fact that people of different cultures and beliefs are on their own paths."

"And all paths lead to the divine," said Josephine.

"It's very much like Francis Bacon's *Idols of the Cave*," said Kim, "where individuals interpret all things based on their own peculiar interests—much like those interested in religion become obsessed with faith, or those who become devoted to art see art in everything."

"Faulty thinking based on these images created in man's mind cause many of our problems," said Mercedes, "including Idols of the Marketplace which gives false significance to words and often causes miscommunication between people."

"I knew it!" cried Cleo. "You don't need words to have thoughts, so dogs *do* think."

"I've always believed you need words to have thoughts," argued Pearl. "Dogs don't think."

"They have thoughts; they just don't have words to communicate them, and according to the *Idols of the Marketplace*, it's the words that screw up the thoughts," Cleo continued.

"I believe you two are arguing over words, so you must be erring based on *Idols of the Marketplace*," said Dede.

"Who wants dessert?" asked Wren, "I've made Vanilla Panna Cotta topped with fresh fruit."

Eleanor sat with Wesley at the dining table playing a game of Clue. "I think Mrs. White did it," sang Eleanor in her operatic voice.

"Don't sing, Gramma," said Wesley.

"Why not? Don't you like my singing?"

"You sound pretty good for an old lady, I guess," said Wesley. "I just can't concentrate when you sing."

"I'm not old you know." Eleanor replied. "I've just been young for a very long time."

Wesley looked at her closely but didn't argue. He moved Professor Plum into the lounge. "I think Professor Plum did it in the lounge with the revolver."

"Oh, Wesley, I think you are right," Eleanor conceded. Wesley opened the confidential envelop and found the cards that confirmed his accusation.

"I win, again." Wesley raised his arms above his head in victory.

"It's never nice to gloat," said Eleanor. "That's very poor form."

"Sorry, Gramma," he apologized. "I'll put the game away to make up for my very bad behavior."

"Deal!" Eleanor went to the kitchen in search of cookies. Feathers flew to the door announcing that Angus had arrived while Wesley raced to let him inside.

"Hey, Buddy.," Angus' greeting was ignored as Bones bounded in almost knocking Wesley down in his excitement. There was lots of petting, licking, and hugging between dog and boy. "Are you ready to go fishing?"

"I beat Gramma at Clue three times," bragged Wesley. "She's getting cookies now."

"Wow, she must be sick. I've never beaten her at Clue," Angus announced. "Maybe you're just good at elimination."

"No maybe about it," said Wesley riding high on the euphoria of confidence.

"I'd better sample those cookies to make sure your Gramma isn't off her game." Angus strolled to the kitchen where he stole a kiss and a cookie.

"Do the cookies pass inspection?" asked Wesley.

"Yup," Angus said as he grabbed a bag of the freshly baked chocolate chip cookies. "We may need these for later."

"See ya, Gramma." Wesley waved goodbye. He was beyond the age for kissing—at least in public.

"I'll drop him off at his house," Angus said as he left for an afternoon out on the river, but not before he quickly placed the fake dog poo near the door.

When they were gone, Eleanor put the Clue game away and sat at the table with a cup of tea. It was a beautiful fall day, bright and sunny, cool and clear, and exceptionally quiet.

Eleanor sighed. It took busy and noisy to appreciate peace and quiet. "Well, Feathers what should we do with this glorious day?" As if the universe had an answer, the doorbell rang.

Faith Strong stood at the threshold with a bouquet of yellow chrysanthemums.

"Faith, please come in," Eleanor said spotting the offensive poo and unobtrusively nudging it out of the way with her foot.

"Mrs. Penrose, I brought these as a sort of peace offering. I'm afraid I haven't been very nice to you," offered Faith.

"They're lovely. I was having a cup of tea, can I get you one?"

"Yes, thank you." Faith followed Eleanor into the kitchen and watched as she poured the tea and put several cookies on a plate.

"Let's go into the living room and get comfortable." Eleanor invited her to sit. "How have you been, Faith?"

"I'm afraid I've been unbearable. Please forgive me I didn't realize it until I witnessed the kindness. It was his kindness that brought me hope that there might be some justice in this life. I'm not used to kindness." Large tears welled up in her eyes and slipped down her cheeks.

Eleanor at first didn't know who Faith was talking about and thought it might be her God.

"Angus brought my mother's remains to me and told me he understood why I did the things I did to hide the truth. Her suicide was a sin—the worst kind—a sin of despair, a lack of faith in God's plan.

My father told me on his deathbed how he found her and buried her to keep her shameful sin a secret. When I dug up her bones, I saw the bullet hole in her head and knew he was telling the truth. He wasn't a perfect man. I've loved him and hated him and thought I could forgive him, but found it difficult to forgive my mother. Angus made me see how someone might feel so low they couldn't live anymore. It wasn't her fault."

By now Faith's face was awash with tears, but Eleanor didn't know what to say to soothe her so she said nothing.

"Angus said he would make everything all right with the police. He said not to worry, that I had been through more than most people could endure and I should let him carry some of my burden. I always believed that God wouldn't let me be tested beyond my strength, but Angus said the world is full of broken people and it's okay to ask for help from someone other than God. He helped me see that I have let kindness and truth leave me. I thought I only needed God in my life, but I need others. The Bible teaches 'Be kind and compassionate to one another, forgiving each other, just as in Christ God forgave you.' I haven't been kind, compassionate, or forgiving. I can do better. I will do better. I will be kind."

Eleanor was touched beyond words that Angus had reached this woman in such a deep and life-changing way. She hardly recognized this Faith as the same woman who sat here just weeks ago. "Faith, I think that's commendable. It's hard to forgive or let go of wrongs suffered at the hands of others. Any time you need to talk, I'm here."

"That's very kind of you, Mrs. Penrose. I'm finding that some of the kindest people are not the ones who profess their faith the loudest. I also wanted to tell you that Hope and I will be leaving as soon as things are finished up here. There is still my father's estate to put in order. I plan to sell his house, but I'm a person of interest in the murder of Jude Thorn and Donnie Gold, so I can't leave just yet. Vivian Thorn and Tonya

Jones think I'm trying to kill them because of what happened in high school. Angus said he would help me prove that I'm innocent. I *am* innocent of killing anyone, Mrs. Penrose, although I'm guilty of many other sins, I'm not a murderer."

Once again Eleanor found she didn't have any words. She wanted to believe Faith but the evidence was pretty damning. What did Angus know that made him so sure Faith was innocent? How did Faith know for sure her father didn't put that bullet in Charity's head? Would a dying man lie?

Faith didn't wait for Eleanor to offer words of comfort or reassurance. She stood and walked to the door. After she left, Eleanor wondered if anything was really solved in Charity Strong's case or if it ever could be.

Angus returned with a bright silver salmon, which Eleanor baked with lemon and butter and served with Potatoes O'Brian and green beans. A blueberry cobbler sat cooling on the counter.

"Maybe you can make salmon cakes and mustard sauce with the leftovers," Angus suggested before he filled his mouth with potatoes.

"Maybe, I could," Eleanor said as she studied this unpredictable version of Angus McBride. He didn't look different and he acted fairly normal. What had prompted him to change his tune toward Faith Strong? "Faith came to visit me today," she began. "She said you were very kind to her and your kindness had softened her heart."

"And you believed her?" Angus almost laughed.

"She was very convincing," Eleanor said, "There were tears and everything. She brought me flowers and told me you were going to help prove her innocence."

"Ellie, one of the things I love about you is your trusting nature. You don't believe the worst about people. You only see the good." Angus took another bite of fish.

"So you don't believe she's innocent?"

"No, I think she's guilty as sin," he said. "I only told her those things so she would let her guard down and slip up. It's a technique often used by police officers. You might recognize it as good cop, bad cop."

"So who is the bad cop?"

"Officer McGraw was out to see her too. He told her he knew she did it and he was going to prove that she's out for revenge on her classmates because of what they did to her in high school. Both Vivian and Tonya have gone to him with complaints about her trying to kill them. He said he's going to be watching her. He doesn't have any proof, of course."

"Angus, I heard someone fired a shot through Tonya's window. Do you think Faith did it?"

"I don't know. The bullet they dug out of the wall in Tonya's house was from the same gun that killed Jude and Donnie. The weapon hasn't been found yet, but who else has a motive?" Angus asked.

"Did Tonya tell you what they did to Faith?" Eleanor asked.

"She's trying to whitewash what they did by saying they were mean to her, teased her about her looks, and accused her of being a slut. Neither one of them is confessing to witnessing the crime we think was committed."

"Did Faith admit she was raped?"

"No, she's way too smart to admit that. It would make their story of revenge more believable because it would give her a stronger motive to get back at them. She claims the journal entries were just stories she made up."

"So she can't kill them now without incriminating herself," Eleanor said. "Do you think she'll give up on getting even?"

"No, she wants justice, but Tonya and Vivian want something too," Angus paused. "Now we wait for someone to make a mistake."

"That's it?" Eleanor asked. "We just wait?"

"No, we eat blueberry cobbler and ice cream."

The coffee group met at the Boat House on an overcast day. They ordered their usual meals and discussed the events of the day.

"I called Richard's mother yesterday," said Josephine. "She's 103 years old now and the home she's in has a breakout of the norovirus so she told me they can't have any visitors or go anywhere. I asked her if she was going crazy and she said, 'No, they won't let me go anywhere.' What a character!"

When the ladies finished laughing, Dede leaned in so they all leaned in. "I have something important I need to tell you. I hope this doesn't make you think less of me."

Everyone leaned in even more. What could this piece of news be that could possibly make any one of them think less of their beloved Dede?

"Mark and I aren't really married," Dede whispered.

As if by plan the ladies all leaned back. "How can that be?" asked Cleo.

"Well I was cleaning out some files last year and came across our marriage license. I noticed the priest hadn't signed it. You know Mark was married before, but what you don't know is that his wife refused to divorce him." Dede paused. "She was mean and spiteful and maybe just a little crazy. They weren't married long and she moved somewhere in Colorado." It was obvious she was upset by the entire incident, but no one spoke so she continued. "I put it away and haven't thought about it until yesterday when I learned that his first wife has died."

"Couldn't you just get the priest to sign it?" asked Pearl. "It may be he simply forgot."

"No, he's dead," Dede said. "You don't understand. We lied because we never told the priest Mark wasn't divorced. I don't know how he knew, but I'm sure he knew and just never signed the paper."

"Well if his first wife is dead now you can get married in the church," Cleo said. "What's got you so upset?"

"I'm just a little worried that it might get out that we've been living together all this time without being married." Dede could see the headlines already: "Mayor Caught in Bigamy Scandal."

"Just go away and get married," suggested Josephine. "We won't tell."

"We can all be bridesmaids," laughed Pearl.

"Did I ever tell you about the time Steve and I went to Saint Kitts on a Caribbean cruise? Blue skies, turquoise waters, and white sand beaches along with the warmth of the tropical sun make it a paradise like no other." Cleo was lost in her memory. "Anyway, we were on Saint Kitts touring the Caribelle Batik compound and there was a 400-year-old Saman tree there. Our guide told us that people from all over the world come to get married under it because legend has it that if two people marry under this tree, they will never part. Steve and I were walking around under the tree. It is huge. Anyway, I passed a woman who was also walking there and just offhand said, 'Would you marry us?' Imagine my surprise when she said she was an ordained minister and she certainly would. It was really strange, but in a good way. She grabbed my arm and put her other hand over my heart and married us under that tree."

"That's quite a story," said Josephine.

"We should all go with you to the Caribbean Island of Saint Kitts," said Eleanor. "No one would ever have to know your secret and then you and Mark would be officially married."

"Well I'm in," said Pearl.

"It sounds wonderful," Dede said thoughtfully. "I'll talk to Mark."

"Do we know anything more about the murders of Jude or Donnie?" asked Josephine.

"No, I guess Faith is our prime suspect," said Eleanor. "Hope and Faith claim they were together but no one believes them."

"I like Tonya Jones for this one," said Dede. "I don't think she was on good terms with her brother."

"Of course, it could be Vivian who killed Jude," said Pearl. "Isn't the spouse always the prime suspect?"

"Vivian has an alibi," Eleanor said.

"What would Tonya's motive be?" asked Cleo. "If not liking your sibling is a reason to kill them there wouldn't be many families intact."

"I think there might be an inheritance involved," Dede said. "I've heard some gossip about her mother investing heavily in the stock market."

"So what would she gain by taking him out?" asked Pearl. "Wouldn't his wife get his share?"

"Not necessarily," said Cleo. "I'm not in my mother-in-law's will. If Steve dies before his mother, her money goes to her grandchildren. I think that's a standard practice to keep the money in the family.

Otherwise I could marry someone else and we could squander the money, or if I died he could leave it to his children instead of mine. Then the family money would be in the hands of strangers."

"Yes, but in this case it would still go to Donnie's children before it would go to Tonya," said Josephine.

"No it wouldn't," said Dede. "Donnie's wife had those two children from an earlier relationship. Tonya's mother might not accept them as family even if they've been part of it for years. I have a feeling her mother is just as mean as Tonya."

"The apple doesn't usually fall far from the tree," said Pearl.

"It would have to be a hefty sum to warrant killing him," said Eleanor.

"How would we ever find that out?" asked Cleo.

"We could go to the Red Shed," said Dede. "I'm sure Tonya hangs out there so we might get lucky and hear something."

"I'm in," said Pearl who liked to play video poker and smoke cigarettes in the back room. The others nodded in agreement.

"Okay, meet at my house at 9:00," said Dede.

Eleanor didn't want Angus to know the coffee group was going to the Red Shed, so she intended to tell him she had a headache and needed to cancel their dinner plans for the evening. She was relieved when *he* called to cancel saying something had come up involving the murder investigation.

The Red Shed was a local hangout for those looking to meet someone. It had sawdust and peanut shells on the floor and cow paraphernalia hung on the walls along with animal hides and mounted heads. The coffee ladies slipped quietly inside and found a table near the back next to the door that led to the video game room. Pearl immediately disappeared to play Keno and smoke cigarettes, much to the wonderment of her friends who understood that Pearl was the kind of person who associated with a variety of people without judgment. They ordered drinks and looked around the bar.

"I don't recognize anyone in here," said Eleanor.

"I'd be amazed if you did," said Dede. "It's not exactly the kind of place old ladies patronize."

"Oh, don't look now but Michael just walked in with Vivian," Eleanor said and they all turned to see.

"He is a handsome man," Josephine said. "I see a lot of Angus in him."

"Vivian's a dish too," said Cleo. "They make a very attractive couple."

"I don't think he saw us," Eleanor said as the two sat at the bar with their backs to them and began canoodling. The amateur detectives sipped their drinks and watched as Vivian made a call on her phone and Michael drank a beer. Before long, the door opened and platinum coiffed Tonya Jones came inside followed by Angus.

Eleanor felt a blow to her solar plexus as they sat down next to Vivian at the bar. Keeping her head down, Eleanor escaped to the game room. There were some things she just couldn't watch and one of them was the man she loved with another woman. Could this be something that came up with the murder investigation?

"Is there a back way out?" Eleanor asked Pearl. "I need to get out of here."

"Sure the door around the corner leads out to the parking lot," Pearl said. "Just let me cash in my winnings."

Eleanor peeked into the bar and saw Delia Parker sitting at a table with Dr. Baxter. Then the door opened and who should sashay in but a beautiful girl with long loose chestnut hair wearing tight blue jeans and a white blouse. Even with the heavy makeup highlighting her sparkling brown eyes, Eleanor recognized Hope Strong.

Meanwhile the other ladies sat and worried.

"How are we going to find out anything now?" asked Dede.

"Maybe we should go and leave the investigating to Angus," said Josephine. "I'm sure he's here on official business."

"Hmmmm, or monkey business," said Cleo who suddenly left the table and sat down at the bar next to Angus.

"Buy me a drink, handsome," she said.

"What are you having, Cleo?" he asked glancing her way but keeping one ear on Tonya's conversation.

"Gin martini, dirty with extra olives," she said.

"Where's Eleanor?" Angus asked as he looked around and spotted Dede and Josephine in their dark corner. When Cleo didn't answer he continued. "Get her out of here. This isn't a suitable place for ladies to frequent."

"I was feeling a little lucky," Cleo raised her voice. "My mother died and left me a tidy sum."

Tonya turned Cleo's way, and whispered to Angus, "Looks like you're going to get lucky tonight."

"I like your date and would like to buy her a drink," Cleo offered leaning in front of Angus and eying Tonya's empty glass. "Back this guy up, too," she told the bartender. "Here's to mothers and their money when they finally share it." Cleo clinked glasses with Tonya and smiled when she saw her chug it down.

"My mother isn't very generous, but I'll drink to yours. How much did she leave you?" Tonya hiccupped.

"My mother wasn't very generous either. We must be kindred spirits. Five million dollars, she left me five million dollars. I can't believe she had that much money. It's unbelievable how she kept all that money and I didn't know it. She never gave me a penny until now." Cleo was on a roll.

Angus sat squeezed between the two rolling his eyes at Cleo's lies.

"That's not unbelievable. I know my mother has twice that amount. She married a rich man who invested in the stock market but she wouldn't help me out to save my life. She gave my brother enough money to start up a business, but me, I got diddly-squat." Tonya leaned toward Cleo and almost fell off her stool.

"Well, here's to us rich bitches," said Cleo as she raised her glass and clinked it to Tonya's empty one.

"To rish bishes," Tonya said. "I'll be one soon."

"Bartender, another drink for my friend." Cleo got up and walked out the front door leaving Angus to pick up the tab.

Dede and Josephine followed. When they got to the car Pearl and Eleanor were waiting and they piled in and drove slowly to Dede's.

"What an absolute waste of time," lamented Eleanor.

"Not for me," declared Pearl, "I won eighty-five dollars."

"I found out that Tonya Jones' mother is worth millions and she resents her brother for getting financial help from her to start up his business while she got nothing," Cleo said.

"That's definitely a motive for murder," said Dede.

It was late by the time Eleanor got home and she was in a very bad mood. When she spied the rubber dog poo by the front door she decided to pay a visit to Angus' house despite the lateness of the hour. As soon as she opened Angus' door, Bones was all over her. She put the doggie doo-doo in the living room and Bones ran outside. Maybe she would take him with her after all, the poor dog needed some exercise and it was comforting to have his company on the walk home. As she walked up the hill, she analyzed the reason for her funk. Was it possible that Eleanor Penrose was jealous? Yes, she was a terrible person, guilty of jealousy, deceit, and manipulation. She was angry at Angus for doing exactly what she planned to do—cancel dinner plans to go to the Red Shed to investigate a motive for murder. Wasn't she taking Bones to her house for the sole purpose of learning the exact time Angus would return home from his rendezvous at the Red Shed? If he even came home tonight. She knew he would come to her looking for Bones. She was almost home when she turned around and began the walk back to Angus' house. Okay, she was still jealous and deceitful but she wouldn't be manipulative. This time when she opened the door she noticed an envelope on the floor that must have been shoved under the door while she was walking home. Eleanor studied it closely knowing it hadn't been there just minutes ago. It was a lovely scented envelope with Angus' name written on the front in a feminine hand. It wasn't sealed. Eleanor opened it and read:

Dear Angus,

I desperately needed to thank you for your kindness the other day. The men I have known have not been kind, but you are a man among men. "Above all, love each other deeply, because love covers over a multitude of sins." "Love is patient, love is kind. It always protects and never fails." Angus, you are patient, kind and you protect me. I believe you will never fail me. You are love and I love you. It may be that you need me to lead you to God as much as I need you to lead me to love.

Yours in love,

Faith

Eleanor stuffed the letter back into the envelope and dropped it on the floor. Then, she locked the door behind her leaving Bones inside. The wind blew from the east causing dry leaves to scatter across the road while a partial moon revealed itself through the swirling nighttime clouds casting shadows that made Eleanor look behind her for someone who wasn't there and stop to listen for footsteps that didn't exist.

She was relieved to step back in her space of peace and safety and lock the door behind her. Switching on all the lights and turning on some music, Eleanor completed her nightly routines and readied herself for bed. She stood at the window looking out at the vast expanse of water below. The constant and repetitive rhythm of the ocean gave her solace as she contemplated the events of the last few weeks. What the heck was she doing? She had invited Faith into her nearly perfect life with her disease and dysfunction. This was no way to live. What she really wanted was a boring peaceful life with Angus by her side enjoying the simple moments that came, surrounded by people of good character and beloved family and friends—not murderers and damaged deranged stalkers. This life of stakeouts, break-ins, and adrenaline-inducing adventure was not for old people. It was not for her. Was she old? What was old anyway, and what did it have to do with taking risks? Nothing. Perhaps Eleanor was just tired of heart-racing thrills. Her friends seemed to enjoy the mental challenge of solving a mystery and so did she, but you could do that while reading a good book. You could experience that terrified feeling in a game of hide-and-seek without welcoming unbalanced maniacs into your life.

Angus had lived with this form of human behavior for most of his adult life mingling with criminals and mental defectives as he worked to put them away from decent citizens. She wondered if he could ever let it go. She wondered if he felt the same way she felt. Weary but unable to sleep, Eleanor poured a glass of wine, lit a candle, turned off the lights, and sat on her couch.

A gentle tapping sound woke her from a light sleep. She moved to the door and made out Angus' fractured face through the stained-glass of the window.

"Did I wake you?" he asked.

"Not really, yes," Eleanor admitted. "Come inside and sit down. Can I get you a nightcap?"

"No, I've had enough to drink tonight. I had to see you to explain what I was doing," he began. "I'm sorry I cancelled our dinner."

"Did you learn anything on your date with Tonya?" Eleanor asked.

"It wasn't a date and I learned that Cleo likes her martinis dirty with extra olives," Angus said. "What were you doing there?"

"We were trying to find out if Tonya had a motive for killing her brother," Eleanor explained.

"Now it all makes sense," Angus said thoughtfully. "Cleo should get an award for acting. I knew she was lying about her mother dying and leaving her five million dollars but Tonya fell for it. Of course, Tonya was three sheets to the wind even before Cleo generously offered her more to drink. By the way, Cleo left me with the bar bill."

"So, what were you investigating?" Eleanor asked.

"Delia asked me to talk to Michael. She thinks he's gotten too close to Vivian and doesn't want him working the case anymore, but she didn't want it to come from her. She's thinking he's not cut out for the PI business."

"Couldn't you talk to him at home? Why go to the Red Shed?"

"Michael hasn't been home. He's more or less moved in with Vivian, which he claims has double benefits, three if you count sex. Vivian needs protection and he can keep an eye on her to be sure she's not the killer. They like the Red Shed."

"I saw Delia there with Dr. Baxter. I'm assuming he's the client that hired them to solve Charity Strong's disappearance." Eleanor wasn't a fool. "Has she told him?"

"Told him what exactly? That it was a suicide or that her husband killed her?" Angus asked, "because we may never know."

"Faith said her father admitted on his deathbed that Charity committed suicide and he buried her to keep her disgrace a secret," Eleanor said. "I didn't know he regained consciousness after his stroke. Do you know if it was possible?"

Angus seemed to mull this information over and shook his head. "I don't know Ellie. What I do know is that Faith Strong is a disturbed woman and you should keep your distance." He raised her hand to his lips. "Your hands are like silk. How are they so small and perfect and soft?" He kissed her palm and stood to leave. "I need to get some sleep. Thanks for taking Bones out. I appreciate it. Can you tell me what the note Faith left for me said? Bones chewed it up."

For one brief second, Eleanor thought about lying but realized it might be important for Angus to know he was the object of a deranged woman's affection.

"She wanted to thank you for your kindness and let you know she loves you," Eleanor said walking Angus to the door.

"I knew it! Ellie, you are an incurable snoop. I can't believe you opened a letter that was addressed to me. You should be ashamed of yourself." Angus pulled her forcefully into his arms and kissed her with a passion that made her knees buckle. Then he walked out the door. Eleanor sighed and watched him disappear into the night before she turned off her porch light. When she reached into the pocket of her robe, she found the rubber dog poo.

Eleanor sat at her desk and waited for inspiration to strike. While she waited, she let her eyes wonder to her crime board filled with victims and suspects:

Charity Strong could have committed suicide. She seemed troubled by a variety of problems including a husband who wouldn't touch her but molested their daughter, accusations of embezzlement from the church, and a pregnant daughter who was the object of gossip. There was also the possibility that she had taken a lover and may have been wracked with guilt.

Reverend Strong might also have killed Charity if she found out about his abuse and misuse of church funds, especially if she threatened to reveal his dark side. Was there blackmail involved? Was he taking money to pay off prostitutes or an angry mistress?

Faith could have killed her mother in a fit of adolescent rage. Her father may have helped her dispose of the body in an attempt to protect his secrets as well as his daughter's crime.

Charity Strong's mystery lover might have killed her if she refused to go away with him. Could it be **Dr. Baxter**?

Vivian Thorn could have killed her husband Jude to end an unpleasant divorce, but what reason would she have to kill Donnie Gold? Besides that, she had an alibi.

Faith Strong might have killed both men as revenge for rape.

Tonya Jones may have killed her brother Donnie for the inheritance, but why would she kill Jude Thorn?

Hope Strong could have killed both men to avenge her mother if she knew what they had done.

Dr. Baxter might have killed Jude Thorn if he had feelings for Vivian. She obviously had feelings for him but she was already getting a divorce so what was the point of all that? Why would he kill Donnie Gold? Maybe Dr. Baxter had just learned about what the two men did to Faith and he killed them to get justice for Charity's daughter. Dr. Baxter hired private investigators to find Charity's killer. What did he hope to prove?

Eleanor remembered the letters she saw on Vivian's desk in Dr. Baxter's office. The ones tied with blue rickrack that matched letters in Charity's box of journals and were delivered to his office by Hope Strong. The contents of those letters might hold the key to unlocking part of the mystery. Eleanor wondered if Delia knew what was in those letters. A quick call was in order.

When Eleanor reached Angus' house Delia had already made tea and welcomed Eleanor inside.

"I was just going over my notes on the murder of Jude Thorn. Angus has taken Bones for an outing. How can I help you Eleanor?"

"I was hoping you could shed some light on Charity Strong's case," Eleanor said as she sat on the leather couch. "I know Dr. Baxter is your client and I was hoping you could tell me if he told you about some letters he had from her."

Before Delia could respond, there was a knock on the door. "Excuse me," Delia rose to answer it.

A somewhat transformed Faith Strong stood on the doorstep with a plate of freshly baked oatmeal raisin cookies. Her hair was loose and she wore a faint trace of lipstick. At first glance, Delia didn't recognize her.

"Oh, I didn't know Angus had company," Faith stammered.

"Did you bake these for Angus?" Delia asked taking the plate. "He's not home now, but I'll tell him you stopped by."

Faith's body literally sagged with disappointment as she stammered her goodbye and stood on the porch while Delia closed the door on her stricken face.

"These will go nicely with our tea," said Delia as she returned to her seat and placed the cookies on the coffee table.

"Was that Faith?" asked Eleanor. "I just got a glimpse of her but she looked different."

"I know. Her hair was different and she was wearing makeup," Delia said. "I didn't figure her for a cookie baker either."

"She's in love with Angus," Eleanor said thoughtfully. "It must have taken all her courage to come here with those cookies and then find us here instead of him . . . how sad for her."

"But lucky for us. These cookies are delicious," Delia said as she took a second bite. "Now, what were you saying about Dr. Baxter and letters?"

"I believe Hope Strong brought him some letters she found in one of Charity's boxes of memorabilia. They were tied with blue rickrack and I think they might contain clues to her death," Eleanor explained.

"He hasn't told me anything about letters from Charity. How do you know he's my client?" Delia asked. "Did Angus tell you that?"

"No, Delia, Angus didn't tell me that. I inferred it when I saw you with him at the Red Shed. I think he was in love with her and continues to be obsessed with her and her disappearance."

"I know nothing about any letters, but I think you may be right about his feelings for her, although he's over her now that we've proved she's dead," Delia smiled.

"I'm not so sure, Delia. I heard him sobbing in his office after those letters were delivered. He hired you to find her killer. That doesn't sound like a man who is over a lost love," Eleanor said. "I hope you haven't lost objectivity in this case. Dr. Baxter is very handsome and charming, but that doesn't exclude him from my list of suspects."

"Do you seriously think he hired us to see if we could find her killer?" Delia frowned.

"I don't know," Eleanor said honestly. "I just think you should heed your own advice about getting involved with your clients. It wouldn't hurt to keep your eyes peeled for those letters."

The coffee group met at the Boat House on Friday. Having received their invitations in the mail, they were excited about the upcoming Halloween party at Eleanor's house.

"I think this will be even more fun than the community celebration. At least it will be more intimate," said Cleo, who could hardly keep her disguise to herself and was bursting to tell her secret.

"I've hired Madam Patruska to do private readings and she said she would facilitate a séance, so be thinking about a dead person we can contact," Eleanor said. "Maybe Mattie May will make herself available."

"Do you need help with the decorations?" asked Pearl.

"Of course," Eleanor said, "I can always use an extra pair of hands."

"Is that a clue to your costume?" asked Cleo. "Are you an octopus or a spider?"

Eleanor rolled her eyes. "I'm not telling."

"We'll know who you are, Eleanor, because it will be at your house," Cleo said. "You'll be the hostess so you'll have to answer the door."

"Detective Cleo, you are so clever," Eleanor remarked. "But has it occurred to you that I may hire someone to answer the door? Maybe Madame Patruska will do that or maybe an early guest."

"I will know who each of you will be," Josephine bragged. "Your shadow selves will be revealed by your choices."

"So you think our dark sides will come out for the party?" asked Pearl.

"Precisely," Josephine answered. "I could tell you in advance who each of you will be, but that might spoil the fun."

"I'm looking forward to this," said Dede, who was thinking she revealed her dark side every day and planned to come as her better self.

Eleanor's mind had already moved on to other things. She knew that Dr. Baxter's office was closed on Saturday and the seed of an idea sprouted in her mind. If she could get her hands on the letters that Hope had returned to him, she would have an insight into his relationship with Charity. Were they love letters? They must have been important to Charity if she kept them tied with a ribbon. Eleanor wondered if the letters were still in his office. She had her lock picks. Could she do this alone? Did she want to? The mere thought of breaking into his office and rummaging through his desk in the dark of night made her heart race. She waited for Dede to say she needed to leave for a meeting, excused herself, and walked with her to her car.

"Dede, I'm going to search Dr. Baxter's office for the letters. Do you want to come with me?" Eleanor knew she would do it no matter how Dede responded.

"When? Dede asked.

"Tonight." Eleanor didn't want time to weaken her resolve. "I'll be at your house at midnight." Dede simply nodded, got in her car, and drove away.

As Eleanor prepared beef bourguignon for dinner with Angus, her mind played out the drama of the break-in she was planning. She visualized herself using the lock picks on the door of Dr. Baxter's office and searching his desk for the letters using her flashlight. Would she dare take the letters? There wouldn't be time to read them there. Should she take pictures of them with her phone or use the copy machine to make her own copies so she could read them at her leisure.

In her mind she imagined a silent alarm alerting Dr. Baxter who caught her in the act and called the police. She saw Angus coming to bail her out of jail and felt the shame of the entire drama as he lectured her and saw the embarrassment it caused her family, not to mention the horrible example it set for her grandchildren.

She spent the afternoon laying out her tools, leaving nothing to chance, going over each detail to insure success. A nap was totally out of the question as she paced the floor, checked on her stew, and worried that she had become an adrenaline junkie. As much as she feared the event, she found she was looking forward to the heart-racing adventure in her future more than not. It made her feel alive. When Angus arrived bearing wine and roses she was eager to get dinner over and move on to the task at hand.

"You seem preoccupied, Ellie," Angus noted. "Is something on your mind?"

"No," she lied. "Do you like the stew?"

"Is that what this is?" he asked. "It's pretty fancy for stew. Just what is this sauce?"

"Red wine," she said. "Do you like it?"

"It's delicious." Angus took a big bite of beef and mashed potatoes.

It was very quiet. Angus chewed and swallowed. "I see you're not drinking. Did you use up all your wine in the sauce?"

Eleanor smiled. "Have you ever known me to run out of wine?"

"No, but you usually have some with dinner."

"I have a headache tonight," she said.

Angus looked at her with concern. "Did you take something for it?"

"Don't worry. I'm just tired and anticipating the Halloween party. I'm sure it will go away after a good night's sleep."

"Then we'll make it an early night," Angus said. "Do you want me to stay over?"

"Oh no," she said too quickly. "I'm not good company I'm afraid."

They finished dinner and snuggled by the fire but there wasn't much conversation or silly banter.

"You know Faith came to visit me today. She brought brownies and we had a very informative talk," Angus said rubbing Eleanor's back.

"She's in love with you," Eleanor said.

"I know. She told me as much. We had an interesting discussion about demons and sex."

"Really?" Eleanor was suddenly distracted from her midnight plan.

"Yes, she believes that sex outside of marriage is a sin, but she can't reconcile it with her belief that it is also a manifestation of love. She offered herself to me in the most obvious way. It was a delicate situation."

"What did she do?"

"She kissed me."

"What did you do?"

"I tried to let her down easy and told her I believed sex outside of marriage was a sin too. Then she told me all about the rape and her father and how she had tried to do penance for all the sex she had because she's never been married but she's had a great deal of sex. She admitted that she had a miscarriage that her father delivered and disposed of and her mother knew nothing about any of it. Do you think I'll go to hell for lying?"

"You will certainly go to hell for lying and for other reasons as well," Eleanor said.

"She thinks sex is love," Angus said. "She's a grown woman with some serious issues."

"How did you leave it?" Eleanor asked.

"Well, I refused her offer of marriage because I'm too old for her but told her we could be friends."

"That was thoughtful of you. Did you offer to get her psychiatric help?" Eleanor asked.

"Actually no, I was sadly flattered that a young woman or any woman would want to marry me since I've been turned down so many times." He looked at Eleanor and hung his head sadly.

"Angus, you are awful. Faith is vulnerable and should not be made fun of in that way. I'm sure she was deadly serious."

"Are you saying she might kill me now that I've refused her advances?"

"You were the one who said she was dangerous," Eleanor reminded him.

"It's more likely that she would kill you, Eleanor. She loves me, but sees you as an obstacle to getting me."

"Did you tell her about us?" Eleanor asked.

"No, but I think she knows somehow. Maybe she's been spying on us. I should probably spend the night to protect you. You know—just in case she wants to kill you."

"Is any of this true? I mean really, Angus, did any of this happen outside of your distorted imagination?" Eleanor asked.

"I can see that you doubt my integrity so I better leave." Angus stood and walked to the door. "Call me if you change your mind or if your 'headache' goes away." Eleanor watched him walk out the door.

He is absolutely maddening she thought as she checked the time and began to dress for her midnight rendezvous with Dede.

Eleanor parked her car along the street near Dede's house and tapped lightly on her door. Dede opened the door before her dog Doogie could react and alert the neighborhood that something was afoot. They decided to walk the few blocks and avoid the possibility of anyone witnessing Eleanor's car near The Lumbar Yard. Neither of them noticed the pickup that followed them at a discrete distance and parked across the street from Dr. Baxter's office even though the streets were relatively deserted this time of night. Eleanor quickly worked the lock on the front door and they were inside within minutes of their arrival.

"You're getting really good at that," Dede said as she glanced around before entering.

"Thanks," Eleanor said.

The front door opened into a small reception area and waiting room with half a dozen chairs lining the walls. Eleanor moved quickly to the space behind the receptionist's desk and into Dr. Baxter's private office. The light from the street entered the room from a single window. Dede quickly closed the blinds while Eleanor searched the desk drawers for the letters. Dr. Baxter was obsessively neat. There was nothing on his desk and each of the drawers was organized so it was easy to see the contents at a glance. Just when Eleanor was ready to give up, she found the one drawer that was locked and used her new lock-picking skills to open it. There among miscellaneous papers were the letters still neatly tied with blue rickrack.

"Jackpot," Eleanor whispered as she held them up for Dede to see. "Start up the copy machine."

Dede was well acquainted with copiers and had no trouble finding the on button. Meanwhile Eleanor opened each envelope and one by one they copied the letters like a well-oiled machine, then tied them with the rickrack and returned them to the drawer. Dede turned off the copy machine and they quickly exited the office.

"Mission accomplished," said Dede.

"I didn't think it would be that easy," said Eleanor.

"Are we going to read them?" asked Dede.

"I think I'd better go home. What would Mark say if he finds me at your house in the middle of the night?" Eleanor asked.

"He won't wake up," Dede said. "He sleeps like a drunken sailor, but it *is* late. Call me tomorrow if you learn anything." They walked back to Dede's house and Eleanor drove to Sand Beach never giving a thought to the truck that followed at a distance.

When she finally arrived home she collapsed exhausted on top of her covers still dressed in her detective uniform and slept until daybreak when she heard the doorbell ring. Eleanor stumbled to answer the door and squinted into the smiling face of Angus McBride.

"Late night?" he asked as he followed Bones inside.

Eleanor fluffed her bedhead and shuffled into the kitchen to make coffee. She didn't feel an explanation was in order.

"I brought your morning paper," he offered laying it on the kitchen counter.

"Thank you."

"Bones and I were hoping you'd accompany us on a walk this morning." Angus eyed her curiously. "Are you up for it?"

"I just need a minute." Eleanor stretched her eyes wide and took in the sun and the glory of a bright October morning. "And a cup of coffee. Would you like one?"

"Always." He sat at the counter and began reading the newspaper. Eleanor excused herself and came back after washing her face and combing her hair. Angus had poured the coffee by then and Eleanor sipped it impatiently wishing she could read the letters she had carefully hidden under her bedroom pillow. "Are you all right, Ellie?"

"I'm fine. You know sometimes it's difficult to get to sleep and then equally difficult to wake up," she said.

"I see. Was there anything in particular that kept you up late?" he asked. Eleanor looked into his green eyes and sensed that he already knew what had kept her up until the wee hours. "Anything you'd like to talk about?"

She considered the possibility that Angus was using his professional detective skills and had come to the conclusion that she was hedging the truth. After all, she didn't usually sleep late while wearing her black stakeout uniform. She realized the clues were obvious, but she wasn't required to tell him everything she did. "No, where do you want to walk?"

Angus finished his coffee. "Let's walk the beach. It's cold but clear and the tide is out."

Eleanor found a warm jacket and put on her walking shoes. As they stepped along the shore Angus took her hand. "You know how much I care for you, don't you Ellie?"

"Yes, and I love you too, Angus."

"You know you can tell me anything."

"Angus, what is it that you think I need to tell you?"

"What were you and Dede doing at The Lumbar Yard in the dead of night? How did you manage to get inside and why are you being so secretive about it?"

"That's a lot of questions, Angus. How do you know I was anywhere last night? Are you having me followed?" Eleanor pulled her hand from his clasp.

"I take care of those I love. You were acting strange last night. I was worried so I followed you, watched you go into Dr. Baxter's office, and followed you home. You know breaking and entering is a crime. You could have been caught and arrested. Dr. Baxter could press charges against you, Ellie. Your behavior is disturbing. You're growing bolder and I'm afraid for you. Tell me you didn't take anything from his office." Angus' concern was palpable. Eleanor took a minute to process his words and recognized the truth they held.

"I'm sorry Angus. I didn't mean to worry you. I think maybe I've become an adrenaline addict. There's a certain thrill I get from snooping. Do you think there's hope for me?"

"No, you are absolutely hopeless." Angus took her hand once more and turned to look into her face. "What did you find last night?"

"Honestly, I did not take anything from Dr. Baxter's office—at least not anything that he'll miss. Dede and I found the letters Hope returned to him and copied them," Eleanor confessed.

"Have you read them?" Angus asked.

"No, I was too tired last night," Eleanor said, "I fell asleep in my clothes."

"I noticed."

"Of course you did. You're a trained professional," Eleanor said. "Angus, do you ever feel it? You know the thrill of the hunt, the fear of getting caught?"

"No, Ellie, I'm an officer of the law. I don't break it. I enforce it. I play by the rules. The only thrill I get is when I catch the perp and they get what they deserve." Angus' face was serious. "I'm beginning to think you have criminal tendencies. I may have to keep you under constant surveillance."

Eleanor felt terribly guilty. She had always been a good citizen and could not explain her brazen acts of criminal activity or the feelings they engendered. "Would you like to come back to my house and read the letters with me?"

"I thought you'd never ask."

Eleanor made a fresh pot of coffee while Angus wiped the sandy paws of Sherlock Bones. After a quick breakfast of scrambled eggs and ham, they sat down together and read the letters Dr. Baxter wrote to Charity Strong twenty years ago.

My Lovely,

How do I begin to explain what you mean to me? From the first time I saw you I felt an exquisite delight that has not paled over time. My eyes couldn't take in enough of your beauty and then when I thought there couldn't be more, you spoke, and your voice was like honey. Yet this was only the shell of something even sweeter that I discovered as we grew to know each other more deeply. To talk with you is knowing myself better - to be with you is the comfort of a soft and soothing touch like being in an all-enveloping cloud of acceptance of who and what I am without judgment. When I look into your eyes, I see myself reflected and it's good.

Everything is good and I want to share it. Every sunset, moonrise, and blossoming flower I want to share with you. Hungry for your thoughts and insights, I wonder what you might say about the color of the sky or shift of the wind. You fill my thoughts day and night. I think I'm in love.

Me

Angus read the letter out loud and sighed. "Dr. Baxter writes a pretty good love letter. Do you feel like swooning?"

"I might, if it was written to me," Eleanor replied.

"He's clever. Not once does he give away her name, or his," Angus noted. "If the letter fell into her husband's hands, there's no proof it was for Charity or from Baxter."

"It's that way with all of these," said Eleanor as she scanned several others. "I wonder how Hope knew they were from Dr. Baxter."

Angus read a few more letters. "There's nothing incriminating here. Just the words of a lovesick man. If you hadn't seen Hope deliver them to Baxter's office, we wouldn't know they were for Charity or suspect that he wrote them."

"I didn't actually see her deliver them. It was more of an assumption based on blue rickrack. Listen to this one." Eleanor began to read.

My Happiness,
You surely are torn, and I know my desires have pushed you to commit acts foreign to your beliefs, but you deserve the kind of happiness you give to me - the kind we give to each other. Our plan to be together is as right and natural as the rising of the sun each day. You can't deny that you feel it too and yet I agree we cannot continue on this path. Choose. If you are not ready tomorrow, it will break me, but I will respect your choice. Everything I feel for

you will be forever with me. Like the roots of a tree grow deep you have embedded your essence in me - you are me and I am you.

Me

Angus' brow furrowed in thought. "Sounds like he planned to run away with her."

"Evidently she didn't choose him," said Eleanor.

"Or maybe she did and someone stopped her from meeting him that day," Angus said.

"That must be what Dr. Baxter wants Delia and Michael to discover. If they tell him she committed suicide, he would feel responsible having pushed her to choose, but if her husband found out she was leaving him and killed her, Dr. Baxter would at least know she chose him."

"He might still feel responsible," Angus said. "The problem is we just don't know what really went down that day."

"So these letters only prove that Dr. Baxter was Charity's mystery man," Eleanor said. "I wonder if she wrote letters to him too." Angus gave her a look that needed no words.

A hunter's moon lit the night as an east wind blew what dry leaves were left from the autumn trees. They scampered over the lane like wild critters and swirled though barren branches competing with the ever constant whisper of the ocean's voice. Eleanor had spent the day decorating her house in preparation for her evening soiree. With the help of Pearl and Cleo the stage was set for a hauntingly good time. The dim lights revealed fall flowers of orange and yellows embedded in pumpkins, candles flickered on the tabletops, and cobwebs hung from macabre decorations that included a skeleton, spiders, and ghosts. The dining table was filled with treats that included mini boo-berry muffins, lady fingers, cocktail sausages wrapped like mummies, cupcakes, and mini torts all decorated in the spirit of the night. The kitchen counter held a variety of beverages and a large punch bowl contained a bubbling concoction created by Cleo who was famous for her witches' brew.

As soon as Cleo and Pearl left, Eleanor hurried to dress for the evening. When she answered the door to her first guest a tall old west sheriff stood on the doorstep. Decked in white from head to toe he glowed in the darkness as he tipped his hat and eyed her from behind his mask.

"Welcome Sheriff," Eleanor said. Her face was disguised by exaggerated makeup and a sparkly white mask. An intricate chorus-girl style headdress with huge billowy feathers over a long black wig capped her head. Overly sequined and brightly colored with lots of colorful beads and bangles, her dress completed her costume. "Why don't you come on into the saloon."

"I really want to kiss you right now," said the sheriff, "but I'm afraid someone watching might get the wrong idea."

"Come in," Eleanor said lifting her mask, "You can kiss me, just don't smear my makeup."

Angus removed his mask, brushed his mustache against her lips, and adjusted his gun belt. "I hope you don't mind that I brought this gun in your house."

"Is it real?" she asked.

Before he could answer, Madam Patruska arrived. She came in her usual psychic attire; wild red hair hopelessly twisted into orderly disarray by a blue scarf covered with silver coins that tinkled musically like a wind chime, an orange tunic embroidered with a multitude of flowers, more scarves and layers of jewelry, a green broomstick skirt, and Birkenstocks. Her face was unadorned, believing her natural beauty was more than enough.

"Happy Halloween!" she cried. "I had so many things to bring I had to drive my car up here instead of leaving it at the wayside like you advised. Can you help me carry them inside?"

Angus helped her with her box of psychic paraphernalia and showed her where she could set up her table while Eleanor greeted a carload of partiers who had carpooled from the wayside. She recognized Josephine and Richard, who dressed as Raggedy Ann and Andy, and watched Cleo trip over her enormous clown shoes as Steve stumbled in behind her in his, their faces painted like Steven King's Pennywise. Two ghosts floated in along with a priest and a nun. Eleanor showed them to the beverages and wondered how long Cleo could wear those shoes before she tossed them aside choosing comfort over style. It wasn't long before another car arrived with a couple of vampires, two skeletons, and the devil with an angel on his arm.

Eleanor lost track of the final guests as she mingled and made sure everyone had what they needed. It wasn't long before the devil took to the piano and played a spine-chilling gavotte followed by *Monster Mash*, which caused Cleo to kick off her clown shoes revealing striped socks and begin to dance with the priest. Soon, there were several odd couples cutting a rug as the devil pounded out a couple of dance tunes and ended with *The Music of the Night* from *Phantom of the Opera*. The Sheriff held the saloon girl tight as they danced.

"Do you know who all these people are?" Angus whispered in Eleanor's ear.

"Careful, you almost knocked the feathers off my head," Eleanor warned as she righted her headdress and glanced quickly around the room, each turn of her head smacking Angus with her feathers. "The dancing nun and priest are Dede and Mark. Cleo and Steve are clowns, and I'm sure the devil is Taylor. Josephine and Richard are the dolls and I think Pearl and Cary are the ghosts."

Angus spotted two skeletons seated at Madame Patruska's table and chuckled. "I think those two are Delia and Dr. Baxter and Michael and Vivian are vampires; of course, Amy is the angel."

"I don't see Nancy and Dennis," Eleanor said. They were Angus' neighbors and long-time friends.

"It's still early," Angus said. The music ended and the two visited the beverage table and mingled with the guests.

"Madame Patruska warned me to take care of my feet," Cleo said as she passed by Eleanor on her way to the cupcakes.

"She evidently noticed the shoes you were wearing," Eleanor said.

"Are you enjoying yourself?" asked Josephine.

"Are you speaking to me?" asked Eleanor.

"I know who you are," Josephine bragged. "It's obvious because your partner looks like the Lone Ranger."

"Really? Do you think that's his shadow self?" Eleanor asked.

"No, Angus is here as himself: hero, Prince Charming, noble knight, and all around good guy," Josephine admitted. "You, on the other hand, surprised me. You do know those saloon girls did much more than dance. But maybe that is your shadow."

"I wouldn't talk if I were you," Eleanor retorted. "You came as a stuffed idiot."

Pearl floated over. "I'm having a terrible time drinking through my sheet. What will happen if I throw it off?"

"That depends on what you have underneath," said Josephine.

"I guess I'll take my drink into the bathroom where I can enjoy it," Pearl said.

"I have a straw somewhere in the kitchen." Eleanor went to get it. They all knew that Pearl liked to sleep in the nude and feared there might be nothing under her sheet.

"We know that's you, Dede," said Pearl, "How rude of you to come as a nun and stifle our fun!"

"You better behave. I have a ruler here and I'm not afraid to use it," Dede warned.

"Stay away from Cleo," Josephine said. "You remember she suffered extreme anxiety at her private school and throws up when she sees a nun."

"That's right," Dede said looking around, "Where is she?"

"I saw her over by the cupcakes," said Pearl.

"Perfect," said Dede as she left to terrorize Cleo. After all, it was Halloween and there were few partiers who were actually afraid of nuns. Eleanor returned with a straw for Pearl.

"I think I was wrong about people coming as their shadow selves," Josephine said. "Looking around I see that your guests are here disguised as who they either want to be, recognize themselves as being, or are afraid of becoming."

"That just about covers everything," Eleanor said. "I think some of them are in the costume that was most convenient. Explain Pearl and Cary in sheets. On second thought . . . don't."

"I think I'll go have my palm read," Josephine said as she wandered away.

Eleanor poured a glass of wine and found Angus chatting with Delia. "Am I interrupting anything confidential?" she asked.

"No, tonight it's all about having fun," Delia remarked.

"Is Dr. Baxter fun?" asked Eleanor.

"I find him quite *humerous*," Delia said tapping her upper arm bone.

"Well, don't let him tell you any *fibulas*," Angus added.

"Do you have a silver bullet loaded in your pistol?" asked Delia. "Because I see a werewolf has entered the party."

"That must be Dennis," Eleanor said. "Please don't shoot him."

"I wonder where Nancy is," Angus said, looking around. It was obvious he was uncomfortable not knowing who was behind the masks. "I've got a bad feeling. You didn't invite Faith, did you?"

"No, I'm sure she wouldn't approve of this pagan celebration," Eleanor said. "Do you feel her demon presence?"

"Who is that in the Grim Reaper get up?" asked Angus.

"I don't know. I didn't see them come in. Maybe that's Nancy," Eleanor answered.

"The fortune teller told me I would find love tonight," Delia said. "I wonder if Dr. Baxter is the one."

"Do you like him?" asked Eleanor.

"I do," she answered.

"I need to go over to the Grim Reaper and check her out," said Angus and he walked away.

"What have you told Dr. Baxter about your findings?" asked Eleanor turning to Delia.

"I've told him the findings are inconclusive," Delia said. "We know she's dead, but whether she killed herself or not is still unknown. It's possible her husband killed her."

"Does it matter to him?" asked Eleanor.

"I know what you're thinking. He's obsessed with a woman who's been lost to him for over twenty years. It's even possible that he killed her, but I don't think that's the case. He's very sweet and romantic. I think he just wants to know if she loved him enough to go away with him. If she killed herself, he may feel responsible."

"If it helps, I don't believe he killed her either," Eleanor said.

"There's Michael," Delia said as she watched him with his trampy vampire partner kissing in the corner.

"I don't know what I ever saw in him," she added. "He's a slut."

"Ouch," said Eleanor. "Are you kicking him out of the agency?"

"You bet," she said with determination. "He doesn't have what it takes to be private. Just look at him. He's disgusting. I can't believe I traded my self-respect for a wink and a couple of dimples."

Eleanor knew what she meant. She was a sucker for good looks and charm too. She watched Angus walk toward her. The Old West never looked so good.

"Eleanor, you need to check out the Grim Reaper. If it's Nancy she's being very mysterious. She hardly looked at me and wouldn't talk to me at all," Angus complained.

"Being incognito gives people the power to act in ways they wouldn't ordinarily," Eleanor said. "Maybe she's always wanted to ignore you."

Angus pulled Eleanor aside and whispered, "I won't tell you what I want to do to you right now. There's something disturbing about it." Eleanor moved toward the Grim Reaper but was intercepted by Josephine.

"I can't believe what Madame Patruska just told me." Josephine was upset. "She said before the night was over I would come face to face with my worst fear."

"What is your worst fear?" asked Eleanor.

"It's death," Josephine confessed.

"Maybe it's time for the séance," Eleanor said as she walked toward the seer.

"Sake a teat, and I'll tell your fortune, Eleanor," said Madame Patruska who often transposed the initial sounds of words.

"I was just thinking it was time for the séance," Eleanor said as Madame Patruska grabbed her hand.

"I see doubt that keeps you from true happiness. Your lifeline is long and your health is good. The love line tells me you have many loves but only two significant ones. Open up to your *half-wormed fish*, if you do not act, you may lose out. Fear is the greatest defeater. Live life like you are going to die tonight. Try something new. Let nothing impede your true desires and stop thinking in ways that trap you in a box of your own making and take flight."

It poured so quickly from her mouth Eleanor was slow to take it all in. "Okay," she said slowly. "Are you ready for the séance?"

Madame Patruska sighed, "Yes."

"How do you want to do it? There are several people here."

"Let's gather everyone in a circle and have them hold hands. The lights are dim already. This is *the pun fart*. I think this will be very revealing."

Eleanor clinked a spoon against her wine glass and waited for everyone to listen for directions. "Please make a circle and hold hands. Madame Patruska will lead a séance as soon as everyone is quiet."

The guests obediently did as they were told and the room vibrated with a sort of nervous excitement. Angus held Eleanor's left hand and when she looked to her right she recognized Nancy Wilson dressed as a witch holding her other hand. Evidently, the Grim Reaper was someone else. Her eyes quickly scanned the circle and found the Reaper between Vivian and Dr. Baxter. Maybe it was Sybil or Mavis.

Madame Patruska put several items inside the circle and lit an incense burner that quickly filled the space with the scent of lemongrass. Madame Patruska began to sway as she welcomed the spirits.

"Good evening everyone. Tonight on All Hollow's Eve, we welcome only good and kind spirits into our circle. Is there anyone we should be calling out to?" There was a long pause until Eleanor mentioned Mattie May's name.

"Mattie May can you hear me? We invite you to join us. Are you with us tonight?" Madame Patruska called. Minutes passed with no response. Madame Patruska offered her invitation again, and after another long wait she said, "Mattie May is not on the other side. We have been sold a *lack of pies*. Someone who knows her well sends his greetings and says she has a surprise. He wishes to get a message to Mattie. He has found his way into the light and is happy. He sends her his love."

Madame Patruska let out a long breath. "He's gone now. Is there anyone else?"

Eleanor thought about Walter but hesitated. "Call on Charity Strong," called a man's voice. Eleanor recognized it as Dr. Baxter.

"Charity Strong, we invite you into our circle. Hear us and tell us what we want to know." Madame Patruska beckoned and then waited patiently for a response. Charity Strong we ask for your presence."

Suddenly the front door blew open and the east wind rushed in bringing with it a small tornado of autumn leaves. There were gasps and a couple of screams as heads turned and the candles went dark.

"Don't break the circle," Madame Patruska warned in a voice that was forceful yet calm. "Are you with us, Charity? Is that you?" The door slammed shut. "She's here and she's pissed." Everyone could sense the fury as it filled the room like a cold wind. Eleanor felt the hairs on her neck stand up and a chill run down her spine. Angus squeezed her hand until it was almost unbearable.

"What causes this anger?" Madame Patruska asked. "Does it have something to do with your death?"

There was a knock that seemed to echo through the house but had no source.

"Ask her if she was murdered," Delia called out, and before Madame Patruska could respond the knock was repeated.

"Who did it? Who killed you?" someone yelled.

"She can't tell you that," Madame Patruska said. "Her knock is one for yes, two for no." Suddenly, the window steamed up and letters spelled out the words: *He did it*. Almost as soon as they appeared, they were gone. Not everyone witnessed them but Madame Patruska did. "Do you seek revenge?" The loud knock echoed again once and then a second time more softly.

Every time she heard the knock Eleanor shivered.

"Are you here for justice?" Madame Patruska asked and was answered with a knock that was softer than before.

"Is there proof of murder?" asked Angus and almost before the words left his mouth the knock came again weaker yet. The window steamed up again and a handprint appeared and then was gone.

Madame Patruska gasped. "She has exhausted her power to be with us. Thank you, spirits, for your presence and your guidance. We will do our best to fulfill your wishes and ease your passing into the next realm. *Eye ball* I mean bye all."

A dim glow from a candle on the floor flickered back to life. The guests broke the circle and began to chatter.

"How did you do that, Eleanor?" asked Nancy who still held Eleanor's hand.

"That was spectacular," said someone else.

"Even I was impressed when the door flew open," admitted Angus. "Did you hire someone to do that?"

Josephine approached. "My heart is still beating as if I'd just run a race."

"Was that for real?" asked Cleo. "Does this mean that Reverend Strong killed her?"

"Do you know more than you're telling us?" asked Pearl.

"What did the handprint on the window mean?" asked Dede.

"I don't have any answers," Eleanor admitted. "Excuse me." She made a direct beeline to Dr. Baxter.

"I just want you to know, Dr. Baxter, that this was not a trick. I would never have made a spectacle of your need to know the answers about Charity. I'm totally at a loss for any of this."

Dr. Baxter stood visibly shaken. "I think she was really here. I could smell her perfume."

"Do you think it means that Mattie is still alive?" a voice from a witch's costume asked.

"Is that you Sybil?" Eleanor asked, turning away from Dr. Baxter.

"Yes, it's me. Was that all a bunch of hooey or is Mattie still alive?"

"I don't know. "Eleanor was almost sorry she'd invited Madame Patruska. The séance was more upsetting than fun. While everyone was talking about the experience, the seer was busy packing up her things.

"Are you leaving?" Eleanor asked her.

"Oh yes, the séance has given me a terrible headache and I'm afraid the night has a *blushing crow* in store for you, Eleanor."

"Was all that on the up and up?" Eleanor didn't believe in communicating with the dead. Sometimes she didn't think it possible to get through to the living.

"I don't want to comment on it. My *zips are lipped*. The experience has to speak for itself. Do you mind if I take some cupcakes home with me?"

"Certainly, help yourself," Eleanor said.

"I'll help you with that," said Angus and he took her box of props and walked out the door.

Most of the guests remained in a state of shock and disbelief, but after speculating about the manner in which

Eleanor and Madame Patruska had perpetrated the hoax, they began to eat and drink and talk about other things. It was evident that only a few actually thought any of it was real. Taylor once more sat at the piano and Michael and Vivian held each other tightly as they danced to a slow love song.

"I don't know how you did it," Angus admitted. "Are you going to tell me?"

"No," she said. Eleanor didn't know how it happened and decided to keep the mystery going. "Someone should have invited Jude Thorn and Danny Gold to the party so we could solve those murders."

"When did you figure out that Charity was left handed?" Angus asked. "Her handwriting didn't give that away."

Eleanor's mind began to grind as she strained to make sense of Angus' remark. The handprint on the window was Charity's left hand and must have been a clue. What did it mean? She stalled, "I didn't guess it from her handwriting either. Usually lefties have a backward slant."

"Well the bullet entered the right side of her skull. I assumed she was right handed, but if she was a southpaw that changes everything." Angus shook his head, "I know better than to assume anything. I'm proud of you Eleanor. Even Delia didn't catch that."

There was no way Eleanor was going to tell the truth at this point so she just smiled and went to mingle with her guests. She approached Dr. Baxter who stood alone by the window evidently looking for signs of Charity's handiwork.

"Dr. Baxter, are you enjoying yourself?" Eleanor asked.

"Yes, more than I thought possible." He turned to face her. "It looks like the weather is taking a turn for the worse." Even in the dark Eleanor could see black clouds swirling from the northwest. The winds had changed direction and a bank of thunderheads marched in from over the dimly lit ocean. "I don't usually believe in the supernatural, but tonight I'm having serious questions about what I believe."

Eleanor was impatient to ask him but didn't want to seem too eager. "So, you're not one of those superstitious people who believes left-handed humans are evil."

"How could I be when I'm left handed myself? Charity and I had that in common. She often joked that she was the only one in her family in her right mind," he sighed. "I still miss her but now that I know she's okay I think I can move on with my life." It seemed he no longer wanted to keep his relationship with her a secret.

"You deserve to be happy," Eleanor said as Delia appeared by his side.

"Let's dance," she invited and grabbed his hand. They danced next to Michael and Vivian, and Eleanor wondered if Delia liked Dr. Baxter or if she was using him to show Michael that other men found her desirable. Whichever was true, Vivian and Michael left the dance floor and went their separate ways. It was the first time Eleanor had seen them apart. The other guests were eating and drinking and growing ever louder. She looked around to see where her coffee friends had gone and realized she still had no idea who the Grim Reaper was or where they had gone. Usually her guests thanked her before leaving, but maybe the séance had frightened this one away prematurely. She walked over to Dede who was standing next to Cleo chatting.

"I've had a breakthrough on Charity Strong's case," she began when suddenly there was a brilliant flash of lightning followed by a tremendous crack of thunder. It made Eleanor flinch and many of her guests gasped.

"It really is a dark and stormy night," said someone in the following silence and then there was the kind of nervous laughter that came after a fright.

"Did you special order this weather?" asked Mark.

"It certainly is appropriate," Dede said.

"Drinks are on me for the rest of the night," said Cary and there was more nervous laughter before another strike flashed and lit the room in an eerie strobe-like way that froze creepy costumed people in a macabre tableau. The following peal of thunder was not as loud and Eleanor was relieved to know the storm was passing quickly.

"What were you saying about a breakthrough?" Cleo asked.

"Oh, we never considered whether Charity was left or right handed, but she was a leftie," Eleanor said.

"So, how is that relevant?" asked Dede.

"If she shot herself she would have held the gun in her left hand and the bullet would have entered the left side of her head, but it didn't," Eleanor explained.

"So someone else killed her. No wonder she was pissed," said Cleo. "First her husband spreads rumors of her stealing funds from the church to support her gambling addiction, and then he kills her and tells everyone she was a cheat who ran off with her lover."

"I'd like to believe it was him, but can we be sure? Is there a way to get prints off a gun after a long period of time?" Dede asked.

"I don't know, but Angus will," Eleanor said as she watched him talking with Michael across the room. Something in the way he moved alerted her. She walked quickly and followed the two men; a diabolical blood sucker all in black and the archetypical good guy all in white, as they stepped outside into the aftermath of a thunderstorm's downpour. Eleanor squinted and made out a dark shape lying in the lane. Angus and Michael were bent over it. She stood under the protection of her porch roof and watched Angus shake his head before he turned and saw her standing there. Before she could move he was at her elbow ushering her inside.

"Ellie, go inside and call 911. Tell them there's been a shooting and we need an ambulance and the police, ASAP. Don't tell anyone else yet and don't let anyone leave this house."

"Angus . . . who?" Eleanor stammered. These were her friends and one of them was lying in the lane.

"It's Vivian. I'm pretty sure she's dead or close to it," he said. "I'm going to look around and Michael's staying with her. Don't let anyone out here." Eleanor watched him walk away down the lane before she hurried inside and made the call.

It seemed like hours had passed as Eleanor's guests sat and waited while each was taken individually into her office and questioned by Officer McGraw about their recollections of the evening. Angus had returned with a black glove he found near Faith Strong's house. Eleanor could hardly keep her eyes open and brewed a pot of coffee to help manage her fatigue. Several guests sat in various rooms and were cautioned not to discuss their observations. Others nodded off. Many of them had rubbed off their face paint to reveal weary faces and droopy, red-rimmed eyes.

The ambulance had arrived quickly, but Vivian was beyond saving. It was eerily quiet after the shock of death had worn off and the night was quickly turning into another day. Angus was busy working with a group of people outside who combed the area for a weapon and took pictures of the crime scene looking for other clues that might shed light on the murder of Vivian Thorn.

As tired as she was, Eleanor's mind worked overtime convicting Faith Strong. She had pieced together her own facts and concluded that the Grim Reaper had to be Faith, who had come uninvited to the party to kill the woman that had tormented her as a young girl. Jude Thorn, Danny Gold, and now Vivian Thorn were all dead and they were sadly linked to Faith and a crime that happened years ago but must have festered into an ugly wound and ended in a brutal killing spree.

Tonya Jones needed protection. Was anyone at Faith's house preventing her from killing again? Eleanor didn't have all the information but she knew the facts weighed heavily against Faith. How did Faith know about the party? How did she know that Vivian would be here? Maybe it wasn't Faith after all? The Grim Reaper didn't seem as tall or thin as the most obvious suspect. Could it have been Hope? Eleanor wondered if Officer McGraw was asking the right questions.

She was sure of one thing and that was whoever came to the party as the Grim Reaper was the killer. Did anyone talk to that person? Maybe someone in this house knew who the killer was. Was it the same person who shot Jude Thorn and Danny Gold? Who else had a motive for doing away with all of these victims if not Faith? One other thing was certain and that was the Grim Reaper was a woman. Eleanor wracked her memory to dredge up something that could help identify this person.

She wore a hooded costume. Her hands concealed by gloves and her face covered by something black—a ski mask perhaps. Not one inch of her skin showed. Eleanor couldn't remember seeing her feet. She was the size of Nancy or Sybil because both Eleanor and Angus thought it was one of them. Perhaps it was a small man. Eleanor couldn't be sure now. Her brain was tired and her thoughts muddled. She got up to get more coffee but Officer McGraw took this moment to invite her into her own office to tell her story. She was able to provide him with a guest list for the party and whatever her security camera had captured of the night's drama.

When everyone had been debriefed, Officer McGraw let them go home but cautioned them not to leave town as they were all possible witnesses in a murder case. Eleanor stood at her door and said goodbye to each guest as they left. Most were eager to get home to bed, too tired to do more than nod or wave. When she closed the door behind the last of them and shuffled into the bathroom she saw her weary face reflected in the mirror and scrubbed it clean wishing the tragedy of the night could be washed away as easily. As tired as she was she lay in bed replaying the night in her mind and fell asleep just as the sun was rising.

The morning brought some comfort in small mundane things like brewing coffee, the daily paper's puzzles, and the company of Feathers who chattered nonstop as if nothing unusual had happened, and for a few minutes, Eleanor forgot about the killing. There was little she could do without getting in the way so she cleaned up the remnants of the party and waited. At one point, she discovered Feathers perched on her discarded headpiece, cooing romantically to the pile of feathers. By the time she finished her tasks, Angus was at her door. He no longer wore his costume and looked freshly showered even though his eyes gave proof of a sleepless night.

"Coffee?" she asked.

"Yes, please," Angus responded. "Are you all right, Ellie?"

"Of course," Eleanor responded.

"It isn't everyday someone is shot outside your house." Angus sipped the rich brew and eyed her carefully over the rim.

"What about Faith? I assume she's your main suspect," Eleanor asked.

"We went over there after Officer McGraw finished here and roused her from her bed. She wasn't happy. Officer McGraw suggested she get a lawyer even though Hope claims they were both home all night. It's just a matter of time before they charge her. Officer McGraw is dead set on it," Angus said.

"You don't think she did it, do you?" Eleanor asked.

"I'm sure she didn't. I looked into the eyes of the Grim Reaper last night and they weren't Faith's eyes. She was wearing mascara and she was too short," Angus said. "I'm thinking it may have been Hope."

"You found the glove near Faith's house. Did you find anything else?"

"Your security camera caught the Grim Reaper in the act, but it didn't reveal their identity—just the shot and the killer running away after throwing the gun in the brush. There was a 38-caliber pistol in the bushes not far from Vivian's body," Angus said. "My bet is it's the same gun used to kill Jude and Donnie, but we'll have to wait for ballistics to prove that."

"If the murderer threw the gun away, does that mean she's finished killing people?" Eleanor said. "If it's Faith taking revenge on those who hurt her, wouldn't Tonya Jones be next on her list?"

"It's hard to say. The killer might have been afraid and threw the gun away just to be rid of the evidence," Angus said thoughtfully. "Someone's going over to Tonya's house this morning to let her know about Vivian. They were friends."

"How is Michael handling this?" Eleanor asked, assuming that Michael spent the night at Angus' house.

"He feels guilty," Angus said. "It was his job to protect her and the first time he let her out of his sight someone shot her. It doesn't make him responsible, but he doesn't see it that way. He told me she was on the verge of telling him something important and thought she was making up the story about Faith trying to kill her because she wasn't really afraid. Now he feels guilty about that too."

"Did he love her?" Eleanor asked.

"No," Angus answered quickly. "He seems more concerned about failing his job to protect her than missing her. There wasn't time to form a deep attachment. Dr. Baxter was more upset by her death than Michael and I think that irked Delia."

"Do you think Dr. Baxter had feelings for her?" asked Eleanor.

"I don't know. He worked with her and obviously knew her well," Angus said. "Now he'll have to hire someone to replace her."

"I'm sure she had feelings for him," Eleanor said, remembering the look of admiration she saw on Vivian's face. "I guess I'll have to take Vivian off my list of possible suspects for murdering her husband."

"I'm surprised you didn't already do that," Angus said. "Her alibi was checked and verified."

"I know, but for some reason I still thought she was guilty." Eleanor furrowed her brow. "That narrows it down to Faith or Hope."

"The fact that they are each other's alibis doesn't lend credibility to their stories. Their relationship makes it easy to believe they would lie to protect each other," Angus said.

"Does Tonya have an alibi for the day her brother was shot?" Eleanor asked.

"Yes, she was visiting her mother who lives in the valley, so there's no way she could have done it," Angus said.

"Could she have hired someone to kill him?" Eleanor asked.

"Maybe, but I don't think she has that kind of money," he said.

Something in Eleanor's mind clicked. "She will when her mother dies if what she told Cleo is true. Maybe she promised to pay the killer later."

"That's not how paid assassins work. Most demand half up front and the rest after the job is done," Angus said.

"What if it wasn't a paid assassin, but a friend or someone who needed money and was willing to wait for it? Maybe Tonya Jones has a lover who did it for her," Eleanor speculated.

Angus didn't say anything more, but the idea that was growing was interrupted by the doorbell and a warning from Feathers who cried, "Ellie get your gun!"

Faith Strong stood in the doorway. "Good morning, Mrs. Penrose," she said with something that might have passed for a smile. "I brought the rental check for November."

Eleanor reached out and took the check while Faith looked beyond her and spied Angus. "Oh, hello," Faith said as she stepped into the house pushing by Eleanor in her attempt to get to Angus. "I didn't know you were here, Angus. I'm afraid I wasn't at my best last night when you came calling, so I wasn't much help. What was all the excitement about anyway? All I understood was that Vivian had been shot, something about a glove, and I should get a lawyer. What does it all mean? Does Officer McGraw think I shot Vivian?"

Eleanor watched as Angus rose and invited Faith to sit down in the living room. "I'm sorry it was so late, but it was important that we talk to you. Vivian was shot and killed last night. We found a glove that the killer was wearing outside your house. I don't have to tell you that it looks bad for you." His voice was gentle and his eyes filled with concern.

Tears welled in Faith's eyes and ran down her cheeks. "I didn't kill anyone! Ever since I came here there has been nothing but death. I never should have come back."

Angus reached out and took her hands. "I believe you, Faith. Can you tell me why anyone would want it to look like you killed Vivian? Have you had any interaction with her since you moved here?"

"No, none at all. The closest contact I've had with her would have been through Jude. I hired him to do the work on my church."

"What about Donnie Gold? Did you see him since you've been here?"

"No, I don't know that I would have even recognized him," Faith said.

"Do you know where Hope was last night?" Angus asked.

"She was at home with me," Faith said without a hint of where Angus was going with this. "You saw her yourself."

"Can you be sure she was home the entire night?"

"I went to bed around ten. I assume she went to bed shortly afterward," she frowned. "You can't think Hope is involved."

"How much does Hope know about her parents?" Angus continued.

"What do you mean?" Faith looked away.

"I know Hope is your daughter, and I know your father is also Hope's father. It must be very difficult for you, but have you told Hope yet?"

"Not yet." Faith began to silently weep. "I'm afraid of what she will think."

"She probably knows something. It's very hard to keep a secret like that without small truths seeping out. It would be best if she learned it from you rather than someone else," Angus advised.

"How would she? Who else knows? Why would anyone tell her such a thing?" Faith stood muttering as she paced. "You belong to your father, the devil, and you want to carry out your father's desires. He was a murderer from the beginning, not holding to the truth, for there is no truth in him. When he lies, he speaks his native language, for he is a liar and the father of lies. Whoever keeps his mouth and his tongue keeps himself out of trouble."

"Nothing is covered up that will not be revealed, or hidden that will not be known." Angus recited.

"Let no corrupting talk come out of your mouths, but only such as is good for building up, as fits the occasion, that it may give grace to those who hear. For God will bring every deed into judgment, with every secret thing, whether good or evil." Faith seemed to answer.

"Then you will know the truth and the truth will set you free," Angus responded in the language Faith understood.

Eleanor watched in awe as Faith sat down across from Angus and looked into his kind eyes. She had no idea Angus was schooled in Bible verses.

"What should I do?" Faith asked putting her fate in Angus' hands.

"Tell me the truth," he said. "Start at the beginning."

Eleanor went to the kitchen and made tea, all the while listening as Faith laid bare her deepest secrets and acknowledged her demons. She retold the horrors of sexual abuse by her father under the guise of prayer and love, the lies she told to protect him, her pregnancies and miscarriage, her confused feelings of love and sex, and jealousy and hatred of her mother who failed her in so many ways.

She confessed her promiscuity, the rape and mistreatment she suffered in high school, the despair of being sent away to live with her grandmother, and the many guilty sins committed in the name of love. Her shame had no limits and her hypocrisy no bounds as she continued to sleep with men while she recited verses against lust.

It was as if a dam broke and all that was darkness burst out in a flood of words and tears. Angus sat patiently as she repeated her story listening for new information or discrepancies in the parts he'd heard before.

"I lied about my father confessing that my mother committed suicide. He never regained consciousness. I found her suitcase full of fancy lingerie and I know he killed her but I convinced myself she deserved it . . . she was going to leave him for another man. She was going to leave us. Daddy was right. She didn't love us. We only had each other. I left him when I thought he was going to start with Hope. I didn't want that. I wanted her to have a good life."

"What do you remember about the day your mother disappeared?" Angus asked.

Faith closed her eyes and exhaled deeply. "It was a Sunday. We went to church, but Mother stayed home with a migraine. There was a potluck lunch afterward so we got home later than normal. She was gone. I knew something wasn't right when we walked in the house. It felt so empty. Father searched every room and told me to check her closet to see if her clothes or jewelry were gone. He wanted me to find her things missing and I did. Then he sat me down and told me she had run off with her lover. It was the story he told everyone after that. I believed it. It wasn't until I found her suitcase while cleaning out the house that I began to suspect it was a lie. Her jewelry and clothes were packed away. She never left. Then I found her in the rose bed. Father was dead. I didn't want to start another scandal so I kept quiet. I planned to bury her with Father after I opened my church."

"Did you kill Vivian, Jude, and Donnie?" Angus asked, knowing she was drained and vulnerable.

"No." Faith didn't waver.

"Did Hope know about them and what they had done to you?" Angus asked.

"Of course not!" Faith had created the role of perfect big sister and maintained it.

"But your grandmother knew," Angus pressed on even though he could see Faith was emotionally spent. "Would she have told Hope any of this?"

"I'm sure I would have known if that were true. Hope and I have a close relationship. She would have come to me and asked questions, but she didn't," Faith persisted.

"Did you know Hope frequently visits a bar in town and meets men there?" Angus asked, remembering her at the Red Shed.

Faith was visibly shaken. "That's a lie."

"She's a grown woman, Faith. Did you think you could keep her under your control forever?" Angus asked.

"No, no, no. 'So I say, walk by the Spirit, and you will not gratify the desires of the flesh. For everything in the world—the lust of the flesh, the lust of the eyes, and the pride of life—comes not from the Father, but from the world.' You didn't lust in your heart for her, did you Angus?"

"No, but I saw her there. There are things you may not know about her. Would she kill for you?" Angus' eyes probed her very soul.

Faith put her head in her hands, "I don't know."

"You need to go in to the station and give your statement to Officer McGraw, Faith. This is serious," Angus said. "No more holding back information to protect anyone else."

After Faith left, Eleanor sat next to Angus. She was amazed at the flood of information he was able to draw out of Faith.

"Do you believe her?" She asked.

"Yes," he replied. "She was very consistent with the facts she told me before, but she's going to need a good lawyer. All the evidence points to her, and if Hope is as innocent of the facts as Faith believes, Faith is the prime suspect."

"There is nothing as deceptive as an obvious fact," quoted Eleanor. Angus simply smiled. For once, he and Eleanor agreed.

The ladies of the coffee group made a visit to Eleanor's that afternoon to learn the latest developments in the case. "We brought dinner," said Dede carrying a pan of lasagna into the kitchen. She was followed by Pearl and Josephine who contributed salad and garlic bread, and Cleo who brought bottles of red and white wine.

Eleanor popped the lasagna in the oven while Cleo opened the wine and poured each of them a generous glass before they retired into the living room and cozied up by the fireplace.

"So what did you find out from Angus?" asked Josephine, looking out over the gray sky and matching sea. Eleanor sipped her wine and recapped Angus' conversation with Faith.

"Does Angus think Faith is the killer?" asked Dede.

"No, he thinks she is the obvious suspect but he said he looked into the eyes of the Grim Reaper and they wore mascara. Faith doesn't wear makeup, although she was wearing it the other day when she brought Angus cookies. He suspects Hope," Eleanor said. "Although Faith claims Hope has no knowledge of her parentage or of the hateful things that were done to Faith in high school."

"You mean Faith hasn't told Hope that she's her mother?" Pearl seemed incredulous.

Eleanor nodded. "She knows," Josephine said with authority. "Hope isn't a little girl anymore. I'd be willing to wager a month's pay that she has figured out the facts by now."

"How would she?" asked Cleo. "They lived far away in Alaska where no one knew anything about them except the grandmother."

"Secrets have a way of surfacing," Josephine said. "Hope is in her twenties, surely by now she's wondered who her father is and with today's technology, it wouldn't surprise me if she hasn't searched for information."

"When we were in their house, someone was looking in the box that contained Charity's journals and letters. Maybe it was Hope," Dede recalled. "Wasn't she the one who took the letters to Dr. Baxter?"

"We don't know if she read Faith's journals, but if she did, it could have been Hope who killed Jude, Donnie, and Vivian," said Eleanor. "She must be really damaged to do that. Faith said she tried to give her a good life."

"It's what we all want for our children," said Pearl, "to give them a good life."

"Faith told Angus she found Charity's suitcase. It was packed with fancy lingerie, a fact that would have repelled Faith. She admitted that her father didn't regain consciousness and never admitted anything. Charity was going to leave her family and go off with Dr. Baxter," Eleanor said. "Faith was angry with her."

"So we can be fairly certain that Charity was murdered by the reverend," stated Dede.

"I'm not so sure," Eleanor said. "Faith said they left Charity home with a migraine and went to church. When they got back Charity was gone. When would he have killed and buried her? We can be certain she didn't commit suicide. A woman doesn't pack a bag full of lingerie and then shoot herself."

"So maybe it was Dr. Baxter who killed her," said Pearl.

"We're no closer to figuring out this case than when we started," sighed Eleanor. "But I'm sure the latest murders are connected to Charity Strong in some way."

"If it wasn't Faith or Hope who killed those people, who else could it be?" asked Cleo.

"My bet is Tonya Jones," said Dede.

"What would her motive be?" asked Josephine.

"The inheritance," said Cleo. "If what she told me was true, her mother had millions to leave her."

"Angus said Vivian and Tonya both had alibis for the times Jude and Donnie were killed," said Eleanor.

"Couldn't they hire someone to do it?" asked Dede.

"Vivian isn't a suspect anymore," Eleanor said, "And Angus doesn't think Tonya had the kind of money it takes to do that."

"I saw a movie once where two people who didn't know each other met on a train and planned to murder each other's spouses," said Cleo. "Maybe that's what Tonya and Vivian did."

It was quiet while the ladies processed this piece of information.

"I like Tonya for the murderer," said Dede, remembering an unpleasant interaction with her.

"Me too," said Cleo. "When Faith came back to town it might have given Tonya and Vivian the idea to put the blame on her."

"You think Tonya and Vivian planned to kill for each other and give themselves solid alibis so they would be above suspicion?" Josephine said. "It's clever. The spouse is usually the prime suspect, but if the spouse is out of town . . . "

"Or at work with her employer who verifies her alibi . . . " added Eleanor.

"So Tonya killed Jude while Vivian was at work, then Vivian would have killed Donnie while Tonya was visiting her mother and Tonya killed Vivian so there wouldn't be any loose ends," Dede speculated.

"They used the same gun and threw suspicion on Faith even pretending to be afraid of her," Eleanor said.

"How would we ever prove such a thing?" asked Pearl.

"Let's pretend to be Vivian back from the dead and haunt Tonya until she confesses," Cleo proposed.

"She'd probably shoot us," said Dede.

"How did they catch the killers in the movie?" asked Josephine.

"I don't remember," said Cleo. "Maybe we should watch the movie and find out."

"I'll Google it," said Dede whipping out her phone.

The ladies sipped their wine while their minds worked overtime trying to solve the problem.

"Ah, one of the killers had a conscience and turned himself in," said Dede.

"I don't think that's going to happen if Tonya is the murderer," said Cleo.

Eleanor remembered the conversation she overheard at the grocery store between Vivian and Tonya and related it to the others. "Tonya told Vivian not to chicken out and to keep her mouth shut. Maybe Vivian had a conscience and Tonya was afraid she wouldn't keep quiet."

"We'll have to think of some way to get her to confess," said Dede.

"We could send her an anonymous note saying we know what she did," said Pearl.

"And . . . " Josephine prodded.

"I don't know, maybe it would prompt her to confess," Pearl said.

"We could pretend to blackmail her and see if she takes the bait," Eleanor said. "An innocent person would just ignore it."

"That could be dangerous," Josephine said. "If she's guilty she wouldn't hesitate to shoot us to keep her secret."

"But she already threw her gun away," said Eleanor, "so she must think she's done with the killing."

"Let's send her a note and see what she does," suggested Dede. "She might be careless and do something stupid."

"What should the note say?" asked Pearl.

"I saw you and I know what you did," said Cleo.

"We could start with that and then send another note later," Pearl said.

"Meet me at the Red Shed and bring $100,000 unless you want the police to know," Cleo continued.

"We'd have to put a time and date on that," said Josephine.

"So what if she comes and just checks out who is there so she can kill us?" asked Dede.

"There would be more people there than us," Cleo said.

"If she showed up it would mean she's guilty," said Pearl.

"I'll get some paper. Should we cut out the letters and glue them on like in the movies?" asked Eleanor.

"Do you have a newspaper?" asked Dede.

Eleanor gathered the materials and the coffee ladies put their plan into action. When they finished their masterpiece read:

I know **what** you and Vivian did. **Bring** $100,000.00 to the **Red Shed** on Friday and **leave** it in a **paper** bag next to the **video** poker **machine** in the back room or **I'll** tell.

"Well, how do we get it to her?" asked Pearl.

"We could pay some little kid to put it in her mail slot," suggested Cleo.

"Let's watch her house and wait until she leaves and do it ourselves," said Eleanor. "That way we'll know it was delivered."

"Let's eat," said Cleo. "When we finish dinner, we can do a drive-by with the letter."

"Good idea," said Dede.

"You don't think this is too juvenile, do you?" asked Pearl.

"Who cares, as long as it gets results?" asked Cleo admiring the artistic merits of the note.

"So what happens when and if she shows up?" asked Josephine. "She might just show up to see who is there."

"She might show up to have a drink," said Eleanor. "Maybe she'll even put a bag by the video machine to see who takes it."

"We'll have to be smart," said Dede. "If she shows up and puts a bag there, we won't take it."

"Suddenly this doesn't seem like a good idea," Eleanor said. "She's smart. She concocted a plan where she's innocent of killing the person she wanted dead, set up Faith, and killed her coconspirator so there are no witnesses. I don't think she's going to leave money in a bag, and I don't think we should show up for her to see us as possible blackmailers."

"Let's think of a better plan then," said Cleo. "Maybe some more wine will help."

Cleo filled their glasses, and they dished up dinner while their unconscious minds continued to work on a solution. "Let's just go visit her mother and tell her what she did. Maybe her mother will disinherit her and she'll do something stupid," Cleo suggested.

"Visiting her mother isn't a bad idea," said Josephine. "She may be in danger. If Tonya wants that money enough to kill for it, she might not want to wait for her mother to die of natural causes."

"Do we know anything about her mother?" asked Eleanor.

"She lives by herself in Beaverton. I think she's still in her own house, but I don't want anything to do with her if she's anything like Tonya," said Dede.

"She might surprise you and defend her daughter," said Pearl. "We couldn't just go there with a lot of accusations."

"If Tonya put this plan into action, she must have killed Jude Thorn. Maybe there is something she left behind that would incriminate her that the police missed," said Josephine.

"Are you suggesting we go back to the Strong house and look around?" asked Cleo.

"No, I'm suggesting we tell Angus about our suspicions and see what he thinks," said Josephine. It was quiet for some time while the idea was processed. It was possible that the trained professionals had already thought of this scenario and dismissed it for reasons the coffee ladies knew nothing about.

"Are you sure Hope isn't the murderer?" asked Pearl. "Maybe we should send both of them the note and see who turns up. I haven't been to the Red Shed since our last visit."

"We would have to leave out Vivian's name and see if Hope shows up at the Red Shed. I like it," said Dede.

"It might be interesting to see if either of them shows up. I'm in," said Cleo.

"I can deliver the note to Hope," offered Eleanor.

"We'll take care of Tonya," Dede said. They finished their wine and began work on the second note. What could possibly go wrong?

After the coffee group ladies left and before Eleanor could deliver the note, Angus rang the doorbell. "Do I smell lasagna?" he asked as he and Bones entered.

"Yes, would you like some?" Eleanor offered.

"Do you have to ask?"

"Aren't Michael and Delia cooking for you, or have they gone home?"

"They're still at the house. From what I understand, they've reconnected after their latest romances fizzled. That's why I'm here; neither of them could ever measure up to your cooking or your company. Even Bones wants to get away from them."

"Are they arguing?" Eleanor asked.

"I wouldn't call it that." Angus wasn't interested in discussing Michael and Delia's relationship.

While Eleanor warmed up the lasagna Angus poured himself three fingers of Crown Royal and loitered in the kitchen. "Did you have company this afternoon?"

"The coffee group came over. You can thank Dede for the lasagna," Eleanor said.

"They must be curious about the shooting," Angus said.

"Of course," said Eleanor. "It was a traumatic event. Are there any new developments?"

Angus didn't answer. He had wandered into the dining area and discovered the letter on Eleanor's dining room table. "Ellie, please tell me you are not planning to give this note to someone," Angus said, alarmed.

"There are some things I'd like to run by you," Eleanor said.

"Like blackmail?" Angus was incredulous.

"Not exactly, we thought we could lure the killer out . . ." she began.

"The killer being . . . " he prodded.

Eleanor put a plate of lasagna and salad down on the table. "That's just what I wanted to run by you. What if Tonya Jones and Vivian Thorn made a pact to kill the people who were obstacles in their lives?

Tonya would kill Jude while Vivian was at work and Vivian would do away with Donnie while Tonya was visiting her mother. Neither would have a motive to kill their victims and each would have an alibi for those they wanted dead. Then Tonya shoots Vivian to tie up any loose ends and hopes the blame falls on Faith who had a reason to get revenge on all of them, leaving Tonya to play the part of the next victim."

It was quiet while Angus processed this information and ate several bites of his dinner.

"That's an interesting idea," he said finally, "but Ellie, you have to promise me you will *not* deliver this note to Tonya Jones. If she did what you're suggesting, she's smart enough to figure out who you are and if she's a cold-hearted killer she wouldn't think twice about hurting you."

Eleanor thought about what he said. "I promise not to deliver the note to Tonya."

Angus finished his meal but was disturbed by Eleanor's promise. He wasn't used to winning so easily.

By the time Friday rolled around, Eleanor had easily delivered the note to Hope and was anxiously awaiting her planned visit to the Red Shed. The coffee ladies met at the Boat House to discuss their scheme and enjoy breakfast with each other.

"How are the plans for your wedding coming?" Josephine asked Dede.

"Mark and I are still talking about it," Dede said.

"I hope you can talk him into going to some tropical island. I really don't care which one but I'd love to vacation in the sun," said Cleo.

"Me too, I need something to look forward to that will get me through the winter," said Pearl.

"Should I invite Angus?" Eleanor asked.

"Absolutely," said Dede, "Unless you don't want him there."

"Tropical islands are very romantic," said Cleo. "If you decide to go alone, you might meet someone." Eleanor shook her head and waved her hand in dismissal.

"So are we still on for tonight?" asked Dede.

"I'm in," said Cleo.

"Me too," stated Josephine.

"I'm looking forward to winning at Keno," Pearl said. "I can play while I keep an eye out for the paper bag."

"How are you going to get rid of Angus? Doesn't he usually stay after dinner?" asked Josephine.

"I don't know. I don't feel comfortable lying to him but I promised I wouldn't deliver the letter to Tonya so I can't tell him I'm meeting you at the Red Shed without looking deceitful. Any excuse I make up will cause him to be suspicious since he already saw the note." Eleanor sighed. "I may have to wait until he leaves, so don't expect me to be on time."

"Eleanor, you *are* being deceitful. Just because you didn't tell an outright lie, doesn't mean you didn't deceive him," Josephine said.

"What would you have done?" Eleanor asked.

"I would have done the same thing," said Cleo.

"Me too," said Pearl.

"What we're doing isn't dangerous. Angus is being overly cautious," said Dede. "What are you making for dinner?"

"I thought I'd make sauteed duck breasts on a bed of red bell pepper and spinach, new potatoes, and string beans," Eleanor said.

"What wine pairs with duck?" asked Pearl.

"A pinot noir is good but I'm thinking a Sangiovese will work tonight."

"If we all came for dinner, I'm sure Angus would leave early," Cleo hinted.

"You better not drink and drive," warned Josephine.

"I'll be sure to curtail my wine consumption," Eleanor vowed. "I better get moving. There are a few items I need at the grocery store."

When Angus arrived with Bones promptly at six with a bouquet of roses, Eleanor had already decided to focus all her attention on him so he wouldn't be suspicious. She greeted him warmly and offered him a generous drink of his Crown Royal. Bones got a liver treat.

As they sat down to enjoy the duck, Eleanor was determined to keep their conversation away from the murder investigations.

"Angus, there's something I'd like to discuss with you," she began. "Mark and Dede are planning a trip to the Caribbean later and I was wondering how you felt about going with them?"

"Really? Angus paused. He'd been to the Caribbean with Margo, his ex, and didn't favor the thought of taking Eleanor there. "Where exactly in the Caribbean?"

"Have you been before?" she asked sensing his hesitation.

"Margo and I spent our honeymoon in Puerto Rico," Angus said. "I don't really want to go back there."

"Oh." Eleanor was taken aback. It hadn't occurred to her that he might say no but could understand why he wouldn't want to stir up old memories of Margo on their honeymoon. Eleanor didn't want that either. They would have been young and in love. No it certainly wouldn't do to have him thinking of a young sexy Margo while he was with Eleanor.

"I didn't mean I wouldn't want to go to some tropical paradise with you, Ellie. I just don't want to go to Puerto Rico." Angus suddenly felt awkward. "Have you ever been?"

"Yes, Walter and I sailed to several of the islands." Eleanor hadn't thought she would be thinking of Walter while on a tropical island with Angus. Walter and Eleanor had traveled to many places together. It would be a shame if she couldn't return to any of them with Angus because it might remind her of Walter. Maybe honeymooning made it more memorable. "Walter and I honeymooned in Paris, but I've been there again with family and friends."

"Are they planning to go to Puerto Rico?" Angus asked.

"I'm not sure. I think St. Kitts was mentioned," Eleanor said, suddenly feeling as if Margo and Walter had entered the room.

"Sure, I'd go to St. Kitts with you," Angus said. "When exactly are they planning this trip?"

"Plans are still in the preliminary stages. Josephine, Richard, Cleo, Steve, Pearl, and Cary might come too." Eleanor took a bite of duck.

Angus looked up with a puzzled expression on his face. "What's the occasion? I mean don't you see enough of your coffee friends already?"

"Mark and Dede want to renew their vows and Cleo suggested they marry under a magical tree on St. Kitts. Legend has it that if you marry under this tree you'll never be parted," Eleanor explained.

"I don't think Mark and Dede will ever let anything separate them." Angus took another bite of duck.

"It's just an idea. I'm not sure they will really do it." Eleanor decided to drop the topic. "They want to be surrounded by their friends when they renew their vows."

Angus suddenly was hit with a thought and blurted, "Are you asking me to marry you, Ellie?" Eleanor was struck dumb.

It was Angus' turn to be uncomfortable. He had jumped to an unfortunate assumption and realized his mistake only after he had engaged his mouth. He knew how Eleanor felt about marriage and had made a promise not to push her but for reasons beyond his control his mind had gone there with little effort and his tongue had followed. Surely it was the memory of honeymooning on a tropical island combined with the references to weddings under magical trees that led him to the conclusion that would also have fulfilled his ardent desire to make Eleanor his wife.

"I'm sorry, Ellie. As tempting as it sounds, I can't marry you right now. I've got a dog who needs me so I couldn't possibly leave him to run off to a tropical island for a quickie wedding. Besides, I'm in the middle of a murder investigation. What would Faith say if she knew that you were trying to take me away from her after I promised to help her? She might come unhinged and try to kill you."

"I hadn't thought of that," Eleanor said, calmly sensing his discomfort by his ridiculous babble. "Why don't you just think about it and we'll talk about it after this case is resolved."

Angus sighed in relief. Eleanor wasn't going to react like she did the last time he mentioned marriage and break off their friendship. "I hope you don't mind if I leave a little early tonight," he said. "Michael and Delia are out tonight and I have my house all to myself. Bones and I plan to watch Trailblazer basketball tonight."

"Oh," Eleanor tried not to appear relieved. "I totally understand."

"The duck was excellent, Ellie. Let me help you with these dishes before I go." Angus stood and cleared the table. They tidied up the kitchen together, each lost in their own thoughts. There was no easy banter or joking and only a swift peck on the cheek as he left. Eleanor had never seen him in such a hurry to leave and wondered if something else was prompting his swift exit, but she had to let it go and get ready for her date with a murderer.

Eleanor arrived at Dede's house ahead of the others and they all drove together to the Red Shed. Pearl staked out her favorite machine in the back room and the rest of them sat at a table in a dark corner where they could easily watch who came and went without being obvious.

"I think we should just drink water," said Cleo. "We need our wits about us tonight."

The ladies were dumbfounded to hear these words from Cleo. "I think it might be okay to have one drink,' Eleanor said. "This is a bar and if we don't order something they might kick us out."

Dede and Cleo went to the bar and put in an order while Josephine and Eleanor took inventory of the patrons. It was still early for a Friday night but several people they didn't know sat at the bar and as they watched from their corner they saw

Delia and Michael enter and sit at a table across the room. It wasn't long before Dr. Baxter came in with Tonya Jones and took seats at the bar. Dede raised her eyebrows and the ladies were on guard watching Tonya's every move carefully, on the lookout for the paper bag. Nothing happened. The music got wilder and the drinkers got louder. The coffee group sipped their drinks and waited. They were all surprised when Hope Strong slipped through the door with a brown paper bag under her arm. Eleanor turned her head away as she passed by their table on her way to the video game room. Cleo's eyes got round, "I can't believe it's her!" she said. Suddenly Hope was at their table glaring at Eleanor.

"I didn't expect it to be you," Hope hissed at Eleanor. "How can you do this to me when you know everything we're going through right now? Faith thinks you're her friend."

Eleanor wanted to reply but was distracted by the sudden appearance of Angus who strode to their table like a man on a mission.

"You too? Hope was clearly upset seeing Angus there. "My sister thinks you're trying to help her and now you're blackmailing me."

"Sit down, Hope," Angus ordered as he pulled out two chairs and sat in one of them. "Tell me what's going on here. Why would we blackmail you? What have you done?"

"I got this note that said you knew that I came here and if I didn't pay $100,000 you would tell Faith."

"What makes you think any of us sent it?" asked Angus who knew Eleanor had.

"Eleanor has seen me here. If Faith finds out I come here, she'll be so disappointed in me. I don't have that kind of money. Please don't tell her. She'll pray for me and make me feel guilty," Hope said.

"She already knows, because I told her I saw you here. Is that the worst thing you've done?" Angus asked.

Hope hung her head. "I don't have to tell you everything I've done."

"A lot of people have seen you here. This is a small town. We're not blackmailers," Angus explained scowling at Eleanor.

Hope ran her fingers through her hair and closed her eyes. "You don't understand what it's like to live with someone like Faith. She's overbearing and controlling."

"You're a grown woman. Get out from under her thumb and live your own life." Angus' voice softened. "It's not a sin to go out to meet people. What's in the bag?"

"Paper, there's just paper in the bag. I was going to put it by the video poker machine and see who took it, but when I saw Eleanor here I assumed it was her. I'm sorry."

"Go home, Hope. Faith already knows about your visits here. She understands. Whoever sent the note has no power over you." Angus and the ladies watched as Hope walked out the door.

"That little act doesn't mean she's not guilty," said Josephine.

"We don't know any more than we did before," said Dede.

"I hope you know that blackmail is a felony." Angus wasn't happy. "I'm putting all of you on notice. If you step out of line one more time, I'm turning you in." His angry gaze fell on Eleanor. "You've made me miss my game."

"Why are you here?" Eleanor asked.

"Someone's got to pull your bacon out of the fire. Hope could file charges against you if she learns it was you. You're not a licensed detective, or an officer of the law. You are committing crimes and could get yourselves in real trouble. I read your note. I suspected you might be here and . . . Michael called me. Now go home." Angus walked out the door leaving the coffee ladies to stew over their reprimand.

"Boy is he bossy," said Cleo.

Dede was imagining the headlines MAYOR FOUND GUILTY OF BLACKMAIL.

"What happened to Pearl?" asked Josephine who peeked around the corner and saw an empty chair at her machine.

"Where did Tonya go?" Eleanor hadn't noticed her leave, but Dr. Baxter sat alone at the bar.

The ladies checked the bathroom and then left the Red Shed by the back door hoping to find Pearl in the car.

"Hurry up and get in," she ordered. "Tonya Jones left this paper bag by one of the poker machines and I took it and came out here."

"You weren't supposed to take it," said Dede. "She might have seen you."

Pearl opened the bag and read the note inside. It said, *Go to hell you bitches.*

"She knows it's us," said Dede.

"Why? Were we the only bitches in there?" asked Cleo.

"Maybe she overheard the conversation with Hope," worried Eleanor.

"She can't prove anything," said Josephine. "If she saw Pearl take the bag, Pearl can say she thought someone left it there and threw it away when she saw nothing was in it."

"She doesn't like me and now she thinks I know what she did," Dede said. "Maybe Angus is right to be cautious. She might try to kill me next."

"Just relax," said Josephine. "She won't do anything that would put her in the spotlight. I think now she wants to be the victim who needs protecting from Faith. She'll lay low if she's smart."

"Besides, she threw her gun away," Cleo reminded her. "She'll have to think of another method to do you in."

"What was she doing with Dr. Baxter?" Eleanor asked. "Do you think they're an item?"

"I don't know," said Dede. "Vivian was Tonya's friend and he seemed upset about Vivian so maybe they were comforting each other."

"I don't like it," Eleanor said. "Something about it feels off."

"You better worry about the something that's off with Angus," said Cleo. "He's scary when he's mad."

"What happened? Why is Angus mad?" asked Pearl who had missed the drama with Hope. They filled her in on the way to Dede's house and then each went their own way home.

Eleanor's mind churned with regret at the way things went down. It was supposed to be simple. One of the suspects was supposed to turn up, not both of them. No one was supposed to suspect the coffee group of blackmail, yet it seemed that both suspects did. Obviously, the snoops were not as clever as they thought they were. Now Angus was angry about her deceit and she had absolutely no excuse. This alone caused her heart to hurt. Nothing about this entire scheme felt right. Dr. Baxter's involvement with Tonya was troubling too. She didn't fit his type, so what were they doing together? Maybe Eleanor had missed something in the letters Dr. Baxter wrote to Charity. She could look at them again. Eleanor drove to her house and only noticed Angus' truck behind her when he pulled into his place. He had followed her home. Probably to make sure she didn't get into any more trouble. Eleanor was in disgrace.

Eleanor read every letter Dr. Baxter had written to Charity Strong three times and couldn't detect anything other than adoration. She didn't think he could kill her and had already taken his name off that list. Now she was sure that Charity Strong's death was connected to the string of murders in some way that involved Dr. Baxter and Tonya Jones. If only she had the letters Charity had written to Dr. Baxter she could know for sure how Charity felt about him, but all she had was speculation. She needed proof; the journals. Eleanor hadn't read all of Charity's journals, but Delia had. Eleanor wondered if Angus still had the box of journals. She wondered if he would ever speak to her again, but Delia might.

The next morning Eleanor woke with a heavy feeling in her chest. Phooey, she should have married Angus when he asked her. In her attempt to be independent and free she didn't factor in that loving someone invalidated all those things whether you were married or not. She was not independent or free as long as his disapproval could make her feel this wretched, but she couldn't face him either. How could she get the information she needed? A walk was in order. She dressed quickly and started for the beach. The November day was cold and drizzly and matched her mood exactly. Hurrying along to keep warm Eleanor completed her exercise in record time and stopped at the post office to pick up her mail.

A letter written in beautiful script caught her attention and she opened it on the spot.

My Dear Eleanor,

Please don't faint or fall dead of a heart attack when you read this. I must apologize for deceiving you about my death, but it could not be helped. Art and I had one chance to be together and we took it even though it may have caused others some distress. I'm sorry for that but I'm not sorry for what Art and I shared. It was the time of my life. Unfortunately, Art died in his sleep three weeks ago. I have spent this time putting his affairs in order and plan to return to Sand Beach before Thanksgiving. Hopefully you have kept my house for me. Please tell my friends that the rumors of my death have been greatly exaggerated. I'll tell you all about it when I return.

Fondly, Mattie May

Eleanor was beside herself. She hurried across the street to Suzanna's to share the news with the Do Nothings. Mavis and Sybil sat at their usual table sipping coffee and looked up in surprise as Eleanor burst rudely into their conversation.

"Mattie's alive!" she said tossing the letter onto the table.

Sybil picked the letter up and read it aloud. "I knew it! I just knew she wasn't gone."

"I don't believe it!" Mavis was in shock, but both women had smiles that lit up the gray November day. "I think it may take me a minute to soak this in."

"We will have to get her house ready for her return," said Sybil. "Eleanor you must evict the Strong women as soon as possible."

"I have to go," Eleanor said, "but I had to let you know." Eleanor left the two chattering about a welcome home party, which Eleanor was sure Mattie would hate, and almost flew up the hill to Angus' house to give him the news forgetting in her delight that she was not in favor at the moment. She didn't think about her appearance until Angus opened the door and saw herself through his eyes; wet and bedraggled, but happy.

"You're welcome," he said as he took in her smiling face. "I was happy to bail you out last night and I know you're sorry and you'll never deceive me again."

"Mattie May is alive and coming back to Sand Beach," Eleanor said shoving the letter into his hands. Bones came bounding to the door to check out the excitement and Delia poked her nose out of the kitchen.

"I'm making pancakes," Delia said. "Are you staying for breakfast?"

"No thank you, Delia. Will you call me when you finish breakfast? I've got to go but I just wanted to share the good news."

As she left, she heard Delia ask, "Who the hell is Mattie May? I hope she isn't involved in this murder investigation."

Eleanor showered, dressed, and made a pot of coffee before Delia showed up at her door. "I hope you don't mind my hopping right over here, but I needed to get away from those men," Delia whined. "I left before cleaning up the kitchen. Their demands and expectations never end. What did you want to talk about?"

"Would you like coffee?" Eleanor asked as she poured two cups.

Delia nodded and followed Eleanor to a cozy spot near the window where they could look out over the gray churning ocean while they sipped their brew. "I wanted to ask you about Charity's journals. Did they reveal anything about a possible love interest?"

"I read them all. She never revealed the name of a lover, but it was obvious that she had a trusted confidante. She felt safe sharing some very private information with this person and referred to them as 'Me'. Although she never said it outright she held this person in high regard, quoting them and praising their intelligence, physical attributes, and advice."

"Do you think it was Dr. Baxter?" Eleanor asked.

"Could be, although he never offered any information or explanation for his interest in Charity, he was clearly in love with her," Delia said. "Why do you want to know? Haven't we already proved that she was murdered by her husband?"

"I just wanted to know if the journals indicated how she felt about *him*. I was hoping there might be a clue that would link Charity and Dr. Baxter to the current murders." Eleanor paused. "Did Angus tell you about my theory that Tonya and Vivian worked together to kill Jude and Donnie?"

"No, but he did tell us about your plan to smoke Tonya or Hope out last night," Delia said. "He seemed unusually bothered by it but I think it was genius."

"Don't you find it odd that Dr. Baxter was with Tonya last night?" Eleanor asked.

"He's single. He can go out with anyone he chooses," Delia stated defensively.

"Yes, but Tonya Jones is mean and vindictive, greedy, and manipulative—just the opposite of Charity and you. Those aren't traits he would find appealing. Let me tell you what I think happened and you tell me if I'm off base." Eleanor explained her theory that mirrored the *Strangers on a Train* plot casting Tonya and Vivian in the starring roles.

"That's an interesting idea," Delia said. "What did Angus think of it?"

"He said the same thing; that it was interesting," Eleanor continued. "Now I think Dr. Baxter is involved in some way, but I don't know how or why."

"And you think this just because you saw him with Tonya last night?" Delia asked.

"If Vivian shot Donnie Gold she must have had help depositing him in the densifier." Eleanor stopped to think. She remembered something the two women said at the grocery store. There was something about having him where they wanted him. "I think Vivian found out something about Dr. Baxter and was using it against him. I bet Tonya and Vivian pulled him into their scheme."

"It's possible, but all conjecture. You don't have any concrete proof that any of this is true," Delia said.

"Do you still have Charity's journals? Maybe there's something in them that was missed," said Eleanor.

"No, Angus took them to the police," Delia said. "I went over them several times, Eleanor."

"What was in the letters tied up with blue rickrack?" asked Eleanor remembering those left in the box that matched the letters from Dr. Baxter. Eleanor didn't want Delia to know she had broken into Dr. Baxter's office and copied his letters.

"I don't remember seeing any letters tied with blue rickrack," Delia said.

Eleanor wondered if Delia's opinion of Dr. Baxter was colored by her obvious infatuation with him. "What's Dr. Baxter's first name?"

"Martin," Delia said. "Martin Evan Baxter. It's quite distinguished don't you agree?"

"M.E.B. could be 'Me,'" Eleanor said, wondering how Hope knew it was Dr. Baxter.

Eleanor was on the phone telling everyone who knew Mattie May the news that she was alive and returning to Sand Beach when the members of the coffee group arrived.

"We came offering support," said Josephine. "After last night, we were worried we might find you in jail on blackmail charges."

"Have you fixed things with Angus?" asked Dede. "If not I brought a cake so you can use it to help atone for your crime."

"Thank you." Eleanor took the cake to the kitchen. "Who wants a piece?"

"Me," said Cleo.

"The situation must be bad if you're not going to use the cake to bribe Angus," Pearl said.

"He can't eat an entire cake," Eleanor said putting large slabs of the chocolatey confection on plates. "I see you are all still alive so nothing sinister happened last night after we left."

"No," said Dede, "but I couldn't get to sleep for the longest time. First I worried about the wedding. Mark convinced me to just have a quiet civil ceremony somewhere out of town. Then there were strange unexplained sounds coming from downstairs. I was sure it was Tonya Jones coming to kill me in my sleep, but it was just Doogie having a midnight snack."

"I had the same kind of night," said Pearl, "only I was plagued by dreams of Tonya coming after the bag that for some reason contained evidence of her guilt."

"I'm disturbed by the fact that Dr. Baxter was at the Red Shed with Tonya last night," Eleanor said. "Do you think he could be involved?"

"You mean romantically?" asked Pearl.

"No, I mean in the murders," Eleanor clarified.

"Why would he want Jude and Donnie dead?" asked Cleo.

"Vivian worked for him. Maybe she knew something about him he didn't want disclosed," Eleanor said.

"So he helped them to keep them quiet . . . " Dede said. "That would explain how Donnie got in the densifier."

"Do you think Dr. Baxter is her next victim?" asked Pearl.

"Maybe Tonya is *his* next victim. There's nothing linking him to those murders if your theory is right," said Josephine. "If both Tonya and Vivian are dead, his secret would be safe and he'd be home free."

"What could Vivian have on him?" asked Eleanor.

"Maybe it's something that involved a patient," said Dede. "I can find out if any of his patients have sued him lately."

"It would have to be something secret or illegal," said Cleo.

"Let's start at the beginning and review what we know about the case with an eye to this new theory involving Dr. Baxter," said Josephine.

"Let's go into my office." Eleanor led them there where they studied her timeline of events in the case.

"The Strong sisters came to Sand Beach to care for their father who had a stroke," Eleanor began.

"No it started before that," corrected Josephine. "Charity Strong was murdered by her husband."

"Charity was having a relationship with Dr. Baxter even before that. His name is Martin Evan Baxter so he's definitely 'Me'. There's no doubt about that," Eleanor said. "Charity's bones were dug up and eventually identified. Hope delivered the love letters to Dr. Baxter, so she knew who Me was. My guess is Faith knew too and told Hope to give the letters back. Jude Thorn was shot. Dr. Baxter was sobbing in his office."

"Somewhere in here Dr. Baxter hired Delia and Patrick to find out what happened to Charity," Eleanor said.

"Okay, he might have done that to keep abreast of what was being discovered about her death. Are we sure he didn't kill her?" asked Cleo.

"The love letters he wrote were very convincing. I think he truly loved her," Eleanor said. "He just wanted to know for sure that she didn't kill herself, and that she chose him over her husband or someone else."

"Can we read them?" asked Dede.

Eleanor pulled the letters from a drawer in her desk and handed them to Dede while the ladies continued to speculate.

"If you really loved someone and they were in an untenable situation wouldn't you want to kill the person that was creating it?" asked Pearl. "I think I would have shot the reverend if I was Dr. Baxter."

"Maybe he did," said Josephine. "Kill him I mean."

Pearl looked at Josephine and rolled her eyes. "It sure took him long enough. Charity's been dead for over twenty years. It wouldn't have helped her at this point."

"I mean maybe he killed her tormentor when he got the chance. Dr. Baxter didn't know Charity was dead for sure until her bones were discovered but he knew how unhappy she was," Josephine said. "He might have believed the stories about her running away with someone else or suspected her husband found out and killed her."

"Besides that, the reverend wasn't shot—he had a stroke," said Dede.

"Maybe that's it!" said Eleanor. "My doctor told me not to let a chiropractor manipulate my neck because it could cause a stroke. Dr. Baxter knows what he's doing. What if the reverend went to him and Dr. Baxter manipulated his neck so he'd have a stroke!"

"Let me Google that," Dede said tapping her phone.

"That makes sense to me," said Josephine. "It may have been a crime of opportunity. Imagine the man who made someone you loved miserable coming to you for help and giving you the opportunity to make him pay. Reverend Strong probably didn't know that Dr. Baxter was Charity's lover."

"If Vivian knew, she could use that knowledge to make Dr. Baxter help her and Tonya eliminate the people who stood in the way of their goals," Pearl said.

"I guess it's okay to tell you this now that both Vivian and Jude are dead, but I was mediating their divorce and it was extremely ugly," Josephine confided. "Jude Thorn was a narcissist—totally charismatic and charming when he wanted to be but unreasonable—and insisted on having everything his way. He played games, caused delays, and would have drug the divorce out until Vivian had nothing left. It would have bankrupted her emotionally as well as financially. His death freed her from a great deal of grief."

"Who could have known? She seemed so happy every time I saw her," said Eleanor.

"As Freud said, 'Unexpressed emotions never die. They are buried alive and come out later in uglier ways,'" Josephine said.

"Okay, it says that a violent manipulation of the neck can result in a tear in the blood vessels that feed the brain. A blood clot can form and later dislodge causing a stroke," Dede stated.

"That means Reverend Strong wouldn't have had the stroke right away but maybe days after his treatment, leaving Dr. Baxter in the clear," said Cleo. "It seems like the perfect crime."

"Except somehow Vivian found out," said Dede.

"So how do we find out if Reverend Strong was one of his patients?" asked Pearl.

"I think it may be time to go to the police," said Josephine. "They can get a warrant for Baxter's records and prove that Reverend Strong had his neck adjusted."

"Maybe they can get Dr. Baxter to turn on Tonya for a lesser sentence," Eleanor said. "I kind of like the man."

"He'll lose his license for sure. You better start looking for a new chiropractor," said Dede.

Eleanor felt more than the satisfaction of fitting one puzzle piece into another. This was like putting the last piece in the puzzle and looking at the whole picture in its perfection. Their suspected scenario had to be the way it went down. It felt right, but they needed proof. Before the ladies left Eleanor's house, they had decided the best course of action was for Eleanor to tell Angus, but for some reason this felt anticlimactic. There would be no heart-pounding confrontation, no chilling terror that ended in resolution, just the police using their boring methods of drudgery, interrogation, and manipulation. Eleanor would have to close the case, stop thinking about it, and quit using her magnificent brain to solve it. Then what? Would there be another murder—another challenging case?

Eleanor wandered into her office, turned on the gas fireplace, and sat at her desk. Feathers flew in and landed on her computer. He looked at her first with his right yellow eye and then with his left.

"It was a dark and stormy night," he spoke in Walter's voice.

She turned on the computer and sat staring at the desktop image, lost in the flow of her thoughts. Then she placed her fingers on the keyboard and began, "There was a full moon the night I killed my husband . . . "

It grew into a dark and stormy night as Eleanor wrote the first and then the second chapter of what would become her first and finest novel. When the doorbell rang she realized the lateness of the hour and stood to find her body riddled with painful aches from sitting so long.

Angus and Bones waited on the porch as Eleanor made her way slowly to the door.

"Are you all right?" Angus asked, studying her closely for signs of something amiss.

"Of course, I'm fine. Come inside." Bones did his happy dance and Eleanor lavished him with strokes and ear scratches while Angus wiped his paws clean. "I truly am sorry about the other night, Angus. I never expected Hope and Tonya both to turn up at the Red Shed. Only one of them was supposed to show, alerting us to the guilty party. Are you going to forgive me?"

"You lied to me, Ellie," Angus said. "I wasn't going to come over here but Bones insisted. He must be hungry for those liver bites."

"You've every right to be hurt, I did lie to you and I can't excuse it. My adrenaline addiction may need a cure." Eleanor felt a chill emanating from Angus. She was certain Margo had cheated and lied to him during their marriage and now he was looking at her as if she were untrustworthy. "Would you care for a drink?"

Angus sighed. He did want a drink but more than that he wanted to be able to feel the way he used to feel about Eleanor. For a long time, he had adored her from a distance, loved her to distraction, and yearned to spend every day with her. She made him feel warm and accepted and whole. His fear was that his own occupation with the ugliness of life had tainted her and just as her positivity and light had brightened his outlook, his darkness had corrupted hers. Now she was obsessed with murder and murderers, and the thrill it gave her disturbed him. He was certain the lie was her way of hiding her obsession the same way a heroin user lies to keep those close from seeing their addiction. Now she had admitted it.

Eleanor poured them both a nightcap and went to start a fire in the fireplace to take away the chill. Angus sat and watched as she lit the match that set the room a rosy hue. Eleanor sat on the opposite couch and made no move to cozy up to him.

"I haven't been able to write for weeks, maybe months," she admitted. "I no longer feel relevant. It's a horrible feeling, Angus. I think I've latched on to this case as a way to give my life purpose."

"Aren't you the woman who told me I'm not my job and it's enough just to be?" Angus asked. "Don't you believe your own wisdom?"

"It's one thing to say it and quite another to live it," Eleanor said. "I am sorry if I hurt you."

"Are you of the belief that what a man doesn't know won't hurt him? I mean are you sorry I found out you lied, or are you sorry you deceived me?"

"I'm sorry I've lost your trust," Eleanor said. "Your friendship is everything to me. I look in your eyes and I don't like the way you see me now."

"I won't deny the fact that I'm disappointed, Ellie, but even more than that is my fear that you're willing to put your life in danger to solve a mystery and you won't even let me in on your schemes. I don't want to lose you, ever. If I didn't love you I wouldn't care, but I do care."

"*A ship is always safe at the shore, but that is not what it is built for.*" Eleanor quoted Einstein.

Angus stood and sat next to her taking her hands in his. "Then bring me with you when you go sailing." Eleanor smiled. Angus drew her close and Bones jumped on the couch in an attempt to be part of a group hug.

Making up was always good and better still when ice cream and chocolate cake were involved. As Angus and Eleanor finished off the last of the raspberry rumble, she told him how her team of amateur detectives had implicated Dr. Baxter in the three murders. He quietly processed the information.

"I can't think of any reason it couldn't have happened that way, but do you have any evidence?" he asked.

"No, we thought the police could get a warrant and find out if Reverend Strong was a client and if he had a neck adjustment," Eleanor said.

Angus feigned surprise. "You mean you didn't come up with a plan to get that information yourselves?"

Eleanor pressed her lips together to keep from saying something she would regret. She *had* thought of going back to Baxter's office and searching through the patient files, but couldn't admit it knowing how Angus felt about breaking the law. If she let him in on that plan, he would nip it in the bud and she needed to keep him in the loop in order to win back his trust.

"The police need probable cause to get a search warrant, Ellie." Angus said patiently. "Although your theory is interesting, it's not enough without some evidence that he committed a crime. Even if they discovered that Reverend

Strong had his neck adjusted that doesn't prove that Dr. Baxter did anything wrong."

"Oh," Eleanor sighed. "So you're saying we have to have more than a theory, any ideas?"

"If there had been an autopsy that might have shown something, but I'm betting he was cremated or buried without one," Angus said. "A pattern of stroke victims leading to Baxter would help, but I don't think he's a serial stroke-inducer. Your theory is that this was a one-time act of revenge prompted by opportunity and followed up by criminal acts committed under duress through blackmail."

Eleanor sighed. "There is nothing easy about this case." Being an officer of the law put restrictions on a detective that an amateur snoop or private investigator didn't need to consider.

"You need to have patience, Ellie," Angus cautioned. "The glove that was found near Faith's house could reveal DNA evidence telling us who the killer is, but these things take time. I told Officer McGraw about your suspicions and I'm sure he'll look into it. He wants this case closed. So far there have been three murders since Faith and Hope have come back to Sand Beach and all the evidence points to one of them. If your theory is true and Tonya killed Vivian to tie up loose ends, she may make an attempt on Baxter too which would help prove that he was involved. On the other hand, if Baxter tries to get rid of Tonya it looks like Faith or Hope committed the killings and Baxter could get away with it."

"Three can keep a secret if two of them are dead," Eleanor said. Angus smiled but it wasn't because he was happy.

The next morning dawned clear and bright. Eleanor made her way to the beach and as she walked, her face turned toward the wind, her mind rehashed the evidence. Something wasn't right. She remembered the box of Charity's journals and the letters tied with blue rickrack. There had to be two sets of letters. Hope had returned one to Dr. Baxter, but where had the other set gone? Delia said she hadn't seen them, but Eleanor was certain they were in the box when she had snooped in Angus' bedroom. Eleanor decided a visit to Angus was in order.

Delia answered the door in her bathrobe. "Good morning, Eleanor," she said. "I'm sorry, but Angus and Michael have gone to the gym to workout. Would you like a cup of coffee?"

"No thank you," Eleanor answered. "I was just thinking about those letters we talked about earlier. I'm sure they were in the box of Charity's journals."

"You mean the ones tied with blue rickrack?" Delia asked skeptically.

"Right," Eleanor replied. "The last time I saw them they were in that box by Angus' bed. I just thought it might be worth a look."

"You want to search Angus' bedroom?" Delia smiled. "I can tell you right now he's not there."

"Very funny," Eleanor said as she followed Delia to his room.

Everything was in order. The bed was made. Clothes were hung neatly in the closet and Angus' slippers were parked beside the bed where Bones used one as a pillow to rest his head. The black dog looked up as Eleanor entered the room.

"Are you missing your daddy?" she said as she bent to pet him. Eleanor gave Bones a quick rubdown and a few ear scratches before she glanced under the bed and caught sight of something that caused her heart to leap in triumph. "Jackpot!" She reached under the bed and pulled out a dirty sock. "Not exactly what I was hoping to find."

"It could have been worse," Delia said. "Bones is obsessed with dirty laundry of all sorts and likes to hide them under the bed."

Eleanor was not deterred by a smelly sock. She lay on her belly and stretched her arm further under the bed pulling out other items of unmentionables.

"Hey, that's my missing lucky underwear," Delia said, grabbing them out of Eleanor's hand.

Eleanor raised her eyebrows but continued to excavate Bone's collection until finally she retrieved what she was looking for—the envelopes tied with blue rickrack. "These fell out of the box and slipped under the bed. I bet Bones pushed them farther back in his attempt to hoard laundry."

"I'm sorry I didn't believe you Eleanor," Delia said. "Let's get some coffee and see what they have to offer."

As soon as Delia saw the handwriting in the first letter, she recognized it. It was strong and dark and slanted back indicating a left-handed writer.

"I can't believe it. These are from Dr. Baxter. He's still telling the same chiropractic jokes that he used in these letters—wisecracks and funny bones. I wonder if she thought he was funny." Delia said.

"They're not the love letters I was expecting," said Eleanor, making a mental comparison to the ones she had discovered in Dr. Baxter's office. "He signed them Doc."

"Well, he isn't really that romantic if you want the truth, but he is fun, and maybe that was enough for Charity. From what I gathered by reading her journals, her life was very serious and her husband dull and authoritarian," Delia said. "A kind soul and an open ear may have been just what the Doc offered her."

"Yes, but if Dr. Baxter wasn't Me, who was?" asked Eleanor.

Delia simply shrugged. "It could have been anyone."

Eleanor hurried home. She needed to process this new information and get some insight from her friends in the coffee group. After reading the love letters from Me, Eleanor knew it couldn't be just anyone.

The coffee group sat in a booth at the Blue Lagoon and ordered lunch.

"I should have known better," said Eleanor. "It seemed so obvious that Me was Dr. Baxter and Charity's lover, but he wasn't. There were two sets of letters tied with blue rickrack. When I saw Hope at his office I assumed she had returned his letters to him, but his letters were signed Doc and contained his signature chiropractic jokes."

"Were his letters romantic in nature?" asked Josephine.

"Yes, but not nearly as deep or poetic as the others," Eleanor noted. "They lacked the maturity of the other ones and they were obviously written by a leftie, unlike the ones we found in Dr. Baxter's office. Delia recognized his handwriting immediately."

"So how does this change anything?" asked Pearl. "Dr. Baxter could still be involved in the murders."

"The love letters were so sincere and tender," Eleanor said. "I was certain the person who wrote them couldn't have killed Charity. Now I suspect Dr. Baxter may have been involved in murder from the beginning. What if he found out about Me and killed him too?"

"Why would he have the letters from Me in his office?" asked Dede.

"Both letters were tied with blue rickrack so maybe Hope did deliver them to him but picked up the wrong ones," Cleo offered.

"I wondered how she could possibly have thought Me was Dr. Baxter," Eleanor said. "Faith might have told her about him, but Faith may not have known what Hope had found in the box."

"It wouldn't be hard to guess Doc was Dr. Baxter if he made reference to chiropractic humor," said Josephine, "so Hope may have made a mistake. She still might not know who Me is, but I bet she knows who her mother is if she read Charity's journals, and that puts her back in the pool of suspects."

"That might explain why Dr. Baxter was crying that day. He probably realized that Charity had another lover who was planning to go away with her," Eleanor said.

"Maybe Tonya and her mean friends were right about Charity," Pearl said. "She had at least two men in love with her and neither was her husband."

"Oh Lordy," said Dede, "What if Me was Tonya's husband—the one who left her. What was his name? Something Blakely. What if Tonya was right and Charity did run off with her husband?"

"Don't forget that Charity was killed so she didn't actually run off with anyone's husband," Cleo corrected.

"But that doesn't mean she wasn't planning to do it," Pearl said.

"So maybe Charity wasn't as wholesome as everyone thought," Cleo said.

"Gladys said they disappeared about the same time," Eleanor added.

"I bet Tonya killed them both," Dede said. "I can't prove it, but I know that woman is evil."

"If this is true," Eleanor said, "is Me buried on the Strong property too?"

"Just when I think we've figured this all out something new comes up!" Josephine moaned.

"I hope you don't expect us to go back to that place and dig up another body," Pearl said.

"There must be a way of finding a buried corpse without having to dig up the entire Strong property," Eleanor said.

Eleanor woke up with a headache. Her neck hurt and she knew it was out of kilter, but she had a date with Angus to explore the possibility of a second corpse.

Eleanor and Angus walked the perimeter of the Strong property with Faith and Bones looking for any depression that might indicate a body was buried beneath the shallow topsoil that hosted a variety of weeds.

"There aren't many places deep enough for a grave, even a shallow one," Angus commented.

"My mother was buried near the house where soil had been brought in for her rose garden," Faith said.

"If Father buried her lover too, it would have to be nearby. He wasn't a strong or physically fit man so I doubt he could have carried someone very far." Faith had given up protecting the man who had altered her life though abuse and offered to assist in the search when Angus had asked. She willingly pointed out the location of her mother's grave and led them through an overgrown landscape bordered by scotch broom and gorse. A chilly November wind blew in from the southwest stinging Eleanor's eyes and causing them to tear.

Angus eyed the terrain skeptically and sighed. "It's difficult to see any depression. The topography is rocky and uneven everywhere. Show me where you found your mother's body again."

Faith led the way to the spot where roses once struggled to survive but now sat fallow. Angus squinted in thought as he once more surveyed the surroundings and noted the clods of broken soil. "This is our best bet. It's possible the person who buried her here may have buried someone beneath her. How far down did you dig?"

"It wasn't deep," Faith said. "I'll get a shovel."

"If Faith remembers the events of that day clearly, I don't think her father had time to kill Charity and her lover and bury them both. He left her, went to church, and when they came back Charity was gone," Eleanor said.

"She may not remember it correctly," Angus said. "Most people make terrible witnesses."

"Do you think there's someone else buried here?" Eleanor asked.

"We'll see. Just remember if we find something we stop and call in the experts," Angus reminded her.

Faith returned with a shovel and Angus began to dig. At first it was easy but as he dug deeper the soil became more compacted. Faith had loosened the ground that fed Charity's roses and then Charity had fed them too. The dog began to dig, but Eleanor held him back afraid he might get in the way. It was a skeletal hand that appeared just as Angus was ready to give up. He drew back his shovel before he could damage any evidence and Eleanor made the call that would bring Office McGraw to the scene.

"There's no way to know who this is," said Officer McGraw as he carefully studied the makeshift grave, "unless you already know."

"Eleanor thinks it might be Gavin Blakely. He disappeared around the same time as Charity Strong. There are some letters that may link him with her romantically," Angus said.

"So you think Reverend Strong killed them both and buried them here?" asked Officer McGraw.

"Possibly," Angus answered.

"Could this be evidence?" asked Eleanor as she held up something gold that caught her eye in the dirt.

Angus took it and rubbed the caked soil away, revealing a gold pin that looked like a nose with a round mouth under it. He put it carefully in an evidence bag.

"I wonder what that's supposed to be," Eleanor said, but no one had an answer.

"It will take a while for forensic experts to get here," said Officer McGraw. "There's no reason for you to stick around."

"I'll stay," said Angus, looking at Eleanor's pale face. "You go home and get some rest."

Eleanor was grateful and took the opportunity to go home. Her headache continued to grow more intense and she suspected a trip to the chiropractor was in order.

Eleanor was surprised to see Tonya Jones sitting at the reception desk in Dr. Baxter's office, but desperate to get relief from the headache that plagued her and thankful that she could be squeezed in at the last minute, she just couldn't concentrate on Tonya.

"Bone giorno," Dr. Baxter greeted. "What seems to be the problem?"

"I think I slept on my neck the wrong way. It's stiff and I have a terrible headache," she explained.

Dr. Baxter listened attentively, and then had Eleanor lie on the table while he sat behind her and kneaded her neck and shoulder muscles. "Yes, you're very tight. Just relax." He began to talk about the weather and ordinary things and then suddenly twisted her head. Eleanor heard a crack. It felt good. He continued to manipulate her head and neck as he spoke about his latest trip to see his family and then quickly snapped her head to the side again. Eleanor remembered what her primary care doctor had told her about the dangers of chiropractic manipulation of the neck and the dangers of stroke, but she could already feel relief. "That should help, but let's make sure everything else is in line," he said.

Eleanor rolled to her stomach while he checked her back, hips, and legs, and then rolled her onto her back again. She looked up as Dr. Baxter crossed her arms over her chest and gave her back a crack. Her eyes widened, not in pain, but in recognition. The pin that he wore on his lapel was exactly the same as the one found at the grave site.

"What is this pin?" she asked innocently, pointing to it.

"It's a vertebra," he responded. "Not everyone's type of jewelry, but I'm rather fond of it. Had a solid gold one once, but lost it. It was a gift from my mother. This one is just a cheap replacement so she wouldn't know how careless I am."

"I see," Eleanor said. It wasn't a nose with a round mouth, but a vertebra. "How long has your gold one been missing?"

"Why do you ask?" He paused in thought. "Have you found one? Mine had my initials engraved on the back."

Eleanor noticed a change in his tone. She stood and stretched and tried to remain calm although her heart was racing.

"It's incredible the way you can make me feel so much better so quickly," Eleanor said, trying to keep her eyes from the pin. "Thank you. I think I'll go for a long walk on the beach now."

"You're very welcome, Eleanor. A walk on the beach would be good, just don't overdo it. Remember I've got your back."

Eleanor left quickly ignoring Tonya Jones, whose malevolent glare followed her out the door.

Eleanor was positive that Dr. Baxter was involved in the deaths of Charity Strong and her lover, Gavin Blakely, but wasn't sure the gold vertebra was enough to pin the murders on him. She drove home, exceeding the speed limit, and stopped at Angus' house. No one was home, so she drove to the grave site on the Strong property. The road was taped off, declaring it a crime scene, but it appeared that everyone had done their jobs and left the area. Eleanor went home and texted Angus with her latest discovery. She didn't expect a reply since Angus didn't always check his phone and sometimes didn't take it with him at all. Eleanor decided a walk would help her sort things out as well as give her body a chance to fall into its natural rhythm.

It was still a windy November day, cloudy with a chance of showers, and Eleanor could see the tide was coming in but there was time for a short walk before it reached its height. She started off with quick steps. Her thoughts turned inward, she failed to see the white pickup parked at the wayside where Dr. Baxter waited. He followed and slowly gained on her as she skipped over the little streams that ran into the sea.

"Eleanor," he shouted, over the roar of the waves. "Stop, I need to talk to you."

Eleanor was momentarily stunned by his appearance. "Dr. Baxter, what are you doing here?"

"I just got a funny feeling when you were in my office. I thought maybe you found some new evidence regarding the murders," he said.

"No, nothing like that," she said turning to look at him.

"You seemed very interested in my pin," he said.

"Well it is very unusual," Eleanor said. She felt fear creep into her mind uninvited. He was big and strong and as she looked around, she saw no one on the beach to help her, only the incoming waves inching inland over the long stretch of sand.

"Tell me what you know," he said, turning his back to the ocean and taking a step toward her.

"I don't know what you mean," she said, stepping back.

"Don't play games with me, Eleanor. I know you've been involved in investigating Charity's death and the murders of Donnie Gold and Jude Thorn. Delia told me . . . "

Eleanor saw it coming and instinctively turned and ran, but by the time Dr. Baxter realized what was happening a sneaker wave swept in, carrying a large piece of driftwood, knocking him to the ground. As it receded, the log twisted and rolled over him pinning the chiropractor beneath it. Eleanor stood frozen by the power and violence of the ocean, but only for a second. She ran to Dr. Baxter who was conscious but totally in shock.

"Help me," he cried. His voice was almost lost in the roar of the surf.

"I can't lift this log," Eleanor said, "I'll need to go for help."

"Don't leave me, please," he begged. "I don't want to die alone."

A smaller wave followed but did not reach them. The tide was coming in and Eleanor knew there wasn't much time to get help. She pulled out her phone and dialed 911.

"You're not going to die," she said, "Help is on the way."

"You're a terrible liar," he said. "I know how bad the phone reception is out here."

"I'll stay with you as long as I can," Eleanor said, kneeling in the wet sand and taking his hand.

"I want you to hear my confession," he said. "I don't want to take this guilt to my grave."

"I'm listening," Eleanor said, leaning down to hear him.

"I loved Charity. I thought she loved me but I found her with Gavin Blakely that Sunday morning. They were going to run away together. I was hurt and angry. Gavin and I fought. I hit him with a two-by-four and he fell to the ground. I didn't mean to kill him, truly I'm not a killer, but he was dead." He stopped to take a deep breath. Eleanor could see that he was in pain, but he continued. "Charity ran in the house and came out with a gun. I think she meant to stop the fighting, but when she realized Gavin was dead, she turned the gun on herself. There was nothing I could do to stop her. I buried them both in the same grave."

Eleanor held his head as another wave rolled in soaking them both but not enough to lift the log.

"I've lived with this guilt for twenty years, thinking I was safe, until Charity's bones were discovered. Tonya and Vivian planned to rid themselves of Donnie and Jude by each killing the other one's problem and making sure they had alibis. When Faith came back they knew it was their chance to put the plan into action and blame her. Somehow they knew I was involved and blackmailed me into helping them. Tonya killed Vivian to keep her quiet. I think she's planning to kill me too."

Another wave rushed in and out, and then another, as Eleanor shivered and Dr. Baxter passed out. Each time a wave moved in, Eleanor feared the log would roll over her too, but she stayed there holding Dr. Baxter's head out of the water until a rescue vehicle arrived and took over the effort. People gathered at the wayside to watch the rescue team as they worked to free Dr. Baxter. Several strong volunteers heaved the log as each wave came, while others pulled at the man trapped under it until he was freed, put on a stretcher, and taken to the hospital.

Eleanor walked to the wayside and saw Angus getting out of his truck.

"Eleanor, what happened?" He took in her shivering body and pale face, and quickly carried her to the cab of his warm truck.

Eleanor was numb with cold and could not speak, so Angus cranked up the heat and raced her home. He stripped her wet clothes as well as his own and crawled under the covers, holding her close until the shivering stopped. Bones was happy to add his body heat to the effort and curled up next to Eleanor as well.

When he was sure her body temperature had returned to normal, Angus warmed some soup and grilled cheese sandwiches, then carried his offering on a tray to where Eleanor slept.

"Wake up, Ellie," he whispered. "You need to eat something."

Eleanor opened her eyes. It was night and all the earlier drama flooded back to her. "He confessed!" She sat up and began to tell Angus everything she knew. Angus, being a patient man listened until she finished, then told her the rest of the story.

The coffee group ladies leaned in over their usual breakfast fair and listened to Eleanor's solution to the twenty-year mystery.

"So Dr. Baxter killed Charity," said Pearl. "Did he also cause Reverend Strong's stroke?"

"No, he only confessed to killing Gavin Blakely, but not the stroke," Eleanor said. "Evidently, he went to see Charity and caught her with Gavin Blakely. The two men got in a fight and he hit Blakely in the head with a two by four and killed him. Charity ran in the house and got a pistol hoping to end the fight. She was so distraught when she saw Gavin dead she shot herself. Dr. Baxter panicked and buried them both, but his chiropractic pin must have fallen into the grave."

"The Reverend Strong wasn't the killer," stated Dede.

"And Dr. Baxter didn't mean to kill anyone," said Pearl, "but what about her being left handed?"

"Faith said her mother was ambidextrous," Eleanor sighed. "Proving once again how thorough one must be to solve a mystery."

"That solves one mystery, but what about the other murders?" asked Cleo. "Are they connected?"

"According to Tonya, the day of the tragedy Vivian drove Tonya to the beach for an early morning run. When they returned to the wayside Tonya spotted her husband's car. She decided to drive it home and leave him stranded because that's who she is. She probably knew he was in love with Charity and suspected he was with her. Both Dr. Baxter and Gavin Blakely parked their cars at the wayside and walked to the top of the hill to protect Charity's reputation. When Gavin didn't come home Tonya spread the rumor that he had run off with Charity because that's what she believed to be true," Eleanor said. "It wasn't until much later when Tonya coveted her brother's inheritance and Vivian wanted her husband out of her life for good that they came up with a plan to kill for each other. Faith's return to Sand Beach prompted them to execute their plan and have her take the blame. When Charity's bones were discovered, Vivian recalled seeing Dr. Baxter's car at the wayside and she and Tonya confronted him and pulled him into their scheme. He was riddled with guilt and confessed to helping Vivian with Donnie by putting his body in the densifier. She never could have done it by herself. Tonya sensed Vivian's mental anguish, saw it as a weakness, and decided to do away with her before she spilled the beans."

"Why did Tonya admit to any of this?" asked Josephine.

"She didn't at first," Eleanor explained. "When the police discovered it was her DNA on the glove left at Vivian's murder scene, they went looking for her. Neighbors told them she was filling in for Vivian at Dr. Baxter's office so they went there and found her shortly after Dr. Baxter had gone to confront me. They said she had planted incriminating emails on his computer pointing to him as the killer. Then she played the victim and told them she feared for her own life."

"I knew she was evil," Dede said, hitting the table for emphasis.

"Angus was there and said it was all he could do to keep a straight face as they listened to her lies, cuffed her, and read her the Miranda rights."

"What about Dr. Baxter?" asked Josephine. "How is he doing?"

"He's alive with a broken leg and lots of bruises. Maybe the court will have mercy on him since he didn't mean to kill anyone."

"I think Dr. Baxter's going to end up in the joint," Cleo teased.

Mattie May sat in her cozy cottage sipping tea with Eleanor as the two looked through photo albums—a distraction from setting things right now that Mattie was home, and Faith and Hope had returned to Alaska.

"This is my son. What a character he was!" Mattie pointed to a picture of a boy holding a fish. He wasn't more than five and his smile was bigger by far than his catch. "I remember one day he was struggling to tie his shoe and he said, 'son of a bitch.' When I asked him to repeat that he said, 'Sing along with Mitch.' So I told him to go outside and get a switch so I could punish him. He was gone a long time. When he finally came in his hands were full of rocks. 'I couldn't find a switch, but here are some rocks you can throw at me.' I loved that face, that smile, that clever little mind. He was hit by a car two days after this picture was taken."

"I'm sorry, Mattie." Eleanor didn't know what else to say.

"Don't fuss, Eleanor," Mattie ordered. "You don't have to worry about me. I've lost plenty in my life but I'm not giving up on it. You never know what adventure is just around the corner."

"I'm just so glad to have you back," Eleanor said. "The Do Nothings aren't the same without you."

"I know you have an appointment to keep so you better get along. I'm driving my car down to Suzanna's to meet with those Do Nothings as soon as you go," Mattie said.

Angus had asked Eleanor to meet him at the top of the hill when she was done helping Mattie. He said he had a surprise for her. As she walked there she looked around at the amazing blue of the sky and listened to the shrill cries of the cloud of gulls circling overhead. It was chilly but one of those rare fall days on the coast when it seemed more like spring. She breathed in the clean scent of the sea and wondered how she would fill her time now that the murders had been solved. Writing didn't create that heart racing thrill that she experienced breaking into a forbidden location or the adrenaline rush she felt talking to someone who might have committed a crime, but it would have to do—for now.

As she approached the meeting place, Eleanor noticed several cars parked at the top. This is where the hang gliders launched. It seemed a perfect day for such an activity and the bright colors of the sails added a festive air as a handful of gliders milled around. She spotted Angus wearing a harness and helmet talking with another man near a bright red tandem glider and watched as one couple took off and flew out over the ocean. Eleanor's eyes followed them as they turned toward the beach and became smaller. Angus spotted her and waved. As she closed the gap between them her heart began to race and her palms to sweat. What had Angus done?

"Ellie, this is Ray. He's been giving me hang-gliding lessons. I hope you're ready for a heart-racing adventure." Angus' words held a dare and his eyes twinkled.

"Let's get you geared up," Ray said as he strapped a helmet on her head and helped her into a harness.

Eleanor was speechless as she listened carefully to Ray's instructions. Her life might depend on it. Everything was happening so quickly she didn't have time to think. She looked up into Angus' familiar face.

"Come fly away with me." He held out his hand and Eleanor took it.

Acknowledgments

I'd like to thank the readers who stop me on the street and ask when my next book will be ready and those who invite me to their book clubs, or pitch ideas and offer to be the murderer in my next mystery. It feels like a community project and adds to the fun of it all.

Thank you to my family, especially Nikki and Jennifer, who are full of creative plots and character suggestions, and a special shout-out to my chiropractor, Dr. Waxter, who keeps me in line, and Diane Colcord, who inspired the grizzly idea of death by densifier.

There would be no book without the editors and publishers at GladEye Press, Sharleen Nelson and J.V. Bolkan, who keep me from going off the rails. Thank you all.

About the Author

Patricia Brown was born in Oregon City, Oregon, and attended Oregon State University, graduating with a degree in elementary education, a career she pursued for 28 years.

She currently resides in a small town on the Oregon coast with her husband, where she dabbles in the arts and enjoys the company of family and friends. *Faith, Hope, Dying* is her fifth novel.

Get all the books in the Coastal Coffee Club Mystery series!

A Recipe for Dying: *The old people are dying, but no one seems to notice—after all, that's what old people do, isn't it? Eleanor and her friends set out to discover what the heck is going on!*

Dying for Diamonds: *When a mean-spirited mystery writer visiting the sleepy coastal town gets murdered, family secrets and the bonds we share are tested.*

Under A Dying Moon: *When a girl washes up on the beach and two women are found murdered, it's up to Eleanor and the gang to solve the mystery.*

Dying to Win: *Eleanor and her band of quirky friends investigate the disappearance of a Hispanic man betrothed to the young heiress of the richest, meanest, man in town.*

Hope, Faith, Dying: *Rumors swirl when sisters Hope & Faith return to their hometown to settle their preacher father's estate, prompting Eleanor and her sleuthing friends to dig up the truth about a decades-old mystery.*

Visit www.gladeyepress.com for details.

COMING SOON from

GladEye
Press

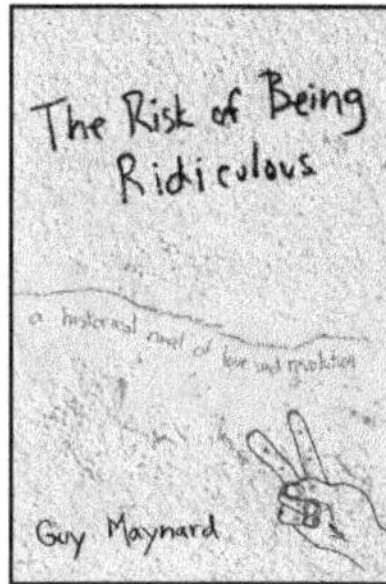

The Risk of Being Ridiculous: A Historical Novel of Love and Revolution
Guy Maynard

Join 19-year-old Ben Tucker for a passionate, lyrical six-week ride through confrontation and confusion, courts and cops, parties and politics, school and the streets, Weathermen and women's liberation, acid and activism, revolution and reaction.

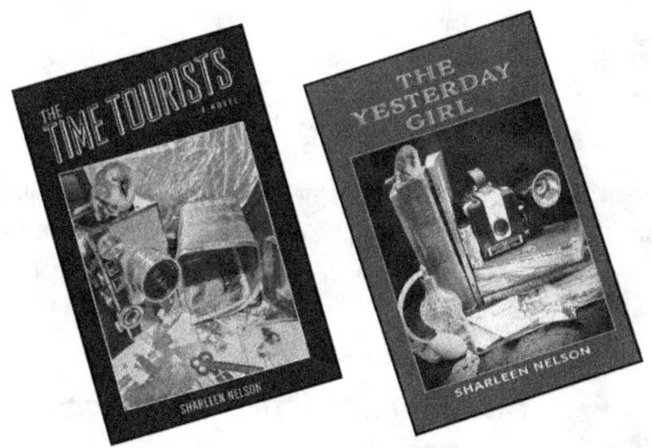

If you enjoyed *The Time Tourists* & *The Yesterday Girl*, you'll love the third book in this exciting time travel series by Sharleen Nelson!

Follow their continuing adventures as Imogen and Simon travel through time. Will Simon find his mother? Will Imogen ever learn the truth about hers? What's Mimi Pinky up to? And what's really going on at the shadowy Daguerreian Society?

Visit www.gladeyepress.com for fantastic deals on all GladEye Press titles.

Follow us on Facebook: https://www.facebook.com/GladEyePress/

GladEye titles can be ordered from your local book store and Amazon.com.

MORE BOOKS FROM GLADEYE PRESS

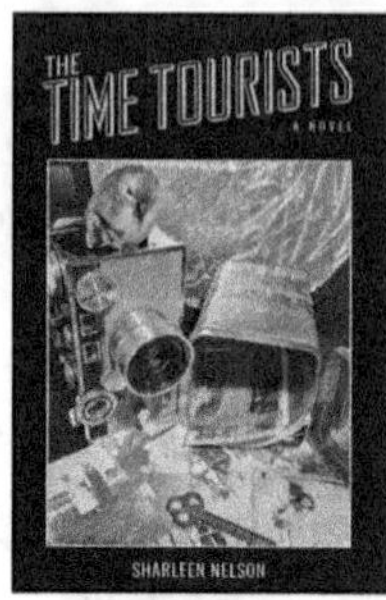

The Time Tourists
Sharleen Nelson

One of only a handful of individuals who can time travel through a still photograph, time-traveling private investigator Imogen Oliver helps people recover lost items and unearth long-buried stories and secrets from the past, all while navigating her own complicated life in the present.

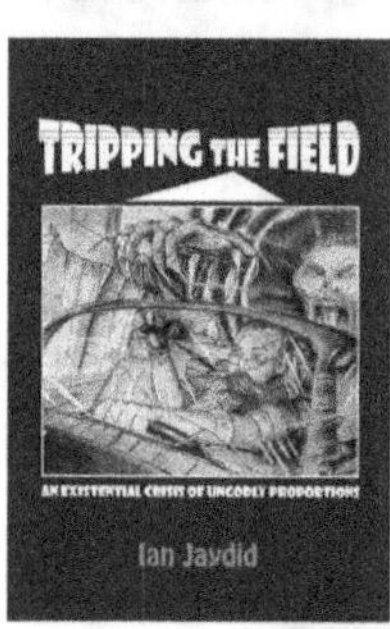

Tripping the Field: An Existential Crisis of Ungodly Proportions
Ian Jaydid

Empiricist scientist, Michael Huxley tumbles, stumbles, strides, and crawls through the jungles of South America, the mountains of Tibet, and the backwoods of Colorado in search of enlightenment and the hope of saving the world from a religious cult that has discovered a dark shortcut to the power of quantum realities.

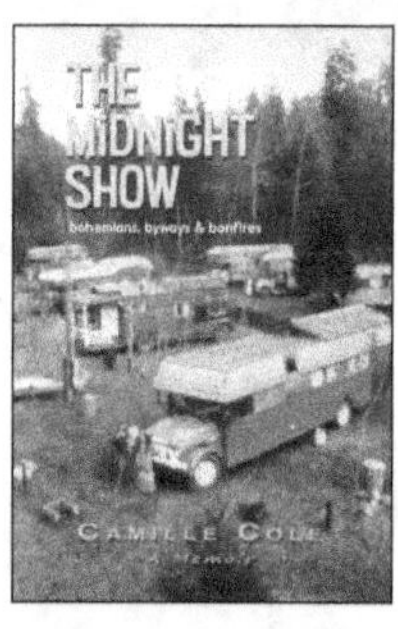

The Midnight Show: bohemians, byways, and bonfires
Camille Cole

During the early days of Oregon's famous Country Fair, the Midnight Show was a stage shared by icons of the counterculture, lovers, children and family, and those of us finding our way through.

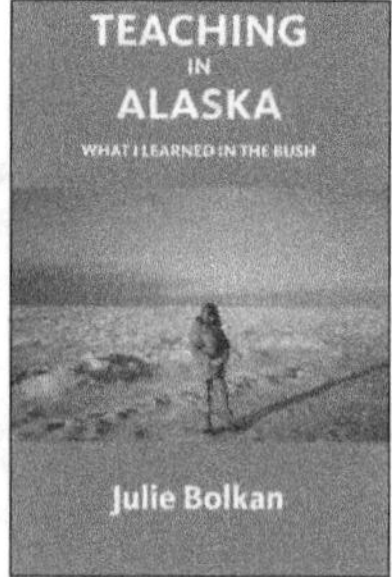

Teaching in Alaska
What I Learned in the Bush
Julie Bolkan

Among the first outsiders to live and work with the Yup'ik in their small villages, this book tells Julie's story of how she survived culture clashes, isolation, weather, and struggles with honey buckets—a candid and often funny account of one gussock woman's twelve years in the Alaskan bush.

 **GladEye Press**

All GladEye titles are available for purchase at www.gladeyepress.com, in book stores, and from Amazon.com

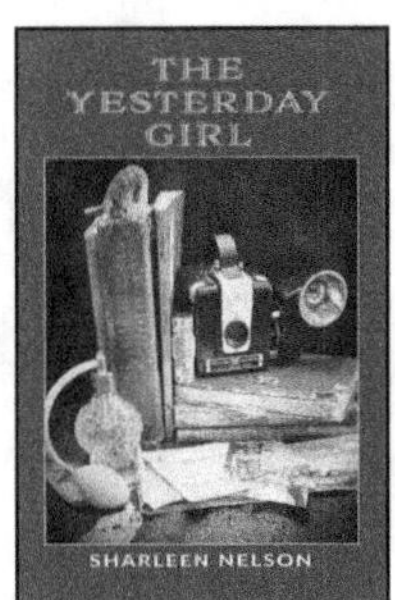

The Yesterday Girl
Sharleen Nelson

In this stand-alone sequel to *The Time Tourists*, time-traveling private investigator Imogen Oliver must once again navigate her complicated life—sometimes learning the hard way that the present can be as dangerous and unpredictable as the past.

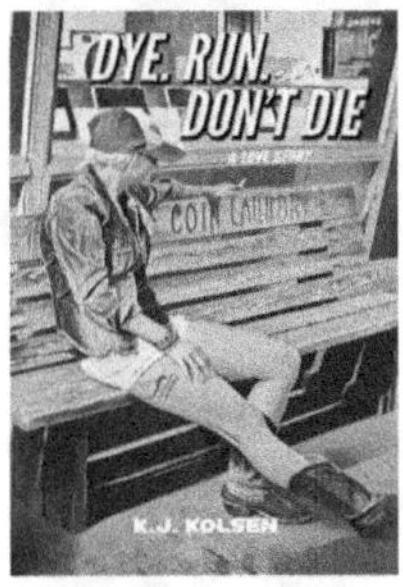

Dye. Run. Don't Die: A Love Story
K.J. Kolsen

Winnie's world is turned upside down when she gets a strange call from her long-estranged mobster father. Chased by shadowy figures, Winnie and her boyfriend Jimmy embark on a wild road trip involving disguises, stolen vehicles, murders, truck-stop perverts, a sex cult, and deadly shoot-outs!

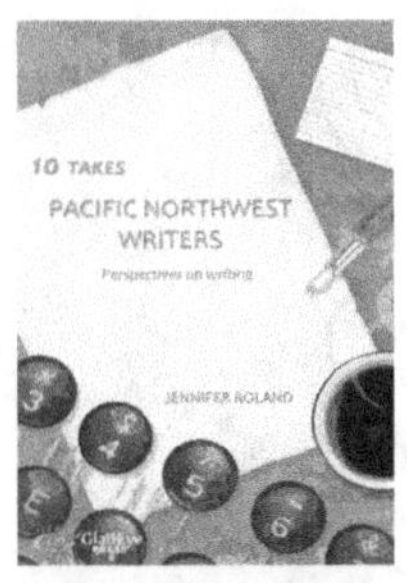

10 Takes: Pacific Northwest Writers—Perspectives on Writing
Jennifer Rowland

From novelists to poets to playwrights, Jennifer Roland interviews a variety of authors who have one thing in common—they have all chosen to make the Pacific Northwest their home.

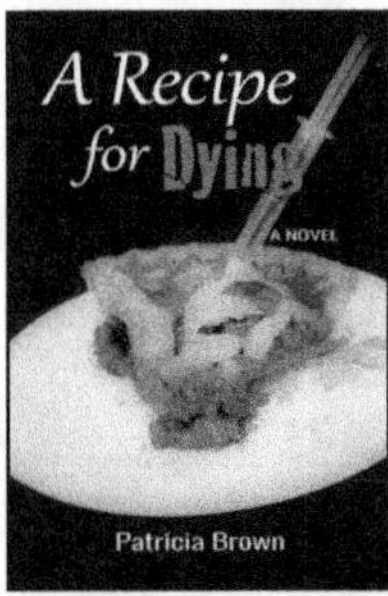

A Recipe for Dying
Patricia Brown

The old people are dying in the small coastal town of Waterton, but no one seems to notice—after all, that's what old folk do, isn't it? Eleanor and her delightful assortment of friends, most whom are getting up in age, set out to discover what is going on. Is it a series of mercy killings, or murder, and is their investigation putting them in danger?